Soul Shares
BACK DOOR
into PURGATORY

BOOK 9

Rory Ni Coileain

For more information contact:
Riverdale Avenue Books
5676 Riverdale Avenue
Riverdale, NY 10471
www.riverdaleavebooks.com

Design by www.formatting4U.com
Cover by Scott Carpenter

Digital ISBN: 9781626015210
Print ISBN: 9781626015227

First edition, September 2019

Prologue

November 15, 2013 (human reckoning)
The Realm

The soft chiming of Aine's water-clock, three hours before dawn, found her in the empty, echoing space between sleep and wakefulness. No sleeping-draught, and no channeling, would have let her sleep soundly tonight, not when she knew what was happening not five minutes' walk from her bower.

Yawning, she sat up and reached for the sheer robe draped across the end of her sleeping-couch; as she settled the robe over her shoulders, she ran a quick channeling through her thick red hair. Nothing elaborate, just enough so as not to arrive at the Pattern-tower looking as if she'd turned and tossed the entire night.

Her fellow Loremasters would know, though. They always did.

Picking up parchment and quill and inkstone, she stepped down from her bower. The grass was cool against her bare feet, the breeze gentle and scented with night-blooming flowers. The light of floating Fire-flies was enough to light her path, but a sliver of the full moon was already showing itself above the distant hills to the east.

Aine shuddered at the reminders of what was to come.

Once, I could have walked between the worlds, as easily as I cross this greensward. Centuries ago, before the Fae and human worlds were sundered, before the Pattern blocked every road from world to world, a Fae who knew the way could step from one world into the next—easily, in the places where the walls between worlds were thin. But a Loremaster could walk where she would, in those days.

When she Faded into the tower, Dúlánc's *tabhse* was waiting for her, kneeling in a meditative pose near the center of the web of the Pattern. 'Ghost' was, of course, not what the eldest Loremaster's image was at all—what Aine saw was a projection of the embodiment of his soul, emanating from the Pattern beneath her feet. Calling him his own *tabhse* was simply a concession to his sense of humor.

She knelt facing the elderly Fae, setting aside her writing implements and arranging the skirts of her robe and night-dress as carefully as if they were the finest gown and she were his guest at a wine-tasting. Only when every last fold was settled to her liking did she meet his gaze. "Is it done?"

His eyes were his answer; his nod merely confirmed it. "The Foreseeing is complete."

"And?" Aine wished she could be as calm as Dúlánc seemed to be, but she had never been much good at that. She was more like Cuinn, the youngest of them, and could not quite keep the edge of her fear from her voice.

"The endgame has begun." The Loremaster sighed deeply, soundlessly. "There are many paths forward for those who must fight; all but one end in chaos, and blood, and two worlds begging in vain to have the twisted evil of the *Marfach*'s tainted magick removed from them."

"All but one?" Aine arched a brow. "And where does that one path end?"

"Darkness. The darkness of our own unknowing." Dúlánc shrugged, the barest lift of his shoulders. "One path would not reveal its end to us, no matter how we pressed."

"Then that is the path our Fae in the human world must take."

"Yes." Dúlánc's voice was thin, even for a *tabhse*, revealing the strain hidden behind the serene eyes. "The one path we cannot see."

Aine glanced up at the sole round window in the row of slits; the moon was not yet visible, but the glow in the night sky heralded its coming. *Her* coming, if Cuinn's tale was to be believed. "Am I to send them a message?"

"Yes." Dúlánc turned his head to follow the direction of her gaze. "And then we must prepare to hold the portal with all our strength. That much we know."

Aine reached for her writing implements; spreading the parchment on the clear stone in front of her, and channeling a few drops of water onto the inkstone, she touched quill to stone, then looked up. "What am I to tell them?"

Dúlánc was silent for the space of a few breaths, his *tabhse* looking around at the brilliant strands of silver-blue wire embedded in the stone of the floor, the strands holding the souls and the bodies of over a thousand Loremasters, who had given up everything else they were to form the last line of defense against the ancient enemy of their race. "We dare not direct them. If we tell them what to do, they will fall from the narrow way, and we—and they—will lose everything."

"It has ever been thus." Actually, the reply that came first to Aine's mind came in Cuinn's remembered voice. *No shit, Sherlock, what was your first clue?* She had never been sure whether the prohibition against giving directions to the Fae of Purgatory was necessary because of the innate nature of the elaborate magickal construct designed to bring the Realm, the human world and the monster seeking to destroy them both into alignment at the perfect time, or because of the essence of Fae stubbornness. Probably both. "Then what shall I write?"

"They do not need to be reminded of what they must do—they need to be reminded of who they are. Or, in some cases, who they have become, since they left us. If they remember, they will do what is needed."

Impossible to keep Cuinn's words, or at least his tone, from her lips any longer. "Could you possibly be any more cryptic? I do have all night, after all."

Dúlánc laughed. "We miss having you among us, *chara*. Very well; listen closely."

Taking her lower lip between her teeth, Aine wrote, in flowing *d'aos'Faein* script:

Osclór, Nartú
Tobar, Soladán
Nidantór, Breathea
Glanadorh, Coromór, Farthor

Scian-omprór, Nachangalte
Crangaol, Síofra
Gastiór, Laoc, Caomhnór
Fánadh, Ngarradh

"Make haste, sister." Dúlánc's voice was even softer than it had been, as she finished writing and blew gently on the parchment; he was fading from view as he spoke. The magickal lights went out, one by one, as he vanished, leaving only the light of the full moon flooding the chamber, nearly centered in the round window.

Aine wondered if her cohorts could hear the hammering of her heart, disembodied as they all were. Leaving quill and stone on the crystal floor, she stood and channeled her mageblade. The sword of pure truesilver, the price of a Demesne's worth, appeared in her hand; bound to her, and to her protection, it was about to be tested as no sword had ever been.

She bent and placed the blade flat on the floor and stepped onto it. The metal was cold and hot at once under her bare feet, surely too slender for her purpose. But she had no choice. Writing directly on and through the Pattern no longer worked; this was their last chance to send a message to the exile Demesne.

And the only way to be sure their missive survived the hammer-winds and passed through the Pattern was for a Loremaster to channel an equal force to drive it through, without being driven through it herself.

The moon cleared the window-rim, burning white surrounded by the blackness of the night. Aine wondered that the full moon had ever seemed benign to her. *Does she hate us, for her captivity?*

A breeze caught at the hem of her robe, playful, teasing. A gust darted up under her gown, then tugged. Tugged harder. Wind circled her, no longer teasing, wrapping robe and nightgown around her legs.

I would have done better naked. Aine clutched the parchment and stared at the floor, waiting. Waiting for the crystal to fall away, for the floor to be full of stars.

A blast of wind rocked her, forcing her to step off the sword-blade. She snatched her foot back and planted it firmly on the hilt of the sword, before she was even aware of the chill of the stone.

Crystal vanished. All that was beneath her now was the Pattern, wire-blades as thin as a thought, capable of slicing soul from soul. And all that was between her and such a fate was the sword on which she balanced, barefoot and buffeted by a captive hurricane.

She had to act now, swiftly, while the way was open, and before she could fall again. She braced herself against winds pushing her this way and that, whirling, their voice a low ragged howl shaking the walls of the confined space, and held the parchment out in front of her. The gale caught it like a sail, tried to wrest it from her.

I have a tempest of my own.

Closing her eyes, she channeled Air. Living magick and elemental answered her summons, welled up from within her and flowed through her and trembled in her outstretched hands. The wind rocked her, battered her—but she was finding its rhythm now, balancing on the sword as if it were an unbroken riding-eagle.

And when the wind blasted upward, she was ready; she spread her hands atop the parchment, palms down, and released her own whirlwind.

The winds fought briefly over the precious sheet, but Aine poured magick into her captive gale, and the Loremasters' message vanished through the deadly lacework.

The wind roared, like a living thing. Perhaps it was. It had been conjured to hunt, and it had been cheated; nothing in the tower looked or smelled or tasted like prey, save the red-haired Loremaster in her lilac robes, balanced precariously on her mageblade.

It was easier with her eyes closed; her body knew what to do, when to push back, when to lean away. She wished she could close her ears, to distance herself from the insane howling of the gale, but she could not spare the concentration for such a channeling.

Surely it's nearly over—

The wind blasted Aine from behind, a stooping gryphon complete with a paralyzing roar. Caught off guard, she fell forward.

And landed on her knees, on cold crystal, in a chamber gone silent and still.

She huddled on the stone, gasping for breath. She had done her part; the Loremasters' message had gone to the human world. It was sealed away now, on the far side of the portal.

Perhaps forever.

* * *

Cape Horn

Wind. Harsh, gusty, bitter cold wind. Warm, though, compared to what they remembered.

Their eyes opened, although they had no memory of closing them. They lay sprawled on a shelf of rock, with stones cutting into their cheek, their naked body. Most of what they could see was a gray blur; squinting made it less blurry but no more colorful.

The crash of surf solved the riddle. More fucking ocean.

How long have we been here? This time the female's voice was relegated to the inside of their shared head.

"Who the fuck knows?" The male had intended to snarl, but realized just in time that loud noises were probably the worst possible idea as far as their head was concerned.

The female ignored him. Of course. *The sun is still in the sky.*

"Which means exactly fucking nothing." He wished she would stop talking. Their head was pounding louder than the surf. Fading sucked, even when the mortal body being force-Faded was dead.

Hsssst.

The male was ready to tell the female exactly how he felt about being shushed—but then he heard what she'd heard. The sound of something being dragged across rocks. Faint, gasping moans.

Maybe something was dragging itself.

Jagged rocks dug into the male's flesh as he struggled up onto an elbow. Ignoring the pain, he squinted down along the shelf toward the ocean.

8

Toward, not at. Fuck him if he was going to look straight at the ocean. None of them could remember their own making, naturally—so none of them could remember how it had been fucked up enough to leave them vulnerable to drowning.

"Dios querido... solo un poco más..."

The male could barely hear the human's voice, but at least now he knew which way to look. The rock shelf fell away off to their left, toward the pounding surf. A battered, bloody mess that the male was pretty sure was a human female clawed her way up the incline, trying to put some distance between herself and the splintered shell of a small boat, half in and half out of the—

Water be fucked. The male returned his attention to the human, who obviously hadn't seen him, or them, yet.

He suddenly realized how very hungry he was.

Look at her. The female's voice had that thick quality it took on when she was desperate to get laid, or looking for one of her orgiastic blood feedings.

"Not much else to look at besides the fucking water." No, the human hadn't heard him—she seemed fairly preoccupied with not dying.

The energy around her, you witless scour of smegma.

The male rolled his eyes, but looked just the same. And blinked, and looked again. The human's skin danced with fractals of light. Not living magick, but something like it.

Life. There was something like awe in the female's voice. Or maybe it was just hunger.

"Do they all have that? Why haven't we seen it before?"

9

He felt the female shrug. *Meat's senses were, no doubt, unequipped to perceive it. But now that he is gone...*

The human continued to drag herself up the slope, oblivious to the presence of the watcher, or watchers. She left bits of herself behind on the rocks, bits that lingered until they were washed away along with the trickles of blood from her wounds by waves coming entirely too fucking close.

It's like watching an ant with only one leg try to crawl out of a puddle of gasoline. The female's voice was dreamy, unfocused.

"How would you know that shit?"

There was a long pause, long enough for the human to make it another couple of feet up the incline. Long enough for the life energy to fade, and spark, and fade again.

Meat must have told us about it once, she replied, almost as if she'd forgotten the question. *It sounds like something he would have enjoyed.*

He'd nearly forgotten the question himself. "Poor Meat."

He could feel the female roll her eyes. *He kept this energy, this beauty, from us. Waste no time feeling sorry for him.*

"I wasn't—"

EAT IT, YOU FOOLS.

The male had almost forgotten what it felt like to have his blood—their blood—turn to ice in his veins.

The obscenity was right, though. If it looked like magick, it probably tasted like magick. And he was hungry. They were hungry.

The human finally saw him when he hitched

himself up to crawl toward her. It was hard to tell what she was thinking; her stare could have been dumbfounded gratitude for rescue, or a silent scream. It was hard to tell, with one of her eyes swollen nearly shut beneath a huge knotted bruise and the other covered with long wet dark hair like seaweed.

But she reached out as he got closer. Even a naked man with filthy dreadlocks, long yellow fingernails, and a hard-on bleeding where it had been cut by the fucking rocks was probably preferable to lying on the slope waiting for the tide to come in.

The male mostly agreed with the human about the tide.

Hurry.

The male didn't bother responding to the female's voiceless hiss. His attention was riveted on the human's hand, reaching up and out toward his own. "That's it. You can do it."

"*Ayuadame...*"

Her rasping plea for help didn't need any translation. Neither did the *Marfach*'s answer.

The male grabbed the human's wrist and pulled. Not a physical pulling—as soon as he touched her, he knew what they all needed, and he took it, sucking in the faint filigree of life-light.

The human screamed, or tried to. Her back arched, her body twisted, her fingers clawed feebly at the air.

Her pain had its own taste. It was sweet.

Too soon, it was over. The human's body went limp, her head hit the rocks with an unmistakably final-sounding thump. Her light died with her.

You killed her too quickly.

The male had no patience for the female's whining. "We're starving, you idiot. We don't have the luxury of fine dining."

Yet.

As meager as it was, this feeding would give them strength for another Fade, let them follow whatever it was that drew them toward their former tool. Somewhere closer to civilization, with more lives to take.

And when Bryce finally led them to the great nexus...

The male cackled.

A whole world of humans to feast on.

And then a Realm of Fae to destroy.

Chapter One

Osclór, Nartú

"You're going to have to keep your head down in order for me to tie off that last—oh, hell." Josh straightened. "I know that look."

Conall sighed. "Sorry, *dar'cion.*" He didn't bother contradicting his partner; it was bad enough that he'd been snapped out of his delicious state of willing submission by a familiar frisson of energy along his spine. "Something's come through the nexus."

Josh went instantly from mildly irritated to wide-eyed alert. "I thought that wasn't supposed to be possible any more."

"I believe I said it was 'highly unlikely,' rather than impossible."

"You were quoting C-3PO at the time. The odds sounded pretty impossible to me."

"Never listen to a golden robot, especially when his head's on backwards." Conall couldn't help smiling, though it didn't last long. "Damn. I don't dare go down there to see what came through." A glance at his erection straining against its cat's-cradle of rope was all the explanation he needed to give. The presence of a Fae, and that Fae's inner store of living magick, near a wellspring shedding untethered magick always produced unfortunate results; the presence of an aroused mage, with his personal magick in a state of hyperactivity, would be the kind of trouble bards wrote songs about. Usually centuries after the fact, once the dust had settled.

"Want me to go check it out?"

"Depends—did Lucien ever get around to installing the lights? You can't see by magick-light, after all."

"He did it last week, he said." Josh wriggled the tip of his smallest finger through a gap in the ropes, finding and stroking Conall's taint.

"Your fingers ought to be illegal."

Conall closed his eyes, focusing what was left of his attention on his memory of the tingle of sympathetic nexus energy. It traced the signature of something small, something non-living, something mostly non-magickal. "It should be safe for you," he said slowly. "But put a shirt on."

"Way ahead of you." When Conall opened his eyes, Josh had already slipped a sweater over his head. "I'll be back in two shakes."

"Shakes of what?"

* * *

The closer Josh came to the bottom of the tight spiral staircase leading down into the nexus chamber, the more his skin crawled. He wasn't afraid—no, his skin was literally crawling. Not only did *Scathacrú* and *Árean* want out from under his shirt, he was pretty sure he could feel the inked vines and flowers covering his shoulder pollinating, with a little help from the bumblebee he'd thought was such a cute touch. And he was very, very happy he'd asked Terry to ink the wolf on his left thigh instead of doing it himself; he had plans for his balls later, plans that didn't involve having them eaten by a tattoo.

What the hell is going on down here?

Coming around the last bend of the staircase gave him a partial answer to that question, at least. The wellspring that had grown to take up about a third of the subterranean chamber's floor had been even more agitated than had become normal for it, since the incident with Maelduin and Terry a couple of days ago. And now the great nexus, the Grand Central Station of ley and elemental energy, was matching it snit fit for snit fit. Where the wellspring threw off what looked—and occasionally felt—like solid shards of living magick untethered from its source, the nexus was spinning off clouds of turbulent ley energy, a miniature hurricane.

Fortunately for everyone—and for the continued structural integrity of the nearly-completed Purgatory over Josh's head—the two energies didn't have any interest in fraternizing, and in fact maintained a DMZ of sorts. Josh hoped the truce held long enough for him to find what he'd come for and get out again.

Squinting into the energy clouds, Josh barely made out what looked like a light-colored patch on the battered black leather chaise at the heart of the nexus. *All this, for that?* He edged closer to the spiraling ley energy, circling to find the spot on the perimeter where he could get closest to the object, whatever it was, without having to step into the nexus. Not that it would be dangerous for him to do so, not really. But he wanted to get in and out before *Scathacrú* figured out that it could probably burn a hole in his shirt and escape.

...not really dangerous?

Chuckling, Josh darted into the cloud. His hand closed around the object on the chaise—heavy paper, from the feel of it. *Areán* shrieked—not out of pain, just for the hell of it, as far as Josh could tell—and *Scathacrú*, never one to take a back seat to its inked sibling, responded with a clicking sound, like a pilot light on a gas stove trying to catch.

Oh, shit.

Josh pivoted on the ball of his foot and ran for the stairs.

* * *

"The next time I have to go down there, would you mind channeling me an asbestos shirt first?"

Conall blinked at the hole charred in the sleeve of Josh's sweater, a hole through which a flash of golden-scaled dragonet-hide was barely visible. "How about a firefighter's jacket instead? And maybe a hat? And suspenders. But no belt."

"My darling horndog." Josh grinned, a sight that never failed to tighten whatever trousers Conall happened to be wearing. Or, in the present case, the loop of rope binding his balls to his cock.

"So glad you noticed," Conall gasped.

"Too tight?"

"Just right." Conall's curiosity was almost as

great as his arousal, but trying to crane his neck to see what Josh was carrying would only make matters worse. Or better. "So what came through the nexus?"

Josh held out a sheet of parchment; the air around it was distorted in an eerily beautiful way, as if something about the parchment, something about its essence, changed from one moment to the next. Or might change. "Only this."

If Conall's hands had been free, he might have pinched the bridge of his nose. "I think I recognize that channeling. Mind bringing it a little closer?"

"Sorry." Josh held the parchment in front of Conall's face. "Better?"

"Yes, thank you." Conall squinted, not because the writing on the parchment was blurry, but because it was unstable. "Dammit. It's *d'aos'faeinen.*"

"Want me to call Cuinn? He can read it—"

"No, no." And not just because of the comments the snarky Loremaster would undoubtedly make when he saw Conall's condition. "Not *d'aos'faein, d'aos'faeinen.* A whole different animal." He started to sigh, but stopped before cutting off circulation to his cock. "The writing itself is unstable—I'm not sure if whoever wrote it did it this way on purpose, or if the *faeinen* is a side effect of coming through the nexus with things the way they are right now, but that doesn't really matter. It takes a channeling to stabilize and read it—I know it, I learned it a couple of hundred years ago, but that makes it a newfangled notion to a Fae Cuinn's age. I don't think he ever picked it up."

By now, Josh barely blinked when reminded of Conall's age, which suited Conall just fine. After 300-plus years of the most stringent self-control he was capable of, it felt wonderful to have a partner who wasn't intimidated by him. Who could treat him... well, like a twink. Take him in hand when the situation called for it.

And the smile on Josh's face was all about taking Conall in hand. Or mouth, or whatever was needful.

"You going to want help with that channeling?"

Damn, his s*cair-anam* even knew the exact vocal pitch that would get him off. "Yes, please."

A Fae's ability to channel magick was strongest when he was aroused. Conall's ability had always been greater than any, even during his centuries of self-denial... and when Josh went to work on him, he was fairly sure the limits of his ability had yet to be discovered.

Conall sucked in a breath through clenched teeth as Josh teased his taint with the tip of his tongue and his cock swelled against its rope cradle. "Damn... you know that's my favorite... but I need you to keep the parchment in front of my face, or I won't be able to read it."

"Sorry, my bad."

"You look about as sorry as Bragan in the Sea King's harem."

"The Sea King had a harem of ginger mages?" Holding the parchment in one big hand, Josh teased at Conall's cock through the spaces left by the rope with the other.

"You. Are. Not. Helping." But, of course, he was. Even his low laughter was helping; Conall could feel magick surging through him like a rip tide, and he hadn't even started the channeling yet.

"Sure I am. If I really wanted to not help, I'd..." The tip of a finger pushing aside the rope and slipping into Conall's eager hole up to the second knuckle finished Josh's sentence for him.

Conall's response was monosyllabic, *as'Faein,* and sublimely filthy. Riding the crest of his arousal, he whispered the first key-words of the channeling and did his best to focus on the writing in front of his nose instead of the fingers teasing his most teaseable places.

"They're pairs of words. Mostly." He sucked in a breath as Josh palmed his cock over the thin ropes. "The first one... *as'Faein,* I think they'd be *osclór* and *nartú.* And fellate me with an oven mitt, there they go."

"No oven mitt handy, I'm afraid." Josh's tone was matter-of-fact, just as Conall's had been. "I'll have to do it the old-fashioned way."

"Wait till I'm done, or I'll never make it to the end of this list." Conall groaned softly, a groan that ended in a strangled laugh at his partner's angelic expression. "And let me concentrate."

"Cheeky minx."

Conall stuck out his tongue, then forced himself to concentrate. "*Osclór* means 'opener' or 'one who opens.' And *nartú* means 'strength.'"

"Odd." Josh traced a fingertip up Conall's auburn treasure trail, until its path was blocked by a half-hitch. "You'd think 'one who opens' would be paired with 'one who closes.' Or 'strength' with 'weakness.'"

"That's awfully linear thinking for a Fae." Carefully, Conall channeled more magic into the parchment. "The next pair is... it looks like an archaic form of *tobar,* and *soladán. Tobar* in *Faen* means a well, but the older form..." Conall blinked. "I will bet you anything you like that it's the *d'aos'Faein* word for 'wellspring.'"

19

"Since only one of us here speaks *Faen*, you could lose that bet and I would never know."

"I'm right. Just accept it." Josh's lips sealed around the head of Conall's cock, and Conall forgot how to breathe for a blissful second or two. "*Soladán—*" He cleared his throat. "*Soladán* means a channel. Like a river, not magickal channeling."

Josh's eyebrows went up, what little Conall could see of them. "A well and a river?"

"No, a wellspring and a... wait." Something about the shape of the words... "Not *a* wellspring, or *a* channel. *The* Wellspring. *The* Channel."

"You lost me."

"No, I didn't, but I may cry if you don't keep licking." Conall let his head drop back with a breathless laugh as Josh's tongue teased at his length. "They're names. The list is a list of names. Lochlann is the Wellspring, with his gift for calling the ley energy."

"And Garrett's the Channel, helping him guide it."

"I could have sworn I said something along the lines of 'keep licking.'" Conall grinned. "So *osclór* and *nartú* should be names, too."

"Maybe they're ours." Fortunately, Josh's free hand more than made up for what his tongue wasn't doing. "You call me your strength."

Conall would have nodded if he could have. "And I'm the one who opens the nexus. Or I was until it went crazy."

Josh frowned, licking up a bead of fizzy Air Fae precum. "Why would the Loremasters use what for all we know might be their last chance to send us a message, to send us a list of our own names?"

20

"Speaking as something of an expert in Fae psychology, it would be a better use of our time to save figuring that out for after I finish translating."

"Roger that."

"I'd rather you roger me."

"Not till you're finished."

Conall squeaked as Josh's thumb slid into him. "Show me the damn parchment again."

Grinning, Josh obliged, and Conall let the magick flow out of him anew, doing his best to focus. "*Nidantór, Breathea.* The... oh, hell. Unraveler? Unmaker? And the Judge, that word's pretty much the same in *d'aos'Faein* and *Faen.*"

"Neither one of those sounds familiar. Unless the Judge is something to do with Fiachra."

Conall shook his head, as best he could. "I doubt it. Fae don't really have what you'd call a judicial system, and the Loremasters wouldn't have any reason to associate police with judges."

"I was thinking more of his Truthsight."

"Oh." Reason and logic were difficult in Conall's situation, but he tried. "Maybe. But that would make Peri the Unmaker, and that makes no sense at all."

"True." Josh stroked one of Conall's swollen testicles with the flat of his tongue, making Conall yelp. "What's next?"

"Quite possibly me passing out."

"The day I exceed your pleasure threshold, the world will be ending around us."

There was nothing to be said to that, because Josh was probably right. "Parchment, please. Erm... this next one's three."

"Rhoann, Mac, and Lucien, then."

"I'm not so sure about that. *Glanadorh, Coromór, Farthor.*" The wavering magick was starting to make Conall's eyes water. "The Cleaner, the... One Who Makes Level? Not sure about that one, it could be the One Who Makes Equal. And the Sentry."

"That could be Lucien." The human fireplug who had been, and would be again, Purgatory's head bouncer had a sixth sense, the gift of his Fae SoulShare, that let him keep police and other ill-wishers out of the club and away from the man and the Fae he loved.

"It could. But the other two don't fit Rhoann and Mac."

Josh slowly worked his tongue into the bend where Conall's drawn-up thigh met his torso, tickling the oh-so-sensitive skin there. "Think we're barking up the wrong tree?"

"Not sure I need that mental image. Coinneach would have way too much fun with it." Conall wasn't sure how he was managing to form words, though long hours of magickal work with his lover and partner and SoulShare undoubtedly helped him concentrate. "Let's leave it for now." He drew a deep, unsteady breath. "*Scian-omprór* and *Nachangalte*. The Blade-bearer and the Unbound."

"Tiernan."

"Or Maelduin." Conall closed his eyes, just for a second, to stop their watering. "*Crangaol* and *Síofra*, the Tree-kin and the Changeling."

"Finally, an easy one." Josh worked his fingers through the binding criss-crossing Conall's chest and pinched his nipple, hard enough to make him yelp. "Fiachra and Peri. And I have to say, I like the Changeling as a name for him. Falcon's a beauty."

"She is."

"I think you just got harder."

"I think you're right." Conall set himself against a wince as the binding around his balls tightened. "Care to get that parchment back here?"

"Sorry-not-sorry."

Conall squinted through another wave of pleasure, at words which disappeared almost as fast as he read them. "Damn. Another three, which makes no sense. *Gastiór*, the Binder, *Laoc*, the Warrior, and *Caomhnór*, the Guardian."

"Well, Mac has to be the Warrior." At 65, with a sort of agelessness gifted him by his SoulShare, Mac was still every inch the ex-Marine.

"Yes, but we already know Tiernan's the Guardian, the Guardian of the nexus." Conall huffed out a short, tight breath. "Maybe these aren't names after all."

"Or maybe the Loremasters are doing something we don't understand. Yet." A soothing hand cupped Conall's ass-cheek, while a decidedly un-soothing thumb traced along his taint. "Don't give up, *d'orant*."

"Never give up, never surrender."

Josh winked. "That's the spirit."

Conall gave himself a moment to enjoy the ripple of delight Josh's smile sent through him. "The last two are *Fánadh* and *Ngarradh*. The Wanderer, and the... damn, I'm not sure. It's similar to one of the older words for the Sundering." The final desperate act of the Loremasters, parting two worlds and walling them off from one another, with a barrier formed of their own essences—a barrier which the Fae of Purgatory had to break down, somehow, without loosing the *Marfach* on the Realm. Which would probably require them to kill the embodiment of evil, a creature legend said could only die if it could be made to forget what it was.

Sure, that was going to happen.

"Can I put this down now? And are you okay?"

"I... yes, I'm all right. Just thinking." The parchment was blank, the magickal wavering gone. "If this was the Loremasters' last message, I'd be considerably happier if I knew what they were saying."

"We can talk it over with the others. Later." The sofa cushions dipped as Josh knelt between Conall's drawn-up legs; Conall couldn't see what his partner was doing with his hands, but the metal-on-metal jangle of a steel-tipped belt being undone was just as telling as the sight would have been.

"Please, yes," Conall whispered, his voice abruptly gone.

It took him a moment to realize why Josh's responsive smile brought effervescent tears to his eyes; he knew the slight curve of his *scair-anam*'s lips much better from the inside, from those times when he Fade-walked into Josh's body to borrow his strength, allowing him to channel magick too powerful for even the greatest Fae mage of the last two millennia to handle alone. *I know you*, that smile said. *I know exactly what you want, what you need. And I want more than anything to give it to you.*

Josh leaned forward, took his weight on his hands, and brushed his lips across Conall's. "Want me to unbind you?"

"No." Conall swallowed a lump in his throat. "Take me. Just like this."

24

Chapter Two

Tobar, Soladán

Garrett slumped against the mirrored wall of the Colchester's elevator, trying to keep weight off his injured leg in a way that didn't make it hurt more and concentrating on not cursing. Well, not cursing too loudly. Not that it mattered, when there was a Fae—and a Fae's hearing—waiting for him.

Lochlann, in fact, was waiting outside the elevator doors when they opened again. *So much for being quiet.*

"What did you do, *grafain*?" His partner's disheveled dark hair hinted at an interrupted nap, but the aquamarine gaze that raked him from head to toe missed nothing.

"Tested the new poles," Garrett muttered.

Lochlann shook his head, and before Garrett could react, his *scair-anam* had picked him up and was carrying him back toward their suite.

"You don't have to do this." Garrett really hated it when his mouth disconnected from his brain without warning.

His Fae didn't bother to answer, unless you counted his low chuckle. The door to their suite was propped open, underscoring the fact that Lochlann had heard him coming, and had probably already diagnosed him before leaving their rooms. At the very least, he'd figured out that there was going to be carrying involved in getting Garrett home.

Not the first time that had happened. But a hell of a lot more pleasant than the first time had been.

"All right, *grafain*, lie still for a minute." Lochlann deposited Garrett carefully on their bed, kissed him on the forehead, and headed for chest of drawers against the far wall. "I'm not really set up for patients here—you're lucky I have an opening."

"And you're lucky I'm too classy to state the obvious."

Garrett's laughter at the slight sashay of Lochlann's delicious ass, and his whistle as the Fae bent to open a drawer, were anything but classy. But damn, they felt good. Lochlann had done it all on purpose, of course, Fae healers did more than channel magick, or at least *his* Fae healer did.

When Lochlann straightened, he had a roll of rubber-backed canvas in one hand and a flat tin that even Garrett's non-Fae nose could tell contained cocoa butter in the other. Shoving the drawer closed with a hip, to the accompaniment of more enthusiasm from Garrett, he unrolled the canvas on the opposite side of the bed and patted it lightly. "Can you wriggle yourself over here, or do you need help?"

"I'd love to take the help, but I think that would make us late for our dinner reservation."

One dark eyebrow went up. "We have a couple of hours yet."

"Exactly."

It was a pleasantly awkward couple of minutes

before Garrett was on the massage cloth—which had actually been on sale online as a portable baby-changing pad—and free of his jeans. Mostly pleasant; there was no way to avoid aggravating his already aggravated thigh muscle in the process.

Lochlann popped the lid off the tin and started running the heel of his hand over the contents in rapid circles, melting the waxy substance inside it. Garrett had never had a masseur use cocoa butter on him before Lochlann; once he'd had to go somewhere on the Metro after a session, and one woman standing near him in the crowded car had turned to her companion, bemused, and said *Funny, I'm craving chocolate all of a sudden.*

"No magick?—not that I'm complaining." Complaining? He'd take and run with any chance to feel Lochlann's hands on him, doing one of the things they did so well. Once he could run, anyway.

"Only if I have to." Lochlann grasped Garrett's leg and eased it out a few inches to one side, gently stroking down the inside of Garrett's thigh with an open palm. "I'd rather not risk waking up the wellspring."

Garrett didn't need to point out the other thing Lochlann was doing a great job of waking up. His cock was already half-hard, the stainless steel ring piercing the underside coming into view. Lochlann rubbing his hands together to spread the warmed cocoa butter around didn't help his condition, either. Or maybe it did. *I suppose it depends on perspective.*

"How did you do it?"

"Just a simple inversion, braking a spiral—aaaaahhhh!" Garrett's head and shoulders came up off the bed as the heel of Lochlann's hand dug in, exactly

27

where all the pain from his torn muscle had accumulated during the cab ride home.

Lochlann didn't say anything. He didn't need to. The tilt of his head and the fractional lift of one brow said *and you didn't warm up first, did you?* perfectly well.

Garrett wished his own eyebrows were half as eloquent. "I didn't think I needed to warm up, not for something that basic." It sounded stupid in his head, even more so when it came out of his mouth.

Lochlann, bless him, didn't press the point. He simply leaned over and placed a kiss on Garrett's abused thigh, before resuming his work. Garrett thought he saw a smile, though.

"Jesus, I think I tore it," Garrett gasped, after a careful stretch of his leg nearly had him climbing a bedpost.

"I think you're right." Unthinking, Lochlann plowed a cocoa-buttered hand through his hair. "I'm going to need to channel to take care of this after all."

Even short of breath and swallowing whimpers, Garrett couldn't help grinning at the thought. Channeling meant calling the ley energy from someplace other than the wellspring directly under them, things being what they were, and calling the ley energy meant his *scair-anam* was going to need some help, of the arousal kind. Fae channeled magick best when they were turned on. *Now there's a real hardship.*

"I know that look." Lochlann's fingertips barely brushed the inside of Garrett's thigh. "Remember, you're the one who reminded me we only have a couple of hours until dinner."

"It's only Thanksgiving. No big deal."

The funny thing was, until he'd met Lochlann, Garrett would have totally bought into those words. Rejected by his family, nothing but a fuckboy to pretty much everyone he knew and an anonymous dancer to those he didn't, and poz into the bargain, holidays had been way up there on his list of things to avoid.

But having someone to share holidays with—to make traditions with—made a difference. And when that someone had literally followed you into death, because he couldn't imagine living without you... that changed you.

Lochlann's half-smile told Garrett his Fae knew where his thoughts had wandered. "Come on, *grafain*. Give me just enough to let me help you. And then..."

* * *

Dinner ended up being frozen pizza and a bottle of pinot noir. It was the best Thanksgiving dinner Garrett could remember.

Chapter Three

Nidantór, Breathea

The music from the dance floor at Piledriver was still pounding in Cuinn's ears when he woke. Well, all right, maybe not in his ears. But his subconscious, definitely. If Fae even had subconsciouses. Most Fae failed to see any point to suppressing anything, and thus had little use for a subconscious.

Unless, of course, a particular Fae had one mass murder and the potential for a couple more on what passed for his conscience.

Cuinn grimaced. Obviously, a night of power metal and his *scair-anam*'s uninhibited dance-floor fornication hadn't been enough to get him the fuck out of his own head for a few hours.

Another exposure to Rian's sublimely talented hands, mouth and ass might set things right, though. Buoyed on that happy thought, Cuinn rolled over to gather up his Prince.

And gathered up about a quarter-acre of cold bed instead.

Wha'fuck, my liege? Wherefore art thou? The mental speech Cuinn shared with his SoulShare was second nature by now.

It took a few seconds for the Prince Royal to answer, long enough that Cuinn started to wonder if there was something amiss.

I'm up on the roof.

From the tightness of Rian's inner voice, there might well be something amiss anyway. Fuck. *You want company?*

Another long silence. *'Sea, if you're willing.*

If I'm... Cuinn reached out with his inner sense and Faded, not bothering with anything as prosaic as clothes, or even a sheet.

His beloved hadn't bothered with either, either. Once Cuinn's eyes had adjusted to the semi-darkness on the brownstone roof, he could make out Rian's naked form easily enough, leaning against the roof's access door. Past the door, and the brick-and-wood frame around it, the buildings of lower Manhattan rose up in their gold-limned beauty. The deeper darkness of moon-shadow shrouded Rian, the nearly half-moon close to halfway up the arch of the sky. Plenty of light for a Fae, and more moonlight than Cuinn wanted.

A tiny flame bloomed out of the shadows; Rian watched the Fire dancing on his fingertip with some bemusement, before raising his clear blue gaze to Cuinn's. "And what's my consort doing clear over on the other side of the feckin' roof?"

"Watching you." Cuinn's voice stuck in his throat.

Rian smiled, a barely visible curve of lips Cuinn loved to see swollen and tender from kisses or bites or stubble burn or an enthusiastic BJ, or any combination thereof. But not tonight. Something was eating at his bondmate, and it wasn't him.

31

Before the Prince Royal could speak again, Cuinn Faded to his side and enfolded him in his arms.

"What's going on?" Cuinn nipped the curve of Rian's ear, tongued the industrial bar piercing it. "Thought you were in bed."

Rian sighed, his breath warm against Cuinn's shoulder—warm as only the breath of a Fire elemental could be. "I thought I'd come out and try to have me a look at the moon. Wrestle with her a bit, like."

The longing in Rian's voice was plain enough, but Cuinn didn't need to ask how the wrestling had gone. His partner's stance, hidden away from the moonlight by the stairwell, told him well enough that this time had been like all the others.

Hell, he didn't even need to ask why Rian had felt the urge to try. Any Fae who had ever come through the Pattern carried with him the sight of the full moon framed in the single window of the Pattern-tower, the trigger to release the magick that brought unimaginable agony. Fae in the human world hated moonlight with a passion, even those like his bond-mate, who wanted to love it.

Of course, moonlight probably hated the Fae right back. Thanks to him.

"Tell me again why you had to go and give me a conscience." Cuinn reached up and worked his fingers through his Prince's thick shock of blond hair, tugging lightly on the forelock that generally curled temptingly down over one blue topaz eye.

Rian's arm slipped around his waist. His lover needed no explanation, he knew what Cuinn meant. "I gave you nothing you didn't give me first."

"Fae don't have consciences. That's a human

32

thing." And Rian had acquired his from his human foster parents, in the years when he'd had no clue who and what he truly was.

"*Íosa, Máire agus Íosef.* You're fecking impossible."

And there was another thing. His Royal beloved was the first Fae of faith in the history of their kind, again courtesy of his foster parents by way of Belfast's Falls Road.

Not quite the first, not exactly. But all Cuinn himself had done in the way of interacting with the divine was murder a goddess' children and then enslave the goddess.

Which brought them right back to where they'd started. Cuinn could barely see the still-rising moon, if he craned his neck just so. And he did, just for a second.

Do you still hate me, Mother Moon?

"Impossible," Rian repeated, but there was amusement in his voice, and he kissed Cuinn's neck as he said it. "But you're a fine distraction, I'll grant you."

"I live to serve." Cuinn wasn't kidding, not entirely. His heart beat for his beloved, before it beat for himself or anyone or anything else.

The Cuinn of two millennia ago—the Cuinn of two years ago—wouldn't have recognized the Cuinn who could think thoughts like that.

The Cuinn of right-this-minute couldn't possibly give less of a shit what the other Cuinns thought, especially not when Rian was going from kisses to nips and pressing an erection into the hollow of Cuinn's thigh. Cuinn turned and pushed his bond-mate back against the brick wall, grinding against him, relishing the scents of musk and smoke.

"Make us a light, there's a sweet Prince." Cuinn backed off just far enough to be able to reach down and cup Rian's sac in the palm of his hand, heft the delicious weight of it. "Let me see you."

He wasn't sure what he'd been expecting—maybe the return of the fingertip-light—but his breath caught hard as the Fire in Rian's eyes flared to light. It wasn't exactly easy to forget that he was bonded to a Fire elemental—the charred holes in the bedsheets when Rian forgot himself after sex were a persistent sweet reminder—but living flames gazing into his eyes had a way of driving the point home like little else could.

"Fuck me hard, consort mine." Rian punctuated his whisper with a hard nip at Cuinn's lower lip.

Cuinn's mouth felt suddenly dry. "You... need it to hurt?"

"Only enough to remind me I'm yours." The fiery gaze turned skyward, for a fraction of a second. "Yours and not hers."

Rian, just short of two weeks old when Cuinn had kidnapped him, hadn't been old enough to remember coming through the Pattern. He couldn't possibly remember his last sight of the moon.

But Rian remembered, of course. No Fae ever forgot.

"Turn around, then." Not waiting for Rian to follow orders—even an immortal Fae could grow old waiting for a Fire elemental to do that—Cuinn took hold of Rian's arm and turned him roughly into the bricks. "Hands on the wall."

Rian complied, his fingers splayed out over the grimy bricks. He wasn't smiling, but the utter satisfaction so plain on his face send most of Cuinn's blood supply straight to his cock. He reached around and gripped Rian's erection, groaning softly at the touch of flame trickling over his fingers.

A high-pitched keening escaped Rian as Cuinn forced his way between iron-muscled ass cheeks and drove his length deep. Or maybe the cry was Cuinn's. Didn't fucking matter, it was beautiful. So sweet, to have to fight for every inch, and to know the fight delighted them both. Cuinn's hips jerked—again, again, winning a few inches each time, jarring the breath from his beloved and sending waves of pleasure along every nerve in his once-jaded body.

"Fuck..." Rian bent over, bracing himself against the bricks, shuddering in time with Cuinn's thrusts. Rian's knees trembled, and so did Cuinn's.

Cuinn leaned forward, too, his hands covering Rian's. "That's the plan, my liege." Bending his knees, he paused, long enough to brace himself—and long enough for Rian to relax a little.

"Shite!" Rian's shout echoed around the rooftop as Cuinn caught him off guard and drilled into him, hard enough to sheath his whole length and drive the younger Fae up onto the balls of his feet and face first into the bricks before he could catch himself. "Oh, fuck, oh, fuck, oh sweet bleeding fuck..." Recited with all the urgency and power of a prayer, in a voice gone suddenly hoarse.

Cuinn would likely have been praying himself, had he been able to find the breath or the inclination for it. But what he was doing, surrendering to the giving and the receiving of pleasure, was probably as close to prayer as any Fae ever came. Any Fae other than his mad consort.

Rian's pleas gave over to a low, keening moan; he clutched at the bricks, his nails bending back and scraping down the wall. "Jesus... take me, damn you, take me..."

"I don't have to, you're mine already—"

He'd meant it as a growl, but he choked back a cry instead, at the sight of a single flame, a Fire elemental's tear, trickling down Rian's cheek. He could feel his bond-mate's joy, his love, as if they were his own.

Because they were.

They came together, gouts of flame painting Cuinn's hand—and, yes, the bricks—as his vision dissolved in golden dazzle and then went momentarily and blissfully black. When he came back to himself, slumped over his Prince and leaning precariously against the wall, he devoted a few seconds to remembering how to breathe... and to making a promise.

When we've done what we have to do... when the Marfach's *dead and the way to the Realm is open... I'm going to free the moon.*

He could think of no other way to give his love the moonlight.

* * *

Pampas de Jumana, Peru

The male felt more than a little bilious as he, and the other selves sharing his senses, looked from the huge figures etched into the plain below to the glowing ley line bisecting the broad valley floor, running past

36

their feet and disappearing into the scrub-covered hills behind them.

This kept us alive. From the time of our exile until our escape. The female sounded as if she were trying not to gag.

"Remember when we let Meat in on the memory of it?" Even shuddering, the male couldn't help smiling, recalling the zombie bouncer's reaction. "He puked. And said it was like... what did he call it?"

BEING FORCE-FED SAWDUST THROUGH A TUBE DOWN HIS THROAT.

The male fought the urge to crouch, to hide. Their monstrous component was getting more vicious every time they Faded, or so it seemed.

Still, they were likely to need that rage where they were going. "That was it. Meat occasionally had a real way with words."

Do you miss him?

The male snorted. "Almost as much as I miss head lice and crabs." The tiny creatures of the human world hadn't liked Fading any more than Meat had.

FEED.

For once, the monster's command wasn't quite enough to make the male move.

The Fae had intended the *Marfach*'s imprisonment to be the worst torment imaginable. Or they hadn't, and it had been a complete fucking coincidence that that was exactly what it had been. Either way, going back to that half-life, even to feed, was more than the male could do.

Until the abomination forced him to his knees and shoved his face into the dirt.

FEED.

"Easy for you to say, you don't have to taste it." But he was as hungry as the rest of them. His hands splayed out over the shifting earth, he steeled himself, closed his eyes, and drew in the ley energy.

Choking, spluttering, gagging, he fell back after only a few seconds. Sawdust wasn't even close.

One vile draw hadn't been enough, of course. The male knew to be more cautious the next time—though a long trickle of the nearly inedible energy wasn't any more palatable than a short flood of it.

By the next attempt, once the edge was off their hunger, the female was in a slightly better mood. Or maybe she was just trying to distract the male and the monster. Either way, the male was cool with it.

Soon we will gorge ourselves on living magick. And death. And pain. This will be nothing but a loathsome memory.

"Doesn't their precious Prince get off on pain?"

The male could feel the female smiling. He thought he could feel the abomination doing the same thing, or whatever it did when it wanted to give the impression it was smiling.

This time, thoughts of the monster didn't make the male gag. It was so fucking good at inflicting pain, while refusing to let the object of its attentions die.

They would all feast on Rian for a long, long time.

Chapter Four

Lasair frowned, probing carefully the one spot Bryce didn't want him to touch and desperately needed him to touch, the dark scar under his rubs marking the spot where Janek's knife had carved out a cozy little nest for a piece of the *Marfach*. "It feels inflamed."

"The fucker's getting closer. Has to be."

The Fae leaned forward and brushed a kiss over Bryce's cheek. "Tell me what you need me to do."

Bryce let out a breath he hadn't realized he was holding in a long unsteady sigh. "What you always do."

Lasair really got a raw deal. Bryce tried to banish the thought, as his Fae lover bent over him and kissed the scar Janek's knife had left. How he could stand to do that, Bryce couldn't imagine—going by his own sensations, what Lasair was doing had to be like sucking from a sewer pipe.

But it helped. The cramping, the feverish cold crawling sensation lessened, every second those incredible lips were on his body. Bryce could breathe again. His head fell back on the pillow, giving him a great view of the hotel room's antique stamped-tin ceiling.

Lasair's fingertips stroked Bryce's ribs, gently but firmly.

The pillow next to Bryce's head dropped suddenly, as if a weight had fallen on it. There was also an unmistakeable scent of sulfur in the air.

Bryce sighed. "Your dog farted again."

Setanta's tail swished frantically across the pillow—faster at the sound of Lasair's chuckle. "He's not farting, *sumiúl*. It's hormones."

"Great, we really need a doggy teenager—hey!" Something very cold and wet landed on Bryce's forehead.

Lasair wasn't even trying not to laugh. Which was okay, actually—as long as the Fae was pressed up against Bryce's body, Bryce was perfectly okay with him laughing all he wanted. But the Fade-hound puppy took Lasair's laughter for approval, and he was wagging his whole puppy butt now.

"You're forgetting how slowly Fade-hounds grow, *sumiúl*." A gentle nip at the rim of Bryce's navel was followed by a long, soothing lick. "We have at least a half-century before Setanta is anything like a teenager. But I think he may be teething."

"One piece of good news after another." This time, Bryce's sour tone was a joke, and everyone present knew it. He'd learned how to adore the puppy even before he'd learned how to adore his *scair-anam*. In fact, he had a sneaking suspicion that he might not have figured out the one without the other. "What did he just..."

Answering his own question, Bryce reached up and grabbed the icy wet washcloth Setanta had dropped on his forehead. "Where did you get this, brimstone-butt?"

The butt-wagging increased in tempo and intensity, as did Lasair's laughter. "I set it out in an ice bucket to get cold when I came in and found you sick. I know it helps."

"Looks like someone else figured it out, too."

The blind puppy flopped down on the bed, his whiskered chin resting on Bryce's shoulder, his tail still fanning the pillow.

"Shall I continue?" Not waiting for an answer, Lasair resumed his stroking, his kissing—activities that would have felt a hell of a lot like foreplay, if only Bryce were feeling better.

Bryce desperately wanted to feel better.

"Close your eyes, *sumiúl*, relax, let me work."

A shock of febrile heat churned Bryce's side, deep under the skin where nothing was supposed to be. He gasped, his head coming up off the bed. Lasair's head came up, too; the Fae checked to make sure Bryce was all right, before glaring at the now-throbbing dark puckered scar, to the accompaniment of a low growl from Setanta. Well, a low puppy growl.

"Couldn't it let you rest for a few hours?" Those perfect hands urged Bryce to lie back down; Setanta helped, too, resting his chin on Bryce's shoulder and pushing.

"I don't think it gives a shit about making me uncomfortable," Bryce mumbled.

* * *

#growling# #pawing at nose# #sneezing#
i think newmaster is laughing. firstmaster smells like frowning. at me?

#whines#
i smell death, death magick. taste it.
#bares teeth#
i want to hunt. but the only death magick is in newmaster. how can i hunt newmaster? no chasing, no delicious fear, no blood, no meat and full belly, not newmaster!

firstmaster says i am too small for that anyway. someday i will show him he is wrong.

"Hey, pup. I was only kidding about the brimstone."

#tail thumping# #love# #ear licking#

"Settle, *tréan-cú*."

#grumbling# firstmaster will not let me even try to hunt.

so I will do what I can.
#ear licking#
#ear nipping#
#love#

* * *

Medellín, Colombia

A white-hot bloom of pain in her head shocked the female to consciousness. A wash of brown blood trickled down the side of her face; magick flooded into the wound as the echoes of a gunshot faded.

I believe we have been shot, she mused.

No one answered.

"*Pendejos*," a male voice snarled. "This is your reward for cheating Cicatrizado."

Soft gasping sobs, two heavy sets of footsteps, the slamming of a door.

Silence, deep and weighty. Except for the sobs.

The female opened her eyes, and beheld beautiful carnage.

Directly in her line of sight lay a dark-haired, dark-skinned human male, most of his face missing. The female suspected from his position that she would find most of his brain soiling her robe. What was left of a child of perhaps six or seven years lay atop the adult; gunfire had nearly bisected the small body.

What little of the sweetness of death remained in father and child was rapidly dissipating; only a trace was left, a trace the female consumed almost instantly.

No fucking way is that enough, the male grumbled. *We spent more than that on healing. If you'd bestirred your pert aristocratic ass ten seconds earlier—*

"Be silent, idiot." The female licked blood daintily from her fingertips, to the accompaniment of labored breathing, choking sobs. Blood like the finest wine.

The female pushed herself up to her knees. Two more bodies lay beside the first two, a woman and the girl-child she had obviously tried to shield with her own body. A plastic-wrapped brick of white powder had burst open and been scattered over her body, along with what looked like currency—although it was now so soaked with blood as to be almost beyond recognition.

Pain and death flowed from the mother in nearly equal measure; from the child came only pain and fear.

None of it was enough to satiate them, not even after the full measure of pain and fear and slow death had been retrieved from the child.

But two lives, and the promise of the feasting to come, would suffice for the next leg of their journey.

Chapter Five

Scian-omprór, Nachangalte

"I think some humans remember the Fae better than you realize." Maelduin had apparently forgotten all about the glass of wine in his hand, and was leaning forward, studying the screen intently. "Your Shakespeare understood *a'gár'doltas* nearly as well as a Fae Royal."

"Remind me what that means again?" Terry was glad Maelduin seemed to be enjoying the DVD of his *Romeo and Juliet*, though it would have been even better if the Fae were appreciating how he, Terry, had looked in the white tights that supposedly put ten pounds on any dancer's thighs.

Maelduin glanced back at Terry, and something in his eyes suggested there might be a fair amount of appreciating going on after all. "It doesn't translate very well, I'm afraid. It has murder in it, but also laughter. But nothing of humor."

"I think I get it." The on-screen him was being stalked by Tybalt, Juliet's older brother, and in this particular performance the role had been danced by a guest artist who had come to the company with a reputation as a bully. A well-deserved reputation.

"And you dance beautifully." The dimple in

44

Maelduin's chin deepened, a sign he was deep in thought. "Do you think I could learn to do that?"

Well, didn't *that* just open Terry's eyes wide. "Dance? You mean... dance? Ballet?"

"Yes." Maelduin touched his forehead to Terry's. "It seems... not unlike what I already know. Only more beautiful."

"It doesn't always involve swords." Terry felt ever so slightly drunk, the way he usually did when Maelduin's attention was focused on him like this. Which meant he probably wasn't making a lot of sense, the way he usually didn't under present circumstances.

Maelduin grinned. "I've seen enough of you in a tutu to have figured that out."

"I think you could be an amazing dancer. With the right teacher."

"That, I will have." Warm soft lips nuzzled Terry's throat, and Terry was sure he could feel a smile. "You, of course."

Terry blinked, his brain doing a great impression of Bambi on the ice. "You want *me* to teach *you*?"

Maelduin looked up, his blue topaz eyes exuding confusion. "Why not?"

"What could I possibly have to teach you? I've seen you dance the blades." Terry's chest ached, breathless with the memory; even knowing his lover had been fighting for his life, the art of the *scian-damhsa* had been poetry in the form of a Fae.

"But I want to learn your art. Your beauty." Maelduin's jaw set, in a way Terry already recognized, a window onto boss-level stubbornness. "And I want to learn from one who loves the art, and who loves me."

"I'm not..."

45

Wait. Wait just a goddamned minute.

Couldn't he, for once, try to see himself as Maelduin saw him?

Beautiful in my own right. Terry's eyes stung. *Loved for who I am.*

He'd learned a lot about Fae in a very short time, since the Pattern had brought him and Maelduin together; his *scair-anam* loved to talk almost as much as he loved to turn Terry's world upside down and inside out. As currently relevant, Terry had learned how Fae coveted beauty. *Coveted* as in *would do absolutely anything to possess,* and make a dragon breathing fire from on top of its hoard look like a rank amateur when it came to keeping it.

And a Fae thought his dancing was beautiful.

A Fae thought *he* was beautiful.

Terry let out a long, slow breath. "Sure. I'll teach you."

It was easy to answer Maelduin's radiant smile with one of his own, and to go boneless in his SoulShare's embrace. On the screen in front of him, his Romeo was bidding Juliet a passionate farewell, but Terry wasn't really seeing the doomed lovers; he saw, instead, a mirrored studio, and himself being held, lifted, spun, by the partner of his dreams. Himself was half hard, too, but that just made the fantasy more fun.

"Are you still here?" The breath of Maelduin's chuckle tickled his cheek.

"Sort of." Terry grinned. "I'm just realizing I'm going to have a hard time concentrating on ballet long enough to teach you anything."

"You don't say." Maelduin's hand 'accidentally' drifted over Terry's groin.

"Tease." Terry managed to uncross his eyes. "How did you ever manage to find a sword instructor who could keep his hands off you long enough to teach you to dance the blades?"

"I didn't, at least not always." Maelduin drew Terry closer. "But most of my teachers were... uninterested... in testing the curse of House Guaire."

Oh, shit. "I'm sorry, I didn't mean—"

A quick kiss cut off Terry's apology. "I know. And none of my teachers ever lasted long, in any event. I learned what they had to teach, and then I was done with them."

"Then how did you get so goddamned good at what you do? A thousand teachers?"

Maelduin snorted. At least, that's what Terry thought the sound was. "I was born a better *scian-damhsa* than most of the teachers in the Realm. The Guaire heritage is good for more than curses."

"That I can believe, having seen Tiernan in action."

"Exactly so." Maelduin laced his fingers through Terry's; that hand had felt amazing in his lap, but he liked it this way, too. "So when I was through with teachers, I went to a mage, and had a *comhrac-scátha* created."

Terry recognized the word. "That purple crystal you keep in the nightstand drawer?"

"Yes." Maelduin's thumb circled Terry's palm, doing a damned fine job of distracting all by itself. "It has a special channeling embedded in it, one that calls forth a mirror image of the one holding it, as long as the *comhrac-scátha* touches bare skin. It was my opponent, my trainer, my last teacher."

47

Terry's heart raced. "Does that mean if you take that stone out of the nightstand bare-handed, there are going to be two of you?"

Jesus, he loved Maelduin's belly-laugh. "For your sake, lover, I could wish it so."

He could feel himself reddening. "There's a reason I don't play poker."

More laughter, and a gentle kiss on his temple. "Before I came through the Pattern, I killed my mirror. One last test of my skill. If you want him back, I will have to have a new channeling put into the *comhrac-scátha*." A silver-blue gleam danced in Maelduin's eyes. "I might be able to persuade Conall, at that."

"I'm not sure I'd survive that." Terry bit his lip, thinking. Or trying not to. "But it might be worth a try. Someday."

"Count on it."

Chapter Six

Crangaol, Síofra

Footsteps in the hall woke Fiachra with a start. *Shit, did I really fall asleep playing Hellmaw's Revenge?* Yes. Yes, he had. Apparently the Fae metabolism wasn't fond of working swing shift.

He touched a button, and the screen went from frozen bleeding fire—or maybe frozen fiery blood, it was hard to tell—to black. *At least I didn't drool on the sofa cushions.*

The footsteps stopped, but not before sensitive Fae hearing made out the distinctive click of stiletto heels. *That's not Peri—it's Falcon.*

A shiver barely had time to race down Fiachra's spine and firmly lodge itself south of his waist before keys turned in the locks and the apartment door swung open. Falcon was humming softly, a smile touching perfectly painted plum lips. She was what other drag queens called a "fish"—a breathtakingly beautiful woman. needing little or no makeup to work what was, even to a Fae, pure magick.

The humming stopped, but not the smile, as Fiachra sat up. "I thought you were working tonight!"

"So did I. Russ had other ideas." Fiachra marveled at the evenness of his voice.

"He did us both a favor, then." Falcon lowered one eyelid a fraction of an inch, in the sexiest wink since the invention of sexy. "Let me go slip into something more comfortable—"

"Wait." Fiachra caught his partner's hand, as Falcon made her way past the sofa.

Dark brows drew together; Peri bleached his midnight hair, but never his brows, because Falcon's hair was always a perfect ebony waterfall and needed eyebrows to match. "Is something wrong?"

"No, nothing." Fiachra could hear his heartbeat pounding in his ears, like wind-driven waves, almost loud enough to drown out the click of five-inch heels against the hardwood floor as he watched Falcon walk around him, tethered by the hand-holding. "I just want to look at you."

Falcon blushed; she didn't let go of Fiachra's hand, but she still managed to make something of a fuss over the rearrangement of her tight skirt as she settled on the sofa next to him, enough of one that she had to break eye contact to make sure the slit was just so. Which was telling—Falcon was the most direct person Fiachra had ever met, with a keen and level gaze that took no shit from anyone.

Falcon was Peri's armor. Fiachra had managed to figure that out during the course of a long, mutually pleasurable, mostly drunken night not long after he had gotten his body back: Falcon kept pain away from a wounded human who spent most of his time as other humans' rental property.

There was just one small problem. Fiachra loved the wounded human. All of him. Falcon as much as Peri. And for Fiachra, as for most Fae, comparatively newly-discovered love was inextricably bound up with that most exquisite Fae art form, lust.

Fiachra had no idea how one went about seducing a human in armor—though no doubt Cuinn could tell him, if he were even slightly inclined to ask.

But he wasn't. He was just going to have to figure it out for himself.

* * *

Peri knew the look in Fiachra's eyes. Funny how it had been the same look when those eyes were blue as arctic ice—he liked it better now, when Fiachra's eyes were even darker brown than his own, but he'd know the look anywhere.

And right now, that look was a complication he wasn't sure he was ready to handle. Not when it was directed at Falcon.

"Let me go change, *aisuruhito*—my feet are killing me." Not quite true; stiletto heels were like bedroom slippers to him, but if he could get out of Falcon's shoes, he could also get out of the rest of her, and be open to what his *scair-anam* so obviously wanted. What he wanted, himself, more than just about anything.

"Please stay."

That got Peri's attention. His Fae was quieter than most, less...well, arrogant. But as a general rule, 'please' wasn't a word any human usually heard from any Fae. Except under certain circumstances, which usually involved being horizontal. Or against a wall. Or in a swing—

Focus. Fool of a Took.

"Here, let me." Without letting go of Falcon's

hand, Fiachra slid his other hand down her silk-stockinged calf and slipped off one silver shoe, then the other. His thumbs whispered against the silk sheathing Falcon's insteps.

"Will you let me in?" The whisper came to Peri in the language of touch the two of them shared—the language they'd found when words had threatened to betray them both. *"Will you let me love the lady of my heart, as well as its lord?"*

Peri couldn't breathe. He'd thought about it—who wouldn't?—about the possibility that Fiachra might want his other side. All that thinking, though, and he still wasn't sure what he thought.

He leaned forward, intending to catch Fiachra's hands in his own, but Falcon's figure-hugging fuchsia silk didn't have enough give. Fiachra, as usual, knew what he wanted, and reached up instead, to clasp Peri's hands.

"You're scared."

"No. Yes." Peri hung his head, letting Falcon's glossy black hair curtain his face. "Hell if I know."

Gentle fingers brushed hair back from his cheek, traced the line of his cheekbone. "I think I understand. The human kind of masquerade isn't a Fae thing, but I get it—

Peri stiffened. "Is that what you think Falcon is? A costume?" The thought stung.

The length of the silence that followed was unusual. In Peri's experience, Fae were almost never at a loss for words, appropriate or otherwise.

"That was the first word I thought of, yes." Fiachra brushed his lips over Peri's forehead. "I thought I got it—got Falcon, what she is to you—

when you told me where she came from. How she was born. But I must have misunderstood."

Every once in a while, Peri realized just how lucky he was. He had a Fae who was willing to admit he was wrong. Occasionally.

"I... probably didn't explain it all that well." Peri sighed deeply, and felt tension go out of him with the expelled breath. "Wasn't that the night I introduced you to sake?"

"I think it was."

God, Fiachra had a sexy smile. It was tempting to lose himself in it, forget about the explanation his SoulShare wanted and deserved. After all, Peri really didn't need to be any more naked than he was about to be with his Fae in a couple of minutes.

Except that he did.

Peri curled his fingers—Falcon's slender, elegant fingers—around Fiachra's hand. "I'm not sure how to explain Falcon. There have been times when she's more me than I am."

"How so?"

There were times when Peri could tell Fiachra was using his truthsight. Like now. Not because he thought Peri was lying, but because he truly wanted, needed, to understand.

"You know how I felt after Yoshi died."

Fiachra nodded. In one of the many bizarre not-coincidences that marked SoulShare relationships, it turned out that Fiachra had been assigned for a while to the investigation of the murder of Peri's best friend since childhood. "You felt guilty. For being the one who lived."

'Guilt' was another one of those ideas most Fae only had any acquaintance with through their human *scair-anaim*. Peri supposed a former Homicide detective understood it a little better than most other Fae. "Yeah. And there was a part of me that was seriously anxious to get me killed because of it."

"I know that."

"Falcon is... the part of me that didn't get caught up in the guilt. Or at least not in the crazy aspects of it." He bit his lip, thinking—though he was careful not to mess up Falcon's perfect lip paint. "Falcon is the part of me I never had to let anyone touch, just because they paid me. The part of me that kept the right to say no."

Fiachra went several shades paler than his usual mahogany. "And here I want to..."

"What?" He'd never seen his Fae so... apprehensive? Uncertain?

"Fuck." Fiachra grimaced. "You know the Fae reputation for dicking around with humans. Taking what pleases us. Sometimes returning pleasure for pleasure, when it suits us. Sometimes not. Sometimes stealing a human from his own world, or hers, and returning them a hundred years too late, or too early—and enjoying the confusion, the heartbreak, as much as the sex."

"Yes, I've read the stories. I went through such a Yeats period..."

"I'm not talking about stories, I'm talking about the truth." Fiachra was talking past Peri, in an odd way, almost as if he were hoping Peri wouldn't connect the words with the Fae speaking them. "Fae can't love, or don't, or won't. Even empathy doesn't matter to most of us. Your consent, or Falcon's, wouldn't matter a damn to the Fae I was when you met me. If I wanted Falcon, she'd be mine. She'd even think it was her own idea."

"The Fae you were—if you ever were—would never have said any of that." Peri was surprised at how steady his voice was. So was Fiachra, if his wide eyes were any indication. "And you turned away from me, back then, when you knew I wasn't sure of you. When you could have had exactly what you wanted with a word, and you knew it."

"I..."

Peri leaned over and brushed Falcon's parted lips across Fiachra's. "You may touch, *aisuruhito*. You, and you only."

Jesus, his eyes... faceted smoky quartz, hunger as pure as a laser and as unapologetic as... as a Fae. Peri felt sweat prickling his forehead; his hand trembled, until he clutched it tighter around Fiachra's.

"You're sure?" Fiachra lifted Peri's hand— Falcon's, actually, those were her silver-gilt nails flashing in the light from the side table—and kissed the back of it. "Your first time would be a poor occasion to fuck up this whole consent thing."

"It's not—"

Yes. Yes, it is. Falcon was quite possibly the most virginal virgin ever.

Fiachra nodded, as if he were reading Falcon's thoughts. "So tell me you're sure."

"I am." Peri took a deep, unsteady breath. "Just... let me stay Falcon. As much as I can, anyway."

His Fae's smile smoldered. "You *are* Falcon. That's why I need you."

Fiachra had never kissed Peri as gently as he now kissed Falcon. Yet there was a profound hunger in his tenderness, as intense as any Peri had ever experienced, maybe more so. And Fiachra's hands, cupping shoulders left bare by the sequined gown, whispering of hidden longings freed at last—had he ever caressed Peri so gently?

No. Peri closed his eyes briefly, long dark lashes brushing his cheekbones. *No. This can't work, this won't work, if I keep comparing how he acts toward Peri and how he acts toward Falcon. I'll end up jealous of myself, wondering which of me he loves better. I need to just be here, now.*

And when he opened his eyes, Peri let go of Peri, and slipped wholly into Falcon. Falcon, whose whole identity was She Who Was Never Touched, wanted the Fae who loved her.

Falcon deserved her happiness.

* * *

Before meeting Peri, Fiachra's rounds in the *rincdaonna*, the human dance, had generally been short and sweet, at least by Fae standards. Peri had changed all that, needless to say.

Falcon...

At least an hour had gone by, not counting the time it had taken to get Falcon out of her skin-hugging silk wrappings. Neither one of them had come yet. Fiachra didn't care. He was pretty sure Falcon didn't either.

He'd wanted Falcon since his first sight of her. He'd had the same reaction to Peri, an instantaneous hard-on and a need that went far beyond the physical. And he loved Peri, in a way no unSoulShared Fae was ever going to understand and he wasn't really sure he understood himself most of the time. Which meant he loved Falcon. As far as he was concerned, that was a no-brainer. And having no brain was something he was rapidly turning into an expert in.

Peri. Falcon. The one he wanted to pleasure, and to receive pleasure from. No matter what was between her legs. His legs.

"Ohmygod, ohmygod..." Falcon's eyes were wide, her breathing sharp and shallow, her words synchronized with the abrupt jerks of her hips.

Peri never swore during sex—not that way. Didn't move that way. Yet Fiachra would have known his lover anywhere, even blindfolded. Or blinded.

Falcon was... himself. Just as Peri was herself.

Falcon's nails dug deep into his ass, and Fiachra officially ran out of patience and philosophy. In fact, he decided, he was going to blow completely sky fucking high in about ten seconds if he didn't hear someone screaming in the kind of pleasure only a Fae and his *scair-anam* would ever know.

"Hold on to something," he growled. "Preferably me."

Fiachra thought Falcon tried to laugh. But what started out as a breathless laugh ended up something else entirely as he arched his back and pinned their cocks together between their bodies.

He wanted to be inside her, yes. But giving Falcon what she wanted was even better than getting what he wanted. Remembering just in time his promise to keep her covered, he braced himself on his elbows and thrust hard, his cock gliding between their bodies. And when his cock slid along Falcon's, it was... fuck.

It was like an electric shock would feel, if an electric shock felt good. Magick, amplifying his pleasure, and Falcon's, and letting him feel both at once.

She was feeling it too. Her eyes were wide, dark wells of need and wonder. She moved with him, undulating, clasping him tighter with legs and arms and hands. "Yes—oh God yes—oh, oh, OH—"

Fiachra hunched over Falcon and froze, clenching his teeth against a shout as his cock went rigid—he wanted to hear Falcon—and her cry, liquid and shuddering, pushed him, pushed them both, over the edge. Fiachra couldn't breathe, didn't care, pistoned against Falcon, her seed enough to slick them both.

Yes... just yes. Perfection.

"Damn." Falcon giggled, her head falling back onto the arm of the sofa. And somehow, there was a hint of Peri in that giggle. "I think I just broke—" Her hands left off their fierce grip on Fiachra's ass, and Fiachra felt her arms moving. "Three nails. Clean off."

Fiachra's smile started at the end of his treasure trail and worked its way up. "That means you have seven to go."

* * *

Orlando, Florida

The scent of death spilled from the door along with the driving, pounding music. So much death, so much pain, enough to sate then all ten times over.

Yet it was all wrong. There was scent, but no substance. None of the power, none of the sustenance they craved.

A promise, nothing more.

The male grumbled inside their head. *Another waste of magick. No one's dead, no one's dying, and in case you haven't been paying attention, so far seven of these idiots have assumed you're a blind drunk drag queen. And they think you're overdoing the goth.*

"Whatever goth is." The female was feeling petulant. Petulant and hungry. They had taken form on a sidewalk, next to the wall of what was obviously a busy nightclub; how they had not been seen while doing so, or accosted before they woke, she could not imagine. How they were to take the next step on their journey was likewise beyond her ken at the moment.

Things should quiet down by sunrise, just like at Purgatory. Somehow, the male was summoning enough energy to leer. She despised him. *You just lie there and let the pretty boys ogle you until then.*

A voice floated out the door over the music, over the false promise of death.

"*La noche es joven, y todos somos hermosos aquí, ¡bienvenidos a* Pulse!"

Chapter Seven

"Whose brilliant idea was it to throw this party so close to the great nexus?" Fiachra looked as if he were trying to stare through the sprung wooden floor, and the concrete under it, and the nightclub under that, and finally the elemental Stone separating everything above it from the nexus chamber.

"Mine, in consultation with my *draoi ríoga*, who says it ought to be safe so long as no one gets into a magickal pissing contest," Rian replied, mildly enough. "It's a bit more comfortable for most of us than the bottom of the Pool in Central Park, none of the basements with wellsprings were large enough for the lot of us, and the laundry room at the Colchester just didn't seem like quite the place for Conclave, no offense to Lochlann or Garrett intended."

Bryce cleared his throat. It sounded like it hurt. "And we need to make plans next to a wellspring because...?" Setanta nuzzled the palm of his human master's hand, where it rested in his lap, and whined softly, tail thumping the side of Bryce's leg and the floor indiscriminately.

This time Conall answered. "Because we want the *daragin* and the Gille Dubh to be able to hear us. Chances are, we aren't going to have the firepower to do everything that needs to be done on our own, and if they have any ideas, I for one would very much like to hear them."

Fiachra and Terry shifted uneasily; the dark Fae in particular made a point of not looking at the silver-blue glow of the newest wellspring. And Cuinn felt rather like he was trying to swallow a golf ball. Which, under other circumstances, wasn't necessarily a sensation he disliked, but these weren't other circumstances.

Rian reached for his consort's hand. "Sorry, *mo chroí*. It's not going to be comfortable for you, I know. But if discomfort is the worst any of us knows by the time this is all over, I'm going to call it a fecking miracle."

"I'm not going to argue with you." Cuinn's smile was a wan imitation of itself. "I don't think the arguing would be quite the sport it generally is, and the mood's all wrong for me to convince you I'm right in the usual way."

A soft snort came from Conall's direction. "This from the Fae who calls me a horndog."

"*Se an'agean flua, a'deir n'abhann, tú—*"

A slight tightening of Rian's grip on his hand cut Cuinn off, very effectively, before his retort could get much beyond "'The ocean is wet, says the river.'" If his Prince was acting Princely, the rubber was about to hit the road, and it probably behooved him to shut the fuck up.

Everyone else seemed to get the message, too; the room went stiller than any room with more than one Fae in it ever got.

"That's well." Rian took a deep breath, let it out

slowly—and the Belfast street kid with long, long legs stretched out in front of him as he sat on a folding chair in the middle of a dance studio so newly finished the paint was barely dry was a Prince Royal from his forelock to the tips of his sneakered toes. "Conall, if you'd be so good as to tell the others what you told me night before last?"

The ginger mage cleared his throat. "Anybody here need a *very* quick and dirty Pattern 101 course, before I get technical?"

Terry, Lucien and Mac all perked up visibly at the suggestion. They didn't speak, but they didn't need to.

"Right, then. The Pattern and the great nexus are basically the wave and the water of the same sea, the Pattern in the Realm and the great nexus about 50 feet under our feet. The Pattern is a kind of channeling no one's done since the days of the Loremasters, a representation of everyplace in the Realm, real enough that what's done to it is done to all of the Realm. It's shot through with the essences of all the Loremasters who made it through the last battle with the *Marfach*, and it was locked down to keep said *Marfach* from touching any of the magick in the Realm. Which basically slammed the door in its then-incorporeal face."

Cuinn wondered just how long a mage would keep talking about magick if one let him.

"The thing is, when the Pattern was locked down, all the living magick in the Realm and the human world had to be on the Realm side, but the ley energy that could become more living magick as needed couldn't be separated from the human world and had to be left over here. Following me so far?"

The three humans nodded—not just them, Cuinn noted, but all the rest of the humans, and even a couple of the Fae. Setanta, too. *That dog is smart enough to worry me. A little...*

"Good. So the Loremasters realized that their solution to the *Marfach* problem couldn't be permanent. Sooner or later, the ley energy was going to have to be reintroduced to the Realm. Their idea of a solution was to leave a hole in the Pattern, one that our slightly oversexed Loremaster here was expected to fill eventually, and turn himself into a living conduit for the ley energy. Only problem was, no one thought to tell him, or his *scair-anam*, what the plan was. And when we found out Cuinn was destined to be a not-very-glorified pipeline, we all decided, fuck that, we're going to do it our own way. Which we did; we blasted a new hole through from the nexus side and bound the energy of the great nexus into it."

Cuinn was trying not to lay it on too thick, but there were some openings a Fae had to take. "Which didn't meet the Pattern manufacturer's specifications. Totally fucked the warranty, in fact."

"Do you mind?"

"Somebody has to hurry you up." Cuinn elaborately smothered a yawn. "The bogeyman's getting closer by the minute, you know."

The look Conall shot Cuinn reminded him of a fusillade of Tiernan's crystal hand-darts—the youngster was too good an actor by half. "As you wish. Our jury-rigged solution saved our Loremaster's pert ass, but it's also the source of our present difficulty." His apple-green gaze now swept the room, gathering in everyone. Even the blind dog. "Ley energy is being forced into the

Realm in a way it wasn't meant to be. I'm sure the Loremasters meant well when they designed the system, but it turns out it doesn't work to have just one entry point into the Realm for all the ley energy of this world. And the Realm's pushing back—living magick is being forced back through the wellsprings, so hard it's becoming untethered from the wellsprings."

"I take it that's a bad thing." Kevin gave the impression that he wasn't listening to his own words, or Conall's for that matter; his attention was all on his *scair-anam.*

"You take correctly." The frown line between the mage's brows said that he, too, was picking up on Kevin's odd vibe. "Living magick needs to be channeled, by a Fae or some other of the *Tirr Brai,* or it isn't safe to be around."

Kevin didn't seem to notice anyone else noticing him. "So channel it."

"It doesn't quite work that way." Conall plowed a hand through his hair, until it looked like a four-alarm fire. "Once the magick's freed, it stays freed."

Rian leaned forward, resting his elbows on his knees, steepling his long slender fingers in front of his nose and resting his chin on his thumbs. Winglike brows drawn together, he could have sat for a portrait of Contemplation. One would never guess that Cuinn himself, Conall, and the young Prince had been up until the wee small hours of the morning had given way to larger ones, talking their predicament into the ground.

"So, *draoi ríoga.*" Rian looked up at Conall, without moving anything but his eyes. "The ley energy's wrecking the Realm. The living magick from the Realm is a danger to the human world. And, not to put too fine a point on things, there's evil embodied and what's left of a feckin' homicidal zombie coming for us. What are we to do?"

Damn, he's good. The Prince Royal gave no sign he knew the answer to the question he'd just put — that this whole harrier-and-hawk show had been carefully choreographed. It was as if Rian waited along with his fractious subjects for the mage's response, and would accept it as one of them. Hopefully stopping a typical Fae free-for-all before it could start.

"We have to do a hard reset. The worlds have to go back to the way they were before the Sundering— coexisting. After all this time, they'll likely be warped slightly out of phase, but that's just as well."

"What about the Pattern?" Josh was the only human who had actually been to the Realm since the Sundering, other than the luckless ones Cuinn had occasionally spirited away from the world they knew for a round or two of the *rinc-daonna*. "The Loremasters won't be able to guard the Realm under those circumstances."

"No, they won't, and we can't afford to let them try. The Pattern will have to come down."

* * *

Rian had to settle what he still thought of as his "Royal face" in place quite firmly, to keep from laughing out loud—or at least indulging in a self-satisfied grin—at the expression on Cuinn's face, as those present gaped at his consort as if he'd taken leave of all his senses at once. Well, most of those present. Rian wasn't entirely certain about the dog's feelings on the matter.

You can forget about the poker face, Your Regalness. I heard that snicker.

Rian had been a choirboy, once, back when he still thought he was human. The expression of baffled innocence still stood him in good stead every now and again. *I haven't a clue what you're on about, beloved consort.*

Get stuffed. In fact, wait till we're done here and I'll do it for you.

Fiachra in particular looked very much like a Fae who had something to say, and was searching for a way to say it that might let him survive the speaking.

"You may as well out with it, Detective. He'll not call you out in the audience chamber." When Rian had been informed he was allowed—but not required—to limit intra-Fae mayhem in his presence, he'd leaped at the opportunity. His Demesne was small enough as it was.

"He won't need to, if he's planning on getting all of us killed at once." Fiachra's arm tightened around Peri's slender shoulders. "We don't know if the Pattern can be unmade, and we *do* know the *Marfach* can't be killed. And if we're seriously considering opening the way back to the Realm, we have no choice but to kill it."

"Oh, the Pattern can be unmade." Cuinn's voice was bland, but Rian could hear the tension his *scairanam* thought he was hiding. "My fellow Loremasters were very clear about that. As clear as Fae have ever been, anyway."

Fiachra cocked a brow at Cuinn. "Why hasn't the *Marfach* done it, then? Or at least tried?"

"Maybe it has." Cuinn could give at least as good as he got in the eyebrow department, not that Fiachra appeared put off by it in the slightest. "But it can't, because I'm the only one who can."

And didn't *that* just center everyone's attention marvelously?

"How do you figure that?"

Rian genuinely couldn't read Fiachra's mood, not a bit. The dark Fae might be curious, he might be stunned, he might be pissed to the wide. And Rian wasn't comfortable with any of those possibilities, most especially the last. "Conall, could I trouble you to finish your part of the tale, before my consort hijacks it completely?"

"Hijack" my ass—

Later. I promise. Cross my heart.

Conall looked as if he could hear every word of the interior dialogue. But the only comment he allowed himself was a slight roll of his bright green eyes. "As you wish, Highness." His glance at Fiachra wasn't quite an apology, but hopefully it would do for one, for a few minutes at least. "There isn't much more to tell. The Pattern's acting to pressurize the flow of ley energy into the Realm, and the flow of living magick back out of it. Think of putting your thumb mostly over the end of a garden hose."

"I swear that was an accident," Josh muttered.

Everyone laughed—even the normally dour Bryce—and Rian silently blessed the brightly-inked human. Josh might not know what was going on, but he had his *scair-anam*'s back regardless.

"So you say." Conall grinned at his partner, making it obvious why a three-centuries-old mage still got carded in every bar in Washington, D.C. and New York City. "We can discuss that later, though. For now... well, there are technical terms that are more precise and less colorful, but think of the great nexus as acting like a log jam in a spring flood, except no one knows where the key log is or what will happen if it moves. And the Pattern's slowly giving way from the Realm side—we know that from Brodulein—resulting in the return of living magick, under enough pressure to untether it."

Terry frowned, in a thoughtful sort of way. "So... you think the only way to solve all those problems is to take down the Pattern."

It was interesting, watching Terry—and Mac, and Lucien—coming to terms with the fact that a great many of the men they'd known for years weren't human. Rian sympathized. It hadn't been easy adjusting to not being human himself, after a lifetime of believing himself such.

"That's part of the answer, yes." Conall raked his fingers through his ginger hair, putting it back to rights—the Fae looked more Irish than Rian himself did, but then Rian wasn't exactly Irish either. "The other part requires killing the *Marfach*, probably at the same time. We don't dare take the Pattern down first, since we know the *Marfach*'s coming for the nexus." The tone of Conall's voice, and the way he glanced at Bryce, made the statement more of a question.

"Damn right it is." Bryce's voice was stretched tight, but he seemed to take comfort from Lasair's arm round his shoulders and the pup curled in his lap. "It feels like it's Fading here in increments, and it needs time to rest up between Fades. Speaking of which, how is it Fading at all? — I thought that was just a Fae thing."

"Not exactly." Fae mages were the closest things the race had to historians, given the nature of their studies; Fae tended not to be overcurious about their own origins, in the same way they saw no need for religion. "Fade-hounds can do it, obviously—"

Setanta's tail thumped against the floor in enthusiastic agreement.

Conall, bless him, didn't turn pale, which would have been a Fae mage's entirely normal reaction to an apex magickal predator, even an adorable puppy. "And some other creatures of the Realm can, too. So it's not a complete surprise if the *Marfach*'s figured out how to do it as well. A pain in the ass, sure, but what's one more of those among friends?"

"One piece still isn't fitting." It was startling to hear Lucien speak; he'd been so quiet until now, he might as well have been a short burly bald statue. "A human is damned lucky to survive a Fade, am I right?"

Most around the room nodded; Kevin shuddered, and Rian winced in sympathy.

"And the monster's Fading every day?"

"Almost. Close enough." Bryce's reply was slightly muffled, as close attention was being paid to his face by a Fade-hound's tongue.

"So what's happened to Janek, the *osti d'épais de marde*?"

The silence stretched out.

Tiernan cleared his throat. "If he's dead, the only regret I have is that I wasn't the one to do it. I had such plans..."

"Don't start regretting just yet—Setanta, will you for God's sake *sit*?"

Bryce's grin made a liar of his rebuke, and the pup was deterred from his face-washing not at all.

"*Tréan-cú...*" There was warning in Lasair's

voice, but Setanta cared as much for that as he had for Bryce's chiding.

Rian clucked softly, the way his mother so often had at his father when his father had gone off on some tale he'd had from his granda instead of finishing the telling of whatever story it was she'd asked him for to quiet their restive child. "Did you have something to tell us of the late unlamented Janek O'Halloran, Bryce?"

"Um. Yeah." Bryce circled Setanta's muzzle with two fingers. "Maybe. I'm still feeling resonance from the Fades. Pain, that is. Would the *Marfach* be feeling pain from Fading if Janek—its meat wagon—is completely dead?"

The utter silence was itself a response, one Rian didn't much care for.

Finally, Cuinn cleared his throat. "There's way too fucking much we don't know. Including the answer to that question."

Peri stirred, from where he was nestled in the curve of Fiachra's arm. "Maybe we're better off if he isn't dead."

Light winked off the gold ring in Tiernan's eyebrow. "How so?—given that carrying my head around by the hair is Janek's peculiar obsession?"

"I hadn't thought of it that way." Peri's hand settled gently over Fiachra's, where it rested on his arm, and for a moment Rian simply stared, delighting in the pattern of light skin and dark. "But if we have to kill it, won't that be easier if at least some of what makes it up is human?"

"Point taken."

Judging from the thundercloud that had taken up

residence over Kevin's dark brows, Tiernan hadn't spoken for his SoulShare. Still, Peri's words offered at least a hint of a way out of the labyrinth they had to navigate. It was up to the Prince Royal to chivvy his subjects down that road, as far as he might.

"We need to plan, gentleFae and *scair-anaim*. As much as Fae can, and accounting for the very real possibility we'll be taken by surprise when the moment arrives."

The ensuing silence was different from the one that had gone before, a thoughtful one. Mostly.

"It'll come down to blades in the end." It was Maelduin who spoke, but his smile and Tiernan's were twins of each other. "Unbinding the Pattern will take all the free magick available, leaving precious little for any fight against the *Marfach*. Not to mention that trying to kill the *Marfach* with magic at the nexus would be like..."

Tiernan picked up the argument without missing a beat. "Like Fourth of July and Guy Fawkes and probably Hiroshima all at once. And it's all going to go down at the nexus, because that's where it's heading. So, blades."

Rian went briefly slack-jawed at sight of the narrow-eyed glare Kevin turned on his *scair-anam*. "If you think you're going to take on the monster that nearly killed your entire race with nothing but the Stone in the hand you have as a souvenir of the last time you went up against it, please explain to me where you plan to sleep between now and then that doesn't involve our bedroom."

Jesus, Mary, and Joseph, it's going to be a long fecking night...

71

* * *

Charleston, South Carolina

Fuck it, the next time I'm doing the gročamchkha *Fading.*

"Be my guest." Hunger had dimmed to a dull ache in the pit of the female's stomach, a sensation that reminded her too much for her liking of long centuries subsisting on nearly inedible ley energy. Even the scent of the false promise—present here as it had been at the nightclub, less profligate but more intense—failed to stir her hunger from ember to flame.

At least this time they were alone, in a cool space filled with tables and chairs, sunlight slanting in through narrow windows high up in the walls and lighting a bright streak along a white tile floor. At the far end of the room stood what something—probably some dead whispered echo of Meat's memory—recognized as a simple altar.

And the promise of death everywhere, taunting her. Taunting all of them.

A voice came to them faintly, through walls and ceiling, a man's rich voice. "All right, brothers and sisters, I know y'all are ready to go home, and so am I, but let's raise up our voices just one more time."

A pause followed, during which the female almost lost interest, distracted by the siren call of future deaths. But then there was music. Meat had once shuffled past the open doors of a church, early in their use of him, and had stopped to listen to something similar, refusing to move on even when goaded. A 'pipe organ,' he had called it.

The female thought she understood, now, why Meat had been so reluctant to leave. Something about this music caught her up, nearly making her forget her hunger.

Then the singing started, many voices in harmony.

O Mary, don't you weep, don't you mourn
O Mary, don't you weep, don't you mourn
Pharaoh's army got drowned
O Mary, don't you weep

Drowned. The male shuddered. *Fuck that noise until it bleeds.*

For once, the female completely agreed with the male.

Some of these mornings bright and fair
Take my wings and cleave the air
Pharaoh's army got drowned
O Mary, don't you weep

"You were saying you wanted to Fade us?"
I can hardly do worse than this, now, can I?

Chapter Eight

Gastiór, Laoc, Caomhnór

"It's beautiful."

What was beautiful, in Lucien's opinion, was the light in his Fae husband's eyes as he studied the huge tank built into one wall of what was going to be the new Purgatory dance floor. Other clubs had cages for dancers; one the three of them had found in New York had glass-walled shower stalls. Purgatory was going to have the biggest *maudite* fish tank anyone had ever seen.

Complete with naked mermen. One of whom— because *le bon Dieu* apparently had a perverse sense of humor—was going to be Lucien de Winter.

Arms went around Lucien from behind, and a chin rested on his shoulder; Lucien didn't need to turn, or even to look down and see the "Semper Fi" tattooed on one forearm to recognize Mac. "Ready to take the plunge, Fuzzball?"

Lucien grunted. "I hope the filters in this thing are up to spec. You know how I shed."

A flash of white reflected in the glass of the tank was Rhoann's grin. "Perhaps we should put a tail on you."

"If the tail didn't have hair, no one would believe it was mine." Lucien couldn't stay grumpy, though, not when Rhoann teased him. "But I think the two of you, not to mention our boss, are out of your minds, if you think our guests are going to be turned on watching me doing underwater barrel rolls."

Rhoann left off studying the tank fittings and took Lucien's hands, running his thumbs lightly over knuckles dusted with short dark curly hair; his slight worried frown was one of the sweetest things Lucien had ever seen. "How could they not be, *laród-ar-Fuzz?*"

Lucien found himself having to swallow an unexpected lump in his throat before he could answer. "I love you, too."

Mac leaned around and kissed the side of Lucien's neck. "He beat me to it. And I'm not even going to tell you how many guys used to come up to the bar and ask me why the bouncer wasn't part of the floor show."

Lucien craned his neck, partly to plant a kiss of his own on Mac and partly to glance at the new bar, the one the workmen had just finished installing last week, to replace the one Mac had presided over ever since Tiernan bought the place. The curved expanse, now taking up the whole back wall of one level of the club instead of being shoehorned into a corner, looked pretty much the same as it always had, from where Lucien stood. But no one had been able to figure out how to replicate the show-stopping feature of the original, the hellish flames dancing under the glass bar top, that seemed to go down and down into an infinite depth. Conall thought he might be able to do it with magick, or maybe Rian could, but nobody wanted to fuck around with magick of any kind near the great nexus, not with the way it and its companion wellspring were acting right now. Good thing he and his husbands had decided to try out the famed nexus chamber when they had—a half-Royal Fae in the throes of erotic overload was the kind of thing guaranteed to short out the entire wellspring network right now.

The fact that their new-found underground garden of delights was now off limits seriously pissed Lucien off. It wasn't forever, though. The three of them could get back to happy business just as soon as they figured out how to kill the monster who had left him for dead behind the bar back in August.

Can't happen soon enough for me. Lucien was a peaceable sort—as peaceable as a nightclub bouncer built like a hairy fire hydrant and married to an only-sort-of-ex-Marine could be, anyway—but he was looking forward to getting his hands around whatever was left of Janek O'Halloran's throat and getting creative.

"I recognize that look." Mac nipped at the top of Lucien's ear.

"What look?" Lucien blinked. "And I could have sworn you're standing behind me."

"You reflect in the tank." Mac's chuckle rumbled against Lucien's back. "At least for now—once you've been for a swim after we open, the glass is going to have... uh, palm-prints... all over it."

Lucien couldn't help snorting. "I repeat, what look?"

Rhoann wrapped his arms around both humans. He could do that—Mac was a good head taller than Lucien, but their Fae had Mac beat by a good four or five inches, and he had arms to match his height. "The look you wore through most of the *bás i'gcuine* last night."

The *Faen* words Rhoann had originally translated for them as "war council" turned out to have meant something closer to "fore-memory of death." The intent of the Demesne of Purgatory had been, more or less, to create the memory of the *Marfach*'s death before it happened. And, like pretty much everything asking Fae to behave in an organized manner, it had gone south from the moment Rian tried calling the group to order. It hadn't helped that Fae who learned English magickally thought the word "brainstorming" was almost as funny as horseradish. Which *was* actually pretty damn funny, once Maelduin had explained it to him.

There had been some great opportunities for glowering, though. Lucien supposed that was the "look" his husbands were on about. "I didn't notice either one of you looking disappointed at the thought of killing the *d'épais de marde*," he grumbled.

"Hell, no." Lucien thought he could feel Mac's jaw clench, where his husband's chin rested on top of his head. "But I'd feel a lot better right now if anyone had had any useful ideas."

"It helps to know that it fears water." There was a smile in Rhoann's voice, one very different from his usual sexy innocence. "I should be able to do something with that."

It hadn't been all that long ago that Lucien had been terrified of water. And trapped in a fuck-ton of it, reliving not-quite-random memories with the *Marfach* on his ass. It was bizarre beyond belief that he was now sharing a soul with a part-time merman, and getting ready to perform as one himself.

And that wasn't even close to being the strangest thing that had happened to him since August.

"Just between you, me, Fuzzball, and the four walls, I think water may be the best chance we have."

Rhoann tilted his head, thinking; when he did that, his crest of blond hair always made Lucien think of a cockatoo. "How does having water between us and the walls help?"

Mac groaned good-naturedly and smacked Rhoann's ass.

"Oh. I am being too literal-minded again." Rhoann rested his chin on the side of Lucien's head Mac wasn't occupying. Lucien was beginning to feel squashed. Squashed between his husbands was one of his favorite feelings, though.

"Don't ever change." A kiss happened somewhere where Lucien couldn't see it. "Seriously, though, I don't think our mages and our blade-dancers have thought this one through. They're still thinking in terms of taking on the *Marfach* here, on this side of the Pattern."

Lucien held back a groan of his own. That particular argument had gone on nearly till sunrise, and parts of it had probably continued past then—neither Kevin nor Terry had been happy with their respective partners' bloody-minded enthusiasm for the idea of taking turns vivisecting the monster, and while Josh had mostly looked resigned to what the royal mage and the Loremaster had concocted, their Prince had obviously been saving a few choice words for Cuinn.

Still... "It's not like we have much a of a choice. We can't even get a skinny whisper through the nexus, we sure as hell aren't going to be able to fit a 6'6" zombie through it."

He could feel Mac shaking his head. "Sometimes the ground dictates your tactics. But sometimes you can't afford to let it."

Lucien shrugged, mostly because he liked the way it felt. "You're the soldier. But I don't think you're going to get Tiernan and Maelduin to listen to you." *Or me*, he nearly added. But that wouldn't help anything. And even Lucien knew it was ridiculous for him to think he had a chance, one on one against the *Marfach*. His protective instincts—the gift of his Fae soul, he'd been told—didn't give a shit about his chances, though. He just wanted to take the *tabarnak de câlisse* down.

"I know." Mac's sigh stirred the curly hairs on the side of Lucien's neck. "But if we can herd the *Marfach* through the nexus without having to get close enough for it to get at any of us, nobody has to risk getting killed, or worse."

Or worse being one of those ideas it would have been impossible for Lucien to get his head around before August. Not anymore, though. And he would be fucked with a chainsaw before he let *or worse* happen to either of his husbands. The monster had caught him flat-footed once before. It wasn't going to do it again.

A kiss on the top of his head startled Lucien; he looked up into cut-topaz eyes and a gentle smile. "My *laród-ar*-Fuzz is troubled."

Lucien rested his head against Rhoann's chest. He was still getting used to the idea of letting somebody else be the strong one—he'd been tight with a Marine since the mid-'70s, but he'd had to hold that Marine up through some incredibly shitty times, and having someone else doing the same thing for him was still new. "Your Fuzzball just wants to put an end to that shitbag. And probably can't."

It didn't surprise him that Rhoann had known where his head was at. He and Mac had always seemed to have that knack with each other, and when the third part of their shared soul had arrived from the Realm, he'd slipped right into that communion like he'd always been there.

And Rhoann wasn't the only one who could head-hop. Clear as day, Lucien could sense the pull the huge water tank behind them had on his Fae husband. "How long has it been since you've been able to sleep in water?"

"Are we counting the time in the bathtub?"

Mac nearly choked, and Lucien only just managed to turn a guffaw into a cough. "That was just maybe the worst idea any of us ever had." Watching Rhoann trying to curl up in the tub in their apartment had been like... well, watching John Cleese trying to get comfortable on top of a coffee table. "No, we're not counting the time in the bathtub."

"Nearly two weeks, then." Rhoann grimaced. "Since the wellsprings became unstable, including the one under the Pool."

Mac rested his hands on Rhoann's shoulders. "That's not good."

Rhoann laughed softly. "Neither is what happens to our wellspring when the three of us are together there. And I have no wish to sleep alone."

"You don't have to." Lucien twisted around to look down into the cock pit. The black leather playground famed in song and story was going to be reborn in the new Purgatory—only this time, its protection from D.C.'s finest was going to rely less on Lucien's sixth sense and Fiachra's truthsight, and more on a state-of-the-art lockdown system—and the furniture had just been delivered yesterday morning. "Mac, d'you think the two of us can fit on one of those sofas?"

"You, me, and half the cast of *Priscilla, Queen of the Desert.*"

It took the two of them—three, once Rhoann caught on to what they were doing—a few minutes, but eventually they hauled one of the sofas up the few steps separating the pit from the rest of the club and positioned it next to the tank. Of course, the only working light switch was all the way over on the other side of the *maudite* room; by the time Lucien found it and killed the lights, Mac had skinned out of his trousers and was mostly finished removing his leg, working by the light of his cell phone.

Rhoann was—of course—watching, fascinated, from inside the tank. Fae had never developed much in the way of technology—hadn't needed to—and Rhoann had thought Mac's C-leg was magickal at first.

But, then, the half-Royal Fae had thought Mac was magickal, too.

That makes two of us.

* * *

Cape Fear, North Carolina

The first thing the male noticed—well, the second, after the pale daggers of sunlight stabbing their way through his closed eyelids—was the

81

uncomfortable way his naked body was sprawled out over jagged rocks.

He debated for a minute over whether to open his eyes first, inviting the light to ream out his eye sockets but giving him a better idea of where they'd all landed this time, or try to sit up, the better to see whatever corner of hell they occupied, and just maybe get an idea of which way food might be.

He wasn't willing to waste more than a minute on that debate, though, because he was fucking starving. They all were. He managed to roll himself onto his side, scraping flesh from his ribs on a spine of rock but not giving a shit, and pushed himself up, bracing himself on one trembling arm.

His hand slipped on wet rock. He fell forward, his arm going into cold water up to the elbow.

The male jerked upright like a child's toy on a string, his eyes wide and staring. His body didn't give a fuck what his eyes were doing; it was preoccupied with scrambling to get as far away from the water surrounding him as possible.

They were all back in their ocean lair, south of the nexus. Not a meal in sight. And the tide was coming in.

What is it? Somehow, the female managed to sound dazed, panicked, and imperious, all at once.

"As Meat would have tried to say, Sheeshush Fuckig Chrish!" The male wasn't sure why he was trying to make a joke of this clusterfuck, other than that it beat the shit out of lying down and dying.

You have done a splendid job for us, as you promised. Not only do we still have no food, but we are surrounded by water.

"I bow to your wisdom, Commander of the Completely Fucking Obvious."

The male's sarcasm was strangely lost on the female. *If superstition had any hold on me, I would say something worked against us.*

"And what might that something be?" Sparring with his other self kept the male from scanning the rising water, remembering the way the ancient Loremasters had almost managed to use their terror of drowning against them.

Nothing in which any of us might believe. The male thought he could hear the female's teeth grinding together—though that was unlikely given her fangs. *Even Meat, were he alive, would want Guaire's head enough to take care for our life.*

"No shit." None of them had ever questioned their meat wagon's obsession—it had been a useful carrot to dangle in front of the poor bastard.

He was used to being ignored by the female. *Unless we move quickly, sheer coincidence is going to kill us.*

"Then let's move." The male's gut clenched, hard; he wasn't sure, but he thought he'd just splashed something on the rocks. A little gift for the gulls. "Now."

Chapter Nine

Fánadh, Ngarradh

"Hey, I like your new digs."

Kevin's head jerked up. *Was I asleep? Nah, couldn't be.* His computer screen hadn't had time to gray out; page 43 of Janet Kilgarten's perfect Memorandum in Support of Motion for Partial Summary Judgment was still staring back at him from the computer screen. "Thanks. I'll probably like them a lot better myself once the new carpet smell fades a little, but any office Art O'Halloran wasn't murdered in is a step up in the world."

Tiernan stepped out of the shadows in the corner, passing the closed door without a glance, to peer out the window as if to make sure he hadn't been seen Fading into Kevin's office. As if some window-washer might have been doing the ninth floor windows at 11:00 at night. "I still don't know what possessed them to give you that office in the first place. Not that I believe in ghosts, but if they exist, that office has a big beefy stage Oirish one with a slit throat."

Kevin shuddered. "Do you mind?"

"Sorry." Tiernan eased a well-formed ass cheek onto the edge of Kevin's desk, his jeans doing a

84

fantastic job of advertising the outlines of every muscle.

"I doubt it," Kevin muttered.

One blond eyebrow went straight up. "Testy." Tiernan turned Kevin's monitor, studied the document on display. "Since when does a partner write his own briefs?"

Kevin shoved the monitor back into place, a little harder than he needed to. "One of our new associates wrote this. I'm just checking it."

"At 11:00 at night?"

Kevin wanted to growl. Or snap. Unfortunately, his innate sense of fairness wouldn't let him do either. That didn't necessarily mean he had to say anything, of course.

"You've been stewing ever since Rian called us into conclave." Tiernan's voice was surprisingly gentle, for him. "What's going on?"

Kevin nearly replied *I don't stew*, but realized just in time how juvenile that would sound. "I'm not happy with how that so-called planning session went." There, that had the advantage of being true, as far as it went.

"Really?" Tiernan manifested a tiny knife from the living Stone of his left hand, and used it to clean the nails of his right. "I thought it went pretty well, myself."

Kevin didn't have to feign a snort. "Really? If I'd been in a room full of humans, I would have called it a meeting of a mutual admiration society. But Fae aren't into that sort of thing."

Tiernan grinned, his attention still on his nails. "True, we usually save our admiration for ourselves. Maybe a circle jerk?"

"Oh, for fuck's sake."

He'd spoken louder than he meant to, apparently; Tiernan looked up slowly, the knife absorbing back into his hand. "What's wrong?"

Kevin took a deep breath; another, when the first one caught in his chest. "We're going to be attacked, probably any day now, by an embodiment of evil that's tried to kill everyone in the Demesne of Purgatory at least once, literally mind-fucked me, and is out to destroy the Realm, and our world along with it if it can figure out how. And all the Fae can manage to do is take turns bragging about how they're going to humiliate and destroy it single-handed." He couldn't help a pointed glance at Tiernan's crystal hand.

"Oh. I get it." Tiernan did a quick Fade; when he reappeared, he was facing Kevin, his long legs dangling over the edge of the desk to either side of the leather captain's chair. "*Lanan*, that's as close to a strategy session as you're ever going to see among Fae. There's a reason we don't have armies, or large-scale wars."

"You don't work and fight well with others." Kevin could feel his face going red with embarrassment at his outburst. "I know."

Tiernan's Stone hand was warm against Kevin's unshaven cheek. "What you heard the other night was a gaggle of rugged individualists who know their lives are going to depend on each other whether they like it or not, and who were letting one another know their respective strengths. What they can be counted on for, when fire comes to stand against dragon's-breath."

"I'm less than crazy about that particular Fae saying." It was hard to stay pissed off, with his husband gently caressing him. Unfortunately, something else was eating away at him, something Tiernan's uncharacter-istically tender touches weren't alleviating in the slightest.

Something he really, really didn't want to talk about. Sooner or later, though, he knew he would.

Tiernan didn't seem to notice anything out of the ordinary. "Even a dragon runs out of fire eventually. A Fire elemental doesn't."

"Great. We can beat a proverb."

"Somebody has a thorn in his paw." Normally, the sexiness quotient of Tiernan's smirk would have completely cancelled out Kevin's dark mood. "Don't forget, we also managed to agree on what needs to be done. I'd call that an accomplishment."

"Spare me. Conall figured all that out weeks ago."

Long fingers gripped the back of Kevin's neck, setting his heart racing despite everything. "Some fancy persuading was still required, if you'll recall. Cuinn was *so* not on board with the idea of unmaking the Pattern, I thought we were going to have to call on Fiachra's special persuasive talents."

"Do you really think that would have worked? On a Loremaster?"

"That's where those talents came from in the first place, so maybe." Tiernan didn't exactly shrug, but the lift of his eyebrows gave the same impression. "We did agree, though, in the end. Unmake the Pattern, so the ley energy and living magick exchange between this world and the Realm will stop fucking up both worlds. And end the reason the Pattern was called into being in the first place."

"Kill the *Marfach*, you mean. Kill something that can't die."

"If you grind your teeth any harder, you're going to get lockjaw." Tiernan's faceted eyes and crystal hand wouldn't let Kevin go. "You weren't this angry at the conclave. What's going on?"

Kevin suspected he knew what a balloon with a slow leak felt like. "I don't suppose there's any chance I can persuade you that you don't want to know?"

"None whatsoever."

Kevin sighed deeply. Maybe getting it off his chest would help, at that. "Just before Maelduin came over from the Realm, I had a... I guess you'd call it a premonition. *Deja vú.* Something like that. So intense, I thought for a second I was losing my mind."

One advantage to having a partner for whom channeling magick was as natural as breathing was that said partner didn't necessarily think you were crazy when you sounded crazy even to yourself. Tiernan just nodded, the hint of a frown putting a line between his blond brows. "What did you see?"

"A sword. You." The single word stuck in his throat to the point where it was barely recognizable. "But... it wasn't so much what I saw, as what I felt." Kevin shivered; his skin prickled, the short hairs rising on his forearms. "Evil. Pure lust for death. Like it felt when the *Marfach* was in me, except it was everywhere."

Tiernan's grip loosened on the back of his neck, became a caress. "Doesn't take a premonition to know the *Marfach's* coming after us, *lanan.*"

"It was more than that. The premonition, I mean. The evil went away. Everything went away. And I was... empty. Alone." Kevin stared at Tiernan, but he didn't see him. He didn't see anything. "I was hollow. Silence, so deep, smothering, I couldn't hear my own heartbeat, or even feel it—"

Tiernan slid off the desk to sit astride Kevin's thighs; the desk chair creaked, but it had been selected because it could hold both of them if the need—or anything else—arose. Kevin leaned into his husband, as strong arms wrapped around him; he could feel the echoes of his shudders in Tiernan's body.

"*Gan cé g'vratheann m'croí,*" Tiernan whispered into Kevin's hair. "Not while my heart beats, *lanan.*"

Unable to speak, Kevin nodded, listening to the reassuring beat of that heart next to his ear.

"You should have said something sooner." Tiernan held him tighter. "Or I should have asked. Fuck me, I could see something was wrong."

Kevin shook his head—not much, he liked it right where he was. "I didn't want to bother you with it. It's ridiculous, a grown man crying over a daydream."

"Crying?" Tiernan pulled back at this, just enough to gaze down at Kevin with narrowed eyes. "And you didn't want to *bother* me?"

Oh, shit. "I... no, I..."

Tiernan's eyes glittered, sharp and bright. "Have you forgotten how to trust me, *m'lanan?*" A finger traced along the line of Kevin's shirt collar, stopped behind the half Windsor of his dark blue silk tie.

Kevin forgot how to breathe, and by the time he finally remembered, sweat was trickling down his temples. "No... but I have a feeling I'll enjoy the next few minutes a lot more if I say 'yes'."

"Say whatever you like." Tiernan tugged at the

knot, gently and teasingly at first, then harder when it refused to yield. "I'll do as I please, and as pleasures you."

Kevin suspected the head of his cock was already peeking up above his belt before the tie was undone; Tiernan's pulling his shirt out of his trousers confirmed his suspicions, and left him breathless again.

"Belt?" he croaked.

"Get it yourself. I'm busy." Tiernan slid Kevin's tie out from under his button-down collar, then undid the top button of the shirt.

"Asshole." Kevin managed something like a little laugh as he fumbled with his belt buckle.

"You tempt me, but I have other plans at the moment." Tiernan pulled on one end of the tie, then the other; the friction of the cool silk heated the skin on the back of Kevin's neck. "No safe word this time—you're just going to have to trust me."

Kevin swallowed hard. Once, Tiernan had misjudged the timing of their breath play, and Kevin had actually blacked out. He hadn't cared much for the experience, so the two of them had agreed on 'spoon' as a safe word. He'd had to use it a couple of times since then, on occasions when Tiernan was in just such a mood as he was right now. Chancy, unpredictable... Fae.

His husband's instincts were dead on, though. Kevin needed this.

Kevin could hear and feel Tiernan slowly wrapping the tie around his hand, just behind his neck and off to his right, as his belt fell open, followed immediately by his trousers. His cock didn't exactly spring free—it was already too large and heavy for springing—but it bobbed. A little.

Then it was trapped between bodies, as Tiernan leaned in and fit his body to Kevin's. Kevin tried to work his hand in between them, but was brought up short by the low, sensual growl in his ear.

"No touching." Teeth closed briefly around Kevin's earlobe. "Your pleasure's mine tonight, remember?"

"I don't think that was ever expressly stated." Lawyers could be brats, too.

Kevin thought he heard and felt a barely suppressed snicker. He might have been imagining it, though, because Tiernan's kiss had nothing of laughter in it; it was hungry, focused, and possessive. Kevin sat back slowly, on a low, shuddering moan, and the incredible kiss followed him. Time didn't exactly stop, but Kevin was definitely paying no attention to it. The kiss, his husband's body against his, the scent of their combined arousal filling him, the sweet painful tension of his erection drove out everything else.

Then the makeshift noose tightened, too quickly for him to steal a breath. And Tiernan arched back just enough to let him wrap a hand around Kevin's cock.

Oh, shit.

Darkness crept in, all around the edges of Kevin's vision. That was all right, though. He could still see what he needed to see, and nothing could keep him from feeling what he needed to feel.

"You're buttoned down tight, *lanan.*"

Kevin's remaining breath left him in a rush. He would never forget those words, the words that had drawn him into the orbit of a Fae, his first night in Purgatory.

"And you're with me because secretly you want someone..."

Damn.

"Someone like me..."

The darkness was almost total; the hand pumping Kevin's huge cock, his *elafantabod*, reached for everything Kevin had left in him.

"...to unbutton you."

Tiernan demanded everything. Kevin's hips slammed up.

And with a guttural cry, he gave everything.

* * *

Tiernan gazed down at Kevin's face, his spent half-smile, his closed eyes, the long lashes forming dark semi-circles over his unshaven cheeks.

His own face was expressionless. His husband shared a Fae soul, which made him just Fae enough to make a Foreseeing a real possibility.

Once, just once, it would be nice not to have bigger things to worry about.

* * *

Union Station, Washington, D.C.

One brief glimpse of a dank, moldy space, windows boarded over. A rusty barrel, charred wood visible through a hole in the side. The scurrying of rats, or tiny monsters falling from a great monster's tail, seeking deeper darkness.

This, too, had once been home.

Now it was oblivion.

Chapter Ten

The light of the rising Moon touches the bark of the *darag*, almost teasingly, in fits and starts through the breeze-tossed branches of the other trees in the oak grove. His Mother's touch gently wakens Coinneach; his awareness stirs, blinks—though his eyes exist as yet only in his mind, and the memory of the *darag*—and peers out into the dappled grove.

* * *

"What memory is this, *m'darag*?"
Laughter, slow and thoughtful. *PATIENCE.*

* * *

The nights are long in Alba, but not as long as they will be when the snow comes, and the cold damp. Night-birds pipe a few hesitant trills, and then fall silent. Only the owls call now, warning small things to hide. Unless it is their time, unless the owl's hunger is greater than their need to continue.

Coinneach stretches, yawns.

A light approaches, warm, flickering, weaving through the grove. Fire. Which means a human—the

Tirr Brai, Fae and *Coin-Sìth* and *eich-uisge,* need no fire to light their way on land or sea.

Coinneach would sigh, had he a body. Humans knew of the *Gille Dubh*, of course. They had legends of the wary, solitary Dark Men of the oaks. Some had more than legends; had met a *Gille Dubh*, had learned something of the ways of their kind, learned what angered them, and what pleased them.

And the bravest among them sometimes came courting.

None have ever come in that way to Coinneach. The local villagers know of him and his *darag*, of course; some leave tokens, small gifts, fresh-baked bread. One old man sometimes comes at dawn, or at twilight, and sits beneath the *darag* in companionable silence, one hand resting on its bark, as if sensing the flow of memories just beneath.

The other, though? Never. Coinneach is—even for a *Gille Dubh*—a lover of solitude. He has the companionship of his *darag*, a closeness no human, no *Tirr Brai*, could imagine. That is enough for him. What more could he need?

He can make out the form of the human, now. Short, fair of skin and dark of hair; young, if he is any judge, but old enough to carry a bow slung over his back, so an adult. The lad carries a fire-bowl in one hand, and a large shell, carefully, in the other. No doubt the shell is full of *uisge-beatha*, the water of life, the distillation of which seems to be a uniquely human gift. The Mothers knew the Fae had never properly worked out the way of it...

Coinneach is not sure how to feel.

The human stops, turns, uncertain. No doubt everything is unfamiliar to him by moonlight.

"My hope? Where are you?"

* * *

"This is not how it was!"
Silence.
"The human gave us no blood. There was never any meaning behind his words." *Surely he never called me his hope...*
Silence.
"*M'darag!*"
PATIENCE.

* * *

The human approaches once again; hesitantly, casting about, studying each tree he passes. He is close enough now for Coinneach to see the way his full lower lip is caught between his teeth, close enough, even, for the scent of his tears to reach the *darag*, and through it to come to Coinneach.

And he is about to pass by, unseeing, unknowing.

Silence is simple. Silence is safe.

Coinneach borrows form from his darag, and emerges from the wood.

For an instant, the human fails to notice the movement behind him. Coinneach reaches out a hand, from which the last of the bark is still flaking away, and rests it on the human's shoulder.

Startled, the human turns, the *uisge-beatha* sloshing in the shell, nearly spilling. Instinctively, Coinneach reaches out to steady the makeshift vessel. His hand covers the human's, dark over fair.

Coinneach looks up, in time to see the human's wide eyes staring at their hands.

95

"You are real," the human whispers. His words are strange, indistinct, but spoken aloud, in a voice deeper than one would expect from his beardless face. Coinneach also hears the words in the rustle of leaves, the play of moonlight that make up the mind-language of *Gille Dubh* and *daragin*.

But Coinneach makes no answer. He does not, because he did not.

* * *

"How is it that what was, is different now?"
PATIENCE—
"You are our patience, *m'darag*. I am not. I am our change, our newness. But even I cannot change what has already been."

A sigh, dappled moonlight and shifting branches. *THIS IS NOT CHANGE. THE GIFT OF OUR COUSIN'S BLOOD OPENS A NEW DOOR INTO OLD MOMENTS.*

"Our cousin? Fiachra?"
Silence, and space for light to dawn.
"He is both Fae and *Gille Dubh*..."
YES. HIS BLOOD GIVES US THE GIFT OF THE FAE TONGUE.

"And the humans of old spoke their own dialect of *Faen*."
YES.
Shivering, as if with a sudden chill.
What did he say?
What is he saying?

* * *

The human offers *uisge-beatha* with an unsteady hand, his gaze locked with Coinneach's. No doubt he finds the eyes of the *Gille Dubh* strange, deep brown flecked with shards of brilliant spring green.

Coinneach cups the human's hand in his own. He admires the shell, larger than anything a fisherman might find off the coast of Alba. A treasure, no doubt. But more precious than the shell is the scent of the *uisge-beatha*. Coinneach takes the offering and sips, sighing softly with pleasure as the potent spirit sings through him.

"Are you pleased?"

Yes, he wants to say. And *you are welcome here.* But he cannot speak, because he did not. He nods, his hand tightening awkwardly around the human's, because the human's eyes ask his approval, as they did when this moment was new.

"I am Donnchadh."

No knowledge of human language is needed to understand this. "Coinneach." His voice sticks in his throat.

The human—Donnchadh—glances around, and carefully sets his fire-bowl on the ground, on bare earth far from the roots of the *darag*. When he straightens, his face is cast in shadow by the shifting flames and coals; he offers the *uisge-beatha* again, but this time his gaze is cast down.

Coinneach drinks, then touches Donnchadh's chin with a fingertip, tilting his face up, from fire-shadow into moonlight. Gently he urges the human to drink, to share the water-of-life. It is not quite the same thing as sharing blood. But it is a sharing, and as such more than Coinneach has known with a human before now.

Donnchadh is startled at the offering, but sips. Coinneach can almost feel the spirit warming its way down the human's throat.

"I am leaving. At sunrise. I am promised to the *draoidhean*, and now that I am of age, I must go."

Coinneach-who-was hears only eagerness, and regret. And, perhaps, a reference to the druids, human folk held in respect by the *Tirr Brai*—especially by the folk of the wood. The humans send only their most perfect to the *draoidhean*, or so the story is told among the *Tirr Brai*. Coinneach is willing to believe the stories are true.

Donnchadh looks around the grove, his smile wistful. "This is where I learned to listen to the heartbeat of the world. And now I am sad to leave it."

Regret, yes. Is the human sorry he offered *uisge-beatha,* in the way of the old promise?—afraid the *Gille Dubh* will see an offer where none was meant?

I will send him on his way. Save his pride, keep my solitude. The thought feels heavy. Coinneach thinks it is the weight of truth. Probably.

Donnchadh takes a deep breath. "I would say farewell to this place properly."

Coinneach raises a hand to stop him.

Donnchadh, though, does not seem to notice; he steps into Coinneach's arms, rests his hand on the *Gille Dubh*'s bare shoulder. "Let me stay with you tonight, until the dawn."

* * *

"If I had understood..."
UNDERSTANDING CHANGES NOTHING.
"It changes me, *m'darag*."

* * *

Donnchadh is daring, bold, yet in a way almost shy; even as he turns Coinneach to face the *darag,* raises his plaid, fumbles to anoint himself with some fragrant oil from the bag hanging from his belt, he murmurs. Soft, needful, broken words, only half understood. Yet wholly understood, then and now.

"Yes," Coinneach whispers, as Donnchadh slowly pierces him. "Yes." His fingers sink into the bark of the *darag*, join with it, wood and *Gille Dubh* together groaning with pleasure.

"Your turn is next." Donnchadh sways, hot friction robbing Coinneach of breath. A hand moves Coinneach's hair from the back of his neck; kisses fall there, small bites. Another hand reaches around, tightly grips Coinneach's shaft.

Faster. Harder. Coinneach's knees threaten to buckle. A strong arm around his waist steadies him.

* * *

"*M'darag...!*"
THE MEMORY DOES NOT PLEASE YOU?
"Why have you waited so long to return this to me?"
IT IS ALWAYS NOW.

* * *

Donnchadh's plaid is unwrapped now, spread out on the ground, covering the tufts of hardy winter grass. The human lies beneath Coinneach, smiling, eyes

99

reflecting the moonlight. Sweat gleams on his brow despite the chill in the air, and his hands are hungry for Coinneach's body.

Coinneach, too, is hungry. He wants every taste of the young man's body, every scent. He wants to see and hear how Donnchadh reacts when each place on his body is touched, tongued, tasted. He savors every moment, understanding at last the allure of this temporary joining.

To the *Gille Dubh*, and their *daragin*, nothing is temporary. Every moment is now, or it can be.

Donnchadh rocks under him, gasping, offering himself. Coinneach braces his knees against the rough wool, takes his weight on one hand, and guides his slick cock to Donnchadh's entrance, probing, testing. He tenses, slides within.

"Please... yes, please, yes..."

Coinneach-who-was understands. Understands the hands, the eyes, the body, the needing.

"Yours, I will always be yours..."

Coinneach-who-is understands the words.

* * *

"Can you not bring him forward in time? Just until the dawn?"

Gentle breeze, the drift of a falling leaf. *HE COULD NOT STAY.*

"No."

AND ONLY OUR KIND CAN TRAVEL THROUGH TIME WITHOUT DAMAGE.

"I know..."

HE MIGHT REMEMBER YOU, WERE HE TO COME TO THIS-NOW. BUT ON HIS RETURN... IN

THEN-NOW HE WOULD FORGET, WOULD LOSE EVERYTHING HE HAS EVER KNOWN, EVERYTHING HE HAS EVER BEEN. WOULD YOU GIVE HIM THAT, IN EXCHANGE FOR WHAT HE GIVES YOU?

A sigh, long and unsteady. "No. Though true kindness might."

* * *

The plaid is wrapped around them both. Coinneach's head is pillowed on Donnchadh's arm; the human's leg is worked between Coinneach's, his pale hand cups Coinneach's dark shoulder. Coinneach closes his eyes as a kiss falls on his forehead.

His own memory of time-bound events is an ephemeral thing, waxing and waning like the Moon, his cradle-mother. But when he returns to the *darag*, this night will join the trove of moments kept by his *darag*, to be re-experienced anew at will, forever.

"Thank you," Donnchadh whispers. "My heart."

Coinneach does not need to understand the words to understand the emotion. And though this moment is as fleeting as any, it is also eternal, and he honors it, returning the words as best he can and seeking Donnchadh's mouth.

Even in the depths of such a kiss, though, he can feel the fire of the coming dawn lick at his skin. He startles, coming up onto an elbow and peering through the trees to the east, toward the glow on the horizon.

Donnchadh follows the direction of his gaze, and sighs. "The stories say your kind cannot abide the sun."

He scrambles to his feet and extends a hand, helping Coinneach to his.

They stand together, the *darag* between them and the sunrise. For the first time, Coinneach is reluctant to return to his tree's embrace; he grips Donnchadh's hard-muscled arms, wishing for an instant that his grasp could be enough to hold the human forever, as some of the *Tirr Brai* have done with humans.

No. This night is his forever, and that will have to be enough.

Donnchadh smiles, his smallest finger tracing the curve of Coinneach's lower lip. "My heart will remember you always." He leans in for one last gentle, lingering kiss.

Then his hands urge Coinneach back against the *darag*. "*Fàilte, mo chridhe.*"

Coinneach's form melts into the wood, just ahead of the first rays of the rising sun.

* * *

"Thank you, *m'darag*."

FOR THE MOMENT?

"For your wisdom, in not taking his memory from him."

Coinneach's awareness settled, down into the roots of the *darag*. In the darkness, those roots twined around and through the place which still held the softly singing memory of the heart buried there thousands of years ago.

The heart did, indeed, remember. Forever.

* * *

Union Station, Washington, D.C.

Silence stared unseeing at its reflection in oblivion.

Redness stirred, rose, fell back.

Or perhaps it was all imagination.

But who was left to imagine?

Chapter Eleven

He. She. It. They.

A swirl of red fog surrounded them all, penetrated them all, a red so dull it was nearly indistinguishable from black.

Every once in a timeless while, a pair of eyes would open, and the red would brighten around them to the glow of a fireplace poker buried in the coals of a wood fire.

"Where are we?" A female voice hung in the not-air long after dark-lashed eyes closed, waiting for someone to hear.

Fuck if I know. A male grumble emanated from bloodshot eyes. *This doesn't look anything like our sweet basement home.*

Another silence, as words awaited an answer.

YOU LOVE YOUR FORMS TOO MUCH.

The grating voice from opal eyes made the sleepers shudder. Yet they listened, eyes opened to glowing slits, trying not to be noticed.

Trying not to be noticed by their own third person. If the monstrosity sharing their psyche could be called a person.

WE EXIST AS SEPARATE BEINGS BECAUSE WE WISH TO. The stomach-churning sound of burning bones was sharpened by hunger. *BECAUSE THE FORMS SHAPED FROM THE FEAR OF OUR PREY AMUSE US.*

We can be whatever the fuck we want.

The monster's laughter was worse than its speech. *TRUE ENOUGH. BUT WE OWE ALL PHYSICAL FORM TO WHATEVER IS LEFT OF MEAT. THE REST IS ONLY IN OUR MINDS.*

So? The male thought he was braver than the female.

Perhaps, though, he was only less intelligent.

It was a long time before the abomination answered.

WE MUST NOT FORGET WHAT WE ARE.

WHAT I AM.

The red fog slowly filled in the silence.

Chapter Twelve

Aine watched the Pattern-tower in the slowly-brightening light, the play of shadows over the stone, the way the subtle colors of the stone shifted as the light changed. Cuinn wrought well, even with no one to guide him.

She was stalling, and she knew it. Better to admire the beauty of the outside of the tower than go inside and subject herself to what the interior had become.

That was unfair to those who waited for her, though. Like them, she had been a voluntary prisoner within those walls for thousands of years—and now that chance, or what passed for chance when one dealt with living magick, had freed her, she was their only contact with the world they were all still fighting to save.

She rested a hand on the chill, rough-hewn granite and closed her eyes, sensing through the stone to the space beyond it. The tower was small—only four Loremasters at a time had been able to kneel on the polished floor to yield up their magick and their souls at the Sundering—yet the interior often gave the impression of being much larger. It *was* larger, in a sense, since the floor represented the whole Realm, and every bit of magick therein.

106

I am still stalling. Grimacing, Aine reached out again, and Faded into the tower, staying as close to the wall as she could.

As soon as the cool semi-darkness had closed around her, she crossed quickly to the cushion she had brought in a handful of days ago and dropped into a wreath position. Not that sitting was any more comfortable than standing, but something about what was happening to the Pattern made it hard to stand upright for long.

Once she was settled, she steeled herself and made herself look around the chamber. If she blinded her magickal vision, she knew, all would be well. She would see the circle of granite blocks, polished on the inside where they were rough on the outside; the torches would be in their brackets, extinguished now because of the harm done by the magick that powered them; the small round window built to frame the moon would frame only a circle of pale dawn light.

But she was not here to be blind to reality.

Magickal vision overlay one reality with another; the floor of the chamber, which looked like black crystal but was in fact a representation of the whole Realm, drawn here and compressed so it could be guarded by the Loremasters who had survived the great battle with the *Marfach*, was swollen and turgid with the uncontrolled influx of ley energy from the human world. The web of silver lines and blue within it pulsed, straining to contain the living magick being created where the ley energy touched the air and soil and living beings of the Realm. Each line was the soul or the body of a Loremaster, stretched to the utmost.

The slightest use of Aine's own magick, or that of

any of the Loremasters, risked upsetting the precarious balance of forces. This ruled out communication by *d'aos'Faen* script written on the interface between the Pattern and the Realm, as they had once managed; still less could Dúlánc manifest and converse with her.

"What news, *chairidi?*" Aine whispered.

Stilling herself, eyes closed, hands resting palms up on her thighs, she waited. Waited for the echoes of 2,000 years spent woven together with her fellow Loremasters to resonate like a harp-string played by the wind.

Their answer was long in coming; the sun brightened, the spot of light from the window moved.

It comes. The words formed themselves within her, as they had when she had lived among them, but fainter. *All we can do is hold, to the very end of our strength.*

"What news of the Demesne of Purgatory?"

More time passed, more sunlight was spent. *We can no longer hear them.*

"Surely they have a plan." Aine's throat tightened. "This was our design from the beginning."

Just for a moment, Aine thought she heard Dúlánc's laughter. *A design untested and flawed. Yet it is all we have, now.* The chorus of voices was weary, yet there was a core to it as unyielding as sun-forged truesilver. *We will not yield. We will stop time itself, if we must, within the Pattern.*

Aine's mouth dropped open. "You will be trapped with it. Forever."

If we must.

How could he be so calm?

But you must be ready if we fail.

108

* * *

"I don't like it down here, Jason. It's creepy. And it's wet."

A girl's voice cut through the fog shrouding the *Marfach*'s mind. All three of its minds struggled toward awareness, grasping the voice like a lifeline.

"Trust me." The voice that answered was light, unctuous. Footsteps approached, two sets, pausing every once in a while to kick away debris. "I used to come down here all the time, between trains, junior year. You wanted to go someplace no one would find us, right? This is it."

Hunger. Starvation.

A nervous giggle. "Yeah. That's what I want. How long do we have?"

"Couple of hours, easy. Capitol tour doesn't end until 4:00, maybe 4:30, then it'll probably take them another 10 or 15 minutes to figure out we aren't with the class." More footsteps. "There used to be a mattress down here..."

"I bet it's as wet as everything else. I say let's do it right here."

A gasp, a groan. "Jesus, Sydney, don't... oh, fuck, yes..."

No words passed between the *Marfach*'s three persons. None were necessary. The male and the female loathed the abomination... but only it could inflict enough agony on their prey to feed them.

To prepare them for Purgatory.

Chapter Thirteen

"I think Setanta is happy you could come out with us tonight."

"And you aren't?" Bryce grinned, watching the Fade-hound pup quest ahead of his masters in his badass truesilver harness and chain leash. They'd had to cannibalize most of the Demesne's remaining truesilver to make them, but it had been worth it; the magickal metal was the only substance capable of keeping Setanta from Fading back to the hotel—or even all the way home, to Greenwich Village—whenever he felt like it.

Lasair made a rude noise. Bryce had never heard a human make it; judging from his experience of Fae lips under other circumstances, he guessed there were slight differences between Fae and human facial muscles, leading to a uniquely Fae embouchure.

The thought lent a slightly wicked curve to Bryce's grin. He'd been spending more time smiling lately. A lot more time. Which was bizarre, considering he'd spent most of the last couple of weeks waiting for the lethal twist in his gut to tell him the monster he'd once been so intimate with had made another Fade-jump.

More Fae than a Fae, Lasair had called him. Once Bryce had realized what love was, he'd treated it as a game, a ritual, a commodity to be won or lost or traded. And unlike his start in life, with all the financial privilege of a fourth-generation investment banking family, he'd started the love game with loose change in his pocket and a pair of deuces in his hand.

Or so he'd thought, until Lasair opened his eyes to what was actually going on around him, and inside him.

The three of them stopped as Setanta cocked a leg beside one of his favorite bushes; the pup never failed to water it, and tonight was no exception.

"You think he knows that's Congress, across the street?"

Lasair frowned. "I thought you told me your Congress was behind us."

Setanta was taking his time about his bush-watering duties; Bryce glanced back over his shoulder at the Capitol dome while they waited for him to finish. "No—well, kind of. They meet in the Capitol, but they have their lairs across Independence and down First Street—"

Cold sweat streamed down Bryce's temples, cheeks and throat, and glued his shirt to his chest. His gut churned and twisted in all three dimensions, and a few it appeared to have invented on the spot. His vision swam; when it cleared, he was on his knees, staring resignedly at his dinner, splattered in the grass behind the overgrown bush.

Setanta whined, standing on his hind legs to nose at Bryce's ear.

"It's here." Lasair didn't bother making it a question; he knelt beside Bryce, an arm around his shoulders, drawing him close.

111

"Yeah." Bryce coughed and spat, then tried to settle against Lasair. He could feel his *scair-anam*'s magick, probing to draw the foulness out of him. "I think... it's been here a while. But more dead than alive. Until now."

Funny thing, though. He felt like hammered dogshit, sure, but he didn't feel nearly as bad as he'd expected to, with the monster on their doorstep and ready to rumble.

Maybe I'm getting used to this.

Bryce had definitely had happier thoughts.

"Can you tell where it is?" Lasair rested his cheek against Bryce's hair.

"Purgatory, I think. Or somewhere nearby."

"*Folathón.*" Lasair grimaced; Setanta, picking up on his master's mood, growled.

Bryce knew how they both felt. All the half-baked plans that had come out of their summit the other night had involved the Demesne getting to the nexus before the *Marfach*.

Wait. Wait justafuckingminute.

"If it was actually at the nexus, we'd know, right? I mean, the world would be ending or something."

Lasair nodded. "You think we might still have time."

"Maybe."

Bryce knew what Lasair's next question was going to be—his Fae was already turning a pale shade of green.

Sure enough, Lasair steeled himself. "How close is the nearest Metro station?"

"I love you. But there's no time for that." Bryce's heart was hammering against his ribs, hard enough to be audible to his Fae lover and their Fae hound, he was sure. "You're going to have to Fade all three of us."

Lasair pulled back just far enough to stare at Bryce. "You're mad."

"I thought you figured that out a long time ago." Bryce's breath caught hard on what felt like a swift kick to the gut; he suspected his half-smile didn't fool his SoulShare one bit.

"I will not kill you." Turquoise eyes narrowed. Even Setanta was getting in on the stern act, lips curling back from what would someday be fangs.

"I'm not asking you to." *I hope.* "One Fade shouldn't kill me."

"I am not convinced."

"I am. Mostly." *I think I need to pick better times to be honest.* "Each time I've gotten sick, since the *Marfach* escaped... I think I've been sharing its Fades. I've gotten... acclimated."

"I would hardly call this acclimated." Lasair inclined his head toward what was left of a medium rare rib-eye.

"I would. Remember how bad it was the first couple of times? How you spent hours getting me to the point where I could sit up without help?"

Setanta whined and licked Bryce's ear. Bryce grimaced apologetically and gave the pup a skritch under his harness.

"Yes." Somehow, the Fae made the single word sound like *I'm still not giving in, so don't get any ideas.*

"We're out of time, Rapunzel." Lasair's enjoyment of the nickname Bryce had given him had been one of the first things to help Bryce to his new understanding of love. "We have to find out what's going on. Then you can take Brimstone-Butt and rally the troops."

"While you do what, exactly?"

"I haven't figured that out yet." *Jesus, my nose should be growing for a whopper that big.* It was perfectly obvious what he was going to have to do. "We'll have a better idea once we get there and see what's going on."

"Seeing without being seen is likely to be... problematic. Especially since the *Marfach* is probably as sensitive to your movements as you are to its."

Setanta crouched in the grass, paws splayed, tail wagging and ears perked up, all hunt-and-play.

Those ears drooped as Bryce and Lasair both said "No." The pup put his head on his paws and whined softly. Bryce thought he could see a faint green cloud emanating from just under Setanta's no-longer-wagging tail.

Lasair picked Setanta up and cradled him tenderly but firmly against his chest. "Stay with me, *tréan-cú*." Bryce wasn't sure what went into being a Master of Fade-hounds, a pack-alpha to a pack of apex predators, but it had something to do with the way his *scair-anam* was talking to Setanta. "Stay. Guard. *Orthú*."

The tiny Fade-hound had learned that *orthú* signaled an unbreakable command, as binding on him as his love for his masters. Even so, he growled softly and licked his canines in frustration.

I guess this means I win. The thought wasn't exactly exciting.

His excitement level didn't matter, though. Not if he could finally do something to make up for 30-plus years of assholery, and just maybe save two worlds.

114

"We don't have to risk our favorite scent hound. Not if we shoot for a landing in the dancers' lounge."

Lasair blinked. "Why not Tiernan's office? The security monitors would show us everything we need to know."

"Tiernan's office is almost directly over the nexus."

"Shit."

When Lasair cursed in English, he was almost as careful and precise about it as Conall. It was almost enough to make Bryce crack a smile. "Precisely. This is going to scramble my innards enough without kicking the nexus in the nuts."

Lasair shook his head, more in a *you're incorrigible* way than in outright disapproval. At least, that was what Bryce hoped.

"We'll make it work." Bryce swallowed a sudden lump in his throat. "We Fade in, find out what the monster's up to, you and the odorous one Fade back out and go collect the cavalry."

"Correction." Damn, Lasair was talking to him exactly the way he'd been talking to Setanta. "We Fade in, I help you recover, and *then* we do whatever else needs to be done." Narrowed turquoise eyes told Bryce exactly what his SoulShare thought of his omission.

"Unless the *Marfach*'s breathing down our necks, in which case you leave me to—"

"No 'unless'." Lasair shook his head calmly. "A choice between your life and my own is no choice."

Damn. Just when I thought I was finally getting the hang of this love thing. Bryce unbuckled Setanta's harness, hoping neither the hound nor the Hound-master noticed his hands shaking.

115

"Why are you—oh." Lasair nodded. "He would not be able to Fade with us if he wore it."

"Exactly." Bryce swallowed hard, forcing down the lump in his throat one more time as Lasair's arms settled around him and Setanta nestled against his chest. "Let's do this. Before someone comes along and finds us."

Lips brushed Bryce's forehead. "Open to us, *sumiúl*."

For once, Bryce did as he was told.

And the world went dark and twisted.

* * *

Bryce was convulsing in Lasair's arms almost before he was solid.

His thoughts filled with dire—but silent—curses, Lasair spared a glance for his surroundings, enough to be sure he'd brought them all to the dancers' lounge behind Purgatory's stage as he'd intended. Then, carefully, he eased Bryce down to the floor; as soon as Setanta had wriggled out from between them, he covered Bryce with his body, the way he always did when Bryce was suffering from contact with the *Marfach*.

Setanta, too, had his usual comfort to offer; the wan light from the phosphorescent telltales plugged into the outlets around the room turned the pup's fur a sickly green and lent his clouded eyes an eerie glow as he gave Bryce's sweaty face a tongue-bath.

Not knowing what else to do, Lasair concentrated as best he could under the circumstances, trying to draw the Fade-sickness out of his *scair-anam*'s body the way he dealt with the *Marfach*'s foul energy.

116

It's working. I think. Bryce's tremors were slowing, his breathing gradually becoming less labored. Setanta's tail thumped softly against the leg of a nearby chair.

Bryce opened his eyes—closed them, barely in time to avoid a tongue-swipe. *Where?* he mouthed, as he cautiously opened his eyes again and tried to look around without moving anything but his eyes.

Lasair lowered his head until his lips brushed Bryce's ear. "Dancers' lounge," he whispered. The lounge's sound insulation had been installed last week—a necessity, if the dancers not on stage were going to be able to relax this close to the monster sound system the new Purgatory was going to boast—but the door was ajar, and unless the *Marfach* was wearing Janek's body, its hearing was probably as acute as that of any other magickal creature.

The Fae could feel Bryce's tight nod echoed all through his still-twitching body. For all his *scair-anam*'s evident suffering, he had obviously been right in his assessment of what had been happening to him since the monster's escape from the Antarctic icecap. He was acclimated to Fading—as much as a human could be, in any event.

Need to find it.

"Are you sure you can—"

By way of reply, Bryce tried to push Lasair off him. Moving a determined Fae would be impossible, of course, unless that Fae allowed it.

Lasair allowed it, reluctantly. In fact, he helped Bryce to his feet, trying not to wince in sympathy with the effort required of his *scair-anam*. Because Bryce was in the right. They had no time to spare for his recovery.

117

The three, Fae, human and puppy, padded down the hallway, around the right angle that would keep light from the dressing room off the dance floor. There would be a curtain at the end of the hall eventually, but for now there was only the chrome rod from which it would hang; they pressed as close as they could to the left wall and inched down the last few feet.

Lasair could hear his own heart pounding, of course, and Bryce's. Even Setanta's, though the pup's hunting instincts had taken over and locked his tiny fangs together, just enough to let him breathe without tell-tale panting.

The crash of shattering glass froze them all where they stood.

"Fuck," a male voice muttered, the single word laden with lust and ire and madness. "It *has* to be here."

Lasair felt as if something had hold of his head, clamping it in an invisible vise, trying to prevent him from moving those last few inches. Whatever it was, it tried in vain; he edged forward just enough to peer around the corner, his arm sliding around Bryce's waist as Bryce came up beside him.

One look was all they needed before falling back. The dreadlocked male aspect of the *Marfach* was behind the bar, frantically searching the back wall in the light from the tell-tales and a strange red glow that might have been coming from the bar, or from the creature itself. The fresh scent of rum told Lasair what bottle had just fallen to the floor; other less fresh scents told him the rum hadn't been the first to go.

Hopefully all of them together were enough to cover the scents of Fae and human and Fade-hound.

Lasair didn't breathe until the three of them had regained the comparative safety of the lounge. He pulled the door most of the way closed and eased Bryce into a chair; Setanta rested his front paws on Bryce's thighs, looking very much as if he wanted to whine.

Lasair empathized.

Bryce motioned, and Lasair ducked his head to put his ear next to Bryce's lips, for once not even noticing the soft tickle of his SoulShare's mustache.

"It's looking for the door to the basement," Bryce whispered.

Lasair nodded. The last time the *Marfach* had been in Purgatory, the only way into the nexus chamber had been through the door behind the bar.

"But we're going to have to get it down there—whatever plans we managed to make the other night all depend on access to the nexus and the wellspring."

Fuck me with an eggbeater.

Bryce let out a breath of laughter, as if he could hear Lasair's thoughts. "I can handle that part. But you and Brimstone-Butt have to get out of here and summon the cavalry."

Lasair pressed his lips to Bryce's ear, the better to keep sound from escaping to be overheard. "If you think I'm leaving you alone with that monster—"

"I managed to live that way for the better part of a year." Bryce gripped Lasair's shoulder tightly. "It would kill you without a thought. I should be able to keep it interested long enough to lead it downstairs. At which point I really, really need you to have alerted the heavy artillery."

Otherwise known as the Defense of the Demesne. They had joked about the name, when making battle plans had been mostly an intellectual exercise, since Rian had flat-out vetoed the notion of having a "proper" Royal Defense. But there was no elite cadre of warriors in the Demesne of Purgatory, and no one person singled out for them to protect.

Lasair had never wanted to shred an attack plan so badly as he wanted to savage Bryce's. Unfortunately, his *scair-anam* was right. "And I have to take Setanta with me."

The puppy's fangs bared in a silent growl as Bryce nodded. "I can't protect him here... and frankly, all it would take is one good fart, and game over."

The wounded expression the blind puppy turned on Bryce was almost enough to make Lasair laugh, even if the Fae did suspect his *scair-anam* was blowing smoke to distract him. "We will go. But if I come back and discover you have taken any unnecessary risks..."

"Me? Never."

Humans set great store by angels, Lasair had discovered, and he suspected Bryce thought he resembled one. "I call bullshit."

There was no more time for banter, though—had never been time to begin with. Lasair brushed his lips across Bryce's cheek and gathered Setanta into his arms. "Keep safe, *m'anam-sciar*."

There was no safety for any of them now; the cold weight in the pit of Lasair's stomach as he and Setanta Faded out was eloquent testimony to that fact. No safety until the unkillable *Marfach* was dead.

* * *

Bryce closed his eyes, just for a second. He needed more than a second, that went without saying, but a second was all he dared to take. He'd recovered from the Fade a hell of a lot faster than he'd expected, which was probably why Lasair had been willing to leave him behind. But Lasair had apparently forgotten about the twisted lump of Bryce's own flesh that was in thrall to the monster, and what that lump did to Bryce when the *Marfach* was anywhere near.

Bryce didn't have the luxury of forgetting.

"Couldn't stay away, could you?" The voice came from immediately behind Bryce and to the right; a broken fingernail caressed his cheek. "Loyalty's so rare a thing, even in ass-puppets.

Shit.

The chuckle behind him turned his fortunately-empty stomach. "You deserve a reward. Maybe we'll make sure you stay dead this time." The voice dropped to a feral snarl. "After you tell us what the fuck you did with the nexus."

"You can go straight to—"

A sharp, brittle chime, wire under tension, shattering glass, cut Bryce off in mid-curse.

Then... nothing.

Chapter Fourteen

The sight of Tiernan in a tux, complete with pearl-gray gloves, never failed to make Kevin's heart skip a beat. Or several.

It also tended to make it difficult for him to buckle his belt, which amused his husband to no end. "Are you really sure you want to go out tonight?"

Kevin stuck his tongue out at Tiernan briefly, before returning his attention to his belt. "You have no idea how hard it was to get tickets to this *Nutcracker*. None."

Tiernan's phone started playing delicious hot jazz. Josh's ringtone.

Tiernan lowered one eyelid in the barest lascivious wink as he peeled off a glove and dug his phone out of his breast pocket. "We'll see if you're still singing the same tune in a few—"

A sound like the "ping" of a wine glass shattering with the force of a soprano's voice fractured the air.

Oblivion followed.

* * *

Some instinct warned Kevin not to breathe. Or maybe it was the couple of inches of water he was lying in face-down that did the warning.

What the hell? Gasping, he pushed himself up onto his elbows, his arms aching with the effort and trembling as they bore his weight. Water streamed down into his eyes; he shook his head, swallowing the bile that rose in his throat with the rapid movement and realizing that the back of his head hurt like a son of a bitch. And he'd somehow lost most of a fingernail, too.

"What the bright shiny fuck?" The voice was Cuinn's, the tone shaken. Kevin managed to raise his head enough to see the Loremaster pushing himself up to his knees, using the black leather chaise in the middle of the nexus chamber for leverage.

The nexus chamber. Minus all the fireworks and unbound magick—and where had *those* gone?—it looked almost banal, like a bathtub with a clogged drain. *What the bright shiny fuck, indeed.*

Groans and curses were coming from all over the room, now.

Rian's head rested on Cuinn's knees, as he coughed and spluttered and swore.

Lucien's distinctive Quebeçois swears were hoarse, vehement and interrupted by coughing, and were not in the slightest mollified by his husbands' wordless murmurs.

Fiachra sat with his back to the wall, cradling Peri's head against his chest; Kevin wasn't sure if Peri was awake. Mascara streaked and ran down Peri's cheeks, and the skirt of a tattered green gown floated around his legs.

Bryce and Lasair and Setanta were huddled in the corner farthest from the nexus, Bryce with the green-around-the-gills look that said he'd been closer to the

Marfach than he could stand, and Setanta whimpering and trembling and worrying at his left front paw.

Lochlann looked the closest to normal of anyone Kevin could see, albeit more bewildered than Kevin had ever seen him as he knelt and stared at the floor, his fingers intertwined white-knuckled with Garrett's.

Conall and Josh were slumped shirtless on the black leather chaise, their poses so perfectly identical as to suggest the mage had just been jarred out of his *scair-anam*'s body.

Coinneach sat on the floor in the middle of the wellspring, his palms splayed out flat on the stone and a spark of panic in his brown-green eyes.

Maelduin crouched on the floor, holding Terry up out of the water; Terry had apparently just been clinging to Maelduin as if his life depended on his grip.

And tiny corpses floated in the water around Terry. Eyeless creatures, all fangs and scaly tails.

Kevin scrambled to his feet, nearly levitating out of the water. "Son of a bitch!" His teeth were chattering; his whole body remembered the sensation of the component creatures of the *Marfach*-monster's tail chewing their way through his guts.

Everyone fell silent; those who could move turned to look up at Kevin, confusion warring with the echoes of anger, fear, pain, sorrow in human, Fae, *Gille Dubh* and blind puppy gazes.

"Sorry," Kevin muttered. "*Marfach* pieces in the water. Freaked me the hell out."

He relaxed unthinkingly back into Tiernan's arms, seeking calm and comfort—so unthinkingly that it took him several seconds to realize Tiernan wasn't actually there.

Heart racing, Kevin turned on his heel, setting the water sloshing and his head pounding. "Where's Tiernan?"

Conall pushed himself to a sitting position, frowning. "Maybe he wasn't taken with the rest of us?"

Fiachra tried to speak, cleared his throat and tried again. "I don't think we were taken." He drew a deep unsteady breath. "That chime we heard—we did all hear it, right?" He waited for nods, and Lucien's *merde alors*, before finishing, "That sounded like a timeslip. You don't forget that sound."

Kevin, like everyone else, turned to look at Coinneach, though Kevin was paying as much attention to the periphery of his vision as to the crouching *Gille Dubh*. Surely Tiernan would be Fading in any second now.

The sound of rustling leaves and the shifting glow of moonlight filled the chamber. Fortunately, Kevin had exchanged blood with Coinneach and his *darag* not long after Maelduin's arrival from the Realm, as had everyone else in the Demesne who hadn't been able to understand *darag*-speech. An affirmation of trust, they'd called it.

"Not a timeslip. None of us have moved in time." Coinneach glanced up briefly, but almost immediately went back to running his hands over the Stone floor, as if searching for something by touch. "This was a different thing, a timewipe."

Kevin squinted at the floor under Coinneach's hands. *It looks as if the wellspring's gone... but it can't be.*

Conall's bright green eyes narrowed. As exhausted as he looked, he was unquestionably in full

125

pissed-off-mage mode. "A few more specifics would be nice."

Instead of answering, Coinneach closed his eyes; his arms stiffened and trembled, as if he were trying to draw something up out of the floor, or put down roots. After nearly a minute of this, he sighed deeply and sat back, splashing into the standing water.

No one so much as cracked a smile.

"The magick of the *daragin* is that of time. Time is our ally, our weapon, woven into our substance. And when we bend time beyond bearing in the service of magick, there is a backlash, a price. A timewipe, defacing the memories of all those too close to the channeling."

Maelduin frowned. "Nothing like that happened when your magick trapped Terry and sent him to Antarctica."

Coinneach shook his head miserably. "That was a great channeling, but nowhere near the power needed to trigger a timewipe."

Several Fae whistled under their breaths. Conall, still frowning, was not one of them. "So you're telling us that you and your *darag* bent time. So severely that none of us remember coming here, or anything that happened here."

"Yes." Coinneach shivered. "That must be what happened."

Things were finally starting to make sense to Kevin. A little. He and Tiernan must have come here together, and then Tiernan had left for some reason, during the time no one could remember.

There was another alternative, though, one that Kevin adamantly refused to let his imagination explore.

One that involved the *Marfach*, and a sword, and darkness.

"How do we reverse the wipe and get our memories back?" It never occurred to Kevin that the timewipe might be irreversible. He had to find out what had happened, or at least give Tiernan time to Fade back from wherever he'd gone.

Again, Coinneach took a while to answer, and when he did the sound was that of leaves dropping one by one into still, cold water. "The timewipe can be chipped away, bit by bit, if those with fragments of memory share what they have."

The *Gille Dubh* had been gazing into the dirty water; now he looked up, pleading and panic in his uncanny eyes. "Let us share, each with all. For the wellspring is gone; I have lost my *darag*, and unless I remember my way back to it, I will surely die."

Chapter Fifteen

"I might be able to start us off." Bryce's voice, as soft and weary as it was, seemed loud in the sudden stillness. "I remember the sound, and what happened right before it—but there's more, I can feel it. Maybe talking it out will help bring back what happened after."

Under any other circumstances, Kevin would probably have laughed at the identical stern expressions worn by Lasair and Setanta as they regarded their *scair-anam* and master. Not now, though. "Try. Please."

Bryce nodded; leaning back into the circle of Lasair's arms, he closed his eyes. "I could tell when the *Marfach* got here—or maybe it just woke up, I'm not sure. The three of us Faded into the dancers' lounge—"

A quick slice of Bryce's hand cut off the ensuing round of exclamations. Kevin wasn't part of the chorus; he was too busy trying to forget what his own accidental Fade had felt like. And, frankly, feeling sympathy for Bryce.

"Do you all mind? I'd like to get this over with." Bryce grimaced. "We found the fucker poking around behind the bar, looking for the way downstairs. I sent Lasair and Setanta to collect the rest of you, while I tried to figure out a way to get the *Marfach* downstairs—"

"So it could feed directly off the nexus?" Conall looked ready to chew nails and shit tacks, as Kevin's Marine sergeant father was fond of saying.

"So what plans you all managed to come up with in between peacock-posturing the other night could stand a chance of being carried out." Bryce opened his eyes long enough to shoot the mage a narrow-eyed glare. "Do you mind?"

"Sorry."

Kevin was pretty sure Conall wasn't.

Bryce sighed. "The *Marfach* found me right after they left..."

* * *

The pain, Jesus God the pain. The *Marfach* had used a piece of one of the broken bottles behind the bar to slash the shit out of the soles of Bryce's feet.

And the red of his blood was mixed with brown.

"Now you can take us to this new entrance. And we'll follow right in your footsteps."

At least the nausea at the thought of what he was about to do kept his mind off the pain as he led the cackling naked male out of the service entrance, through the new hidden door, and down the stairs. Or maybe it was the pain keeping his mind off the nausea. Whatever.

He felt the ward snap and shatter when his blood, mingled with the *Marfach*'s pollution, touched it. The way was left standing open; there was no going back now, even assuming he could catch the leering lecher behind him off guard and run off on his lacerated feet.

Unless, of course, he was willing to admit he didn't stand a fucking chance against the monster alone...

"What the fuck did you do to the nexus?" the male roared.

Bryce hadn't seen the nexus for a couple of weeks, and he didn't see magick well at the best of times, but even so, he was appalled by the sight at the bottom of the tight spiral stairs.

The air over the wellspring looked as if it was thick with tiny razor blades—blades that went invisible when edge-on, and could barely be seen the rest of the time. He wasn't sure what those blades would do to the skin of someone who couldn't channel, and he sure as hell had no desire to find out.

The nexus itself... all Bryce could think of was a hurricane. Or the ghost of one, anyway. Complete with hell's own lightning.

And if it looked this bad to him—

Bryce turned. The *Marfach*'s arm was thrown up to shield his eyes. Its eyes. What the fuck ever.

No time to plan, no time even to think.

Bryce slipped past the creature, ignoring the wrenching in his gut and the screaming of his feet.

It was much easier to apply a choke-hold from behind, after all.

"What in the—"

Bryce grabbed his right wrist with his left hand and used all the strength of both arms to tighten his hold on the *Marfach*'s throat. He really ought to be lifting it off its feet, too, but it was a hell of a lot heavier than anything its size had any business being, and it didn't budge. Other than to thrash around and try to throw him off, anyway.

Time for phase two.

Gritting his teeth against the bile he knew was

about to rise in his throat, Bryce opened up the sinkhole inside him and started to drain the *Marfach*'s clotted evil energy.

Even choked screams from the *Marfach* were enough to make Bryce's ears bleed. Grimly he clung to the monster, doing his damnedest to shut out everything except the task at hand.

With any luck at all, he'd live long enough for the Fae he loved to be the one to kill him.

* * *

Lasair's expression was as grim as Kevin had ever seen it. "You made a promise, *sumiúl*."

"No, I didn't." Bryce tilted his head back against Lasair's chest, the image of exhaustion. "I kept my mouth shut when you asked me to make one. And even if I had agreed, you only asked me not to take unnecessary risks. This was a necessary risk."

Rian held up a hand, cutting off whatever Lasair's retort would have been. "Did that bit of the tale jar anything loose for anyone?"

Lasair arched a brow. "Indeed, Highness."

Kevin winced.

As did several others, including Bryce. "Sorry, Rapunzel." Bryce's hand covered Lasair's, where it rested on his side. "I know you needed me to promise."

Lasair sighed deeply, bowing his head until his cheek brushed Bryce's dark hair. "I did. And you needed..."

"For you to have a chance to live." Bryce's eyes opened to dark slits, just enough to let him glance around the room. "All of you."

The silence that followed was broken only by the soft sloshing of the water.

Finally, Lasair dropped a kiss in Bryce's hair. "I will tell what I remember, and see where the tale leads."

* * *

"How would you like to learn orgasm denial?"

One of the most entertaining aspects of Fading—entertaining when matters were less urgent, anyway—was the ease with which one could drop into the middle of a conversation. Josh's voice, coming from the bedroom and pitched in an intimate register, was perfectly audible to Fae hearing even from the middle of the living room, where Lasair and Setanta had taken form.

As was Conall's groan. "I can't even think about that so close to the nexus right now. I'm having to use every *féin-dúltú* trick I picked up in 300 years as it is—I haven't dared have so much as a wet dream for a week now."

Well, at least that problem was about to be solved.

Lasair raised his hand to rap gently on the bedroom door.

Instead of a knock, a sound like frozen air shattering pierced his eardrums.

Setanta howled, a pitiful cry of puppy distress.

"What the hell?" The door slammed open and bounced against the bedroom wall. Josh was sitting up in bed, his tattooed hawk and dragon starting to peel themselves from his body; Conall had apparently just vaulted out of bed wearing nothing but an expression

132

of horror, probably at the fact that he had just channeled magick, if the conversation he had just overheard was any indication.

Lasair had no time for any horror other than the one undoubtedly going on under their feet. "The *Marfach* is headed for the nexus chamber, and Bryce is with it."

Conall went pale as paper.

"He sent me to summon everyone. Starting with the two of you." Even as he spoke, Lasair realized it was going to be impossible to follow his *scair-anam*'s orders. He could no more continue to leave Bryce alone with the monster than he could shape-shift.

Josh picked up a pair of jeans from the floor. "You'd better get down there, *d'orant*. I'll follow on foot—"

"Wait."

Josh paused, one leg in his jeans; Conall had already pulled on a rumpled pair of sweatpants, and his narrowed gaze indicated a lack of inclination to wait for anything.

"What?" the two chorused, one mildly, the other sharply.

Setanta whined softly; Lasair rubbed gently behind one soft ear as he replied, "Bryce is alone with the *Marfach*. When I agreed to be the one to summon the Defense of the Demesne, I told him not to put himself at unnecessary risk. I am as sure as I can be that he ignored me."

Conall and Josh exchanged a long, unreadable look. Slowly, Josh nodded. "I'll do it."

The red-haired mage appeared to be trying very hard not to frown. "Do it quickly, *dar'cion*. There's a limit to how much I can accomplish without you—and when it comes to containing the *Marfach*, that limit isn't anything worth sending to the Queen's table, not if you want to impress her."

Skirting the foot of the bed, Josh took Conall into his arms and kissed him, quickly but not hastily, a kiss so thorough and so sensual as to send magick rolling off the abruptly aroused mage in palpable waves. "That ought to hold you till I'm done here."

Conall's contented sigh turned into a yelp as *Areán* and *Scathacrú* detached themselves from Josh's skin and settled onto Conall's pale, slightly freckled chest and arm.

"I'll be damned." One corner of Josh's mouth turned up. "They've never done that before."

"They tickle." Conall tiptoed and nipped Josh's chin. "Hurry up and come get them."

* * *

The second rush of unlocked memories—memories that couldn't possibly be his—left Kevin dizzy and disoriented, in a way Bryce's human memories hadn't. He started to slide down the wall to sit on the floor, but remembered the water on the floor just before gravity would have committed him. "Rhoann, could you do something about the water?"

The blond-crested Fae started. "I... yes. Of course." Touching his fingertips to the water, he closed his eyes. A lattice of light spread outward from his fingertips, visible even to human eyes, skimming the surface of the murky water; when it faded, the water was gone. Even Kevin's trousers were dry.

Of course, this meant the tiny corpses surrounding Terry, all chitinous teeth and barbed tails, were left high and dry. Kevin gritted his teeth and looked away.

The *Marfach* had been here. And now it wasn't. And neither was Tiernan.

"Who's next?" he croaked.

Conall glanced uneasily around the room. "I think that would be me."

* * *

He'd suspected—no, he'd known—that Lasair wasn't going to do the prudent thing. If prudence was even a workable concept any more; the *Marfach* warped logic, sense and practicality around itself the way a black hole toyed with gravity. Still, Conall couldn't help but be a bit pissed off when he arrived at the top of the spiral stairs alone.

The roaring from the bottom of the stairs left him little time to be pissed off. Barefoot, and still more than half-hard from Josh's perfect kiss, he raced down the stairs, following a trail of brown bloodstains toward the uncanny light below.

The juxtaposition of beauty and hellscape in the nexus chamber was like a belt sander applied directly to a Fae's hypersensitive senses. Swirling clouds like the mist foaming off Niagara Falls rose in a lightning-shot column over the nexus; the untethered magick of the wellspring was a slow-motion cyclone of potentially lethal glitter.

And the *Marfach*, in its filthy matted male form, lay on its back, howling with rage, on top of Bryce, who had an arm around its throat and was slowly draining fouled magick from it. Lasair and Setanta stood just out of range of the creature's flailing limbs, each trying to find a place to leap into the fray.

Idiots, all of them.

And Conall included himself in that category. "Let go, Bryce!"

He didn't dare tap directly into the ley lines, not here at the unstable center of everything, but the clouds over the nexus were almost as potent an energy source as the lines would have been. Plenty for what he had to do first, anyway.

He drew in the mist of ley energy, his arousal alone enough to convert it to living magick, leaving him light-headed and bizarrely giddy.

How do I get it off Bryce without letting the magick touch it? Conall hadn't seen the world-shaking battle that had preceded the Sundering, of course, but Cuinn had gotten drunk one night in Purgatory and had let himself be persuaded to try to describe it. Conall had no interest in being hauled into the very maw of evil with a binding made from his own twisted, warped magick, and even less interest in suiciding before he and his magick could be turned against the rest of the Demesne.

Air. Air was his element, his ally. He was no elemental like Rian, nor even half of one like Rhoann, but he knew air with nearly the intimacy of a lover.

Channeling all the magick he could hold alone, he called out to the air—specifically, to the air in the *Marfach*'s lungs. *Thar amaic*—come away, come out of the monster, leave it to its own ruin. *Thar amaic*.

Come away it did, and the *Marfach* kicked and thrashed and would have cursed, but it needed air for that. And when the kicking and thrashing grew weaker, Conall summoned the wind, a great blast of air like a fist that knocked the monster to lie against the far wall, twitching like a broken toy.

This couldn't last long, though. Conall could feel the magick pouring out of him, and without Lochlann there was no way to replace it as fast as he lost it, and without Josh there was no way to control the channeling to spend it more slowly. A different channeling was called for, one that would only deplete him if the *Marfach* tested it.

He traced an arc in the air with a fingertip, whispering urgently to the air to tell it what he wanted and setting the channeling free. It took most of his remaining strength not to fall to his knees as he let go of the channeling that was draining him; he dared not let the *Marfach* see his weakness when it woke up.

Hurry, Josh, dammit.

* * *

Josh had drawn Conall close at some point during the mage's sharing, and now rested his cheek on Conall's ginger hair. "I'm sorry I took so long, *d'orant*."

Conall shook his head—gently, so as not to force Josh to move. "I wasn't the only one who needed you."

Kevin's jaw was starting to hurt from keeping his teeth so tightly clenched. *When did you call us?—did you tell Tiernan not to come?*

Rian cleared his throat. "I'm guessing my consort and I were your next call, though I don't remember receiving it." The young Prince Royal's mouth twitched in what looked like the precursor to a wicked smile. "Good job you called when you did, though, because a few minutes later and the two of us would have arrived in something less than a state of grace."

Cuinn's laugh was short and harsh. "The call was perfectly timed for us to do exactly that, *dhó-suil*. And frankly, I could have used a few more minutes' worth of the Royal mouth, considering what was waiting for us..."

* * *

Cuinn's erection had made it nearly impossible to button his jeans before he and his liege Faded. The sight greeting him on his arrival in the nexus chamber, however, would have been the buzzkill to end all buzzkills without Rian's arms around him from behind, his Fire-warmed breath in Cuinn's ear.

Tell me what you need from me. Rian's Belfast lilt, mind to mind, was ordinarily enough to give Cuinn a hard-on all by itself, accompanied as it usually was by unspeakable pleasures.

Now? *Brain bleach, for starters.*

If I had any, t'would be yours.

Cuinn could feel Rian's shudders—even a Fae raised in the human world, with no inkling of the existence of his race's mortal enemy, reacted instinctively to its presence. The male form of the *Marfach* was kneeling on the floor at the edge of the wellspring, clawing at the Stone, its curling yellowed nails splintered down to the nailbeds and bleeding. It snarled incoherently, eyes wild.

Conall stood in one of the small clear spaces

between the nexus and the wellspring. He didn't seem to be actively channeling, yet he also didn't seem to be nervous about the fact that there was nothing between him and agonizing death other than four or five yards of air. Hell, even Setanta, standing guard over Bryce and Lasair on the far side of the chamber, didn't seem all that worried.

Holding Rian's hand, Cuinn edged toward Conall between Scylla and Charybdis, the proverbial rock and the proverbial hard place. Sure, he was going to have to assay the wellspring, or the nexus, or most likely both, before too long, but there was no sense in diving into either before he had to—his mother hadn't raised any fools.

Well, yes, she had. But hopefully he'd learned a thing or two in a couple of thousand years.

"Mind bringing me up to speed, Twinkle-britches?"

He thought he'd spoken mildly enough, but apparently the mage's nickname still had the power to irk him. "*Céd d'chacairt tabh i'r den chosa, a's ná iarr orth sluasad a'fál ar isacht.*" Which translated, roughly, as *pull your shit-cart around back of the stable, and don't ask to borrow a shovel.*

Cuinn caught some serious side-eye from his liege lord, as Rian stepped carefully around him on his way to see what he could do to help Bryce and Lasair.

Well, maybe pissing off the master mage while he was busy holding off an evil force bent on destroying two worlds wasn't such a hot idea at that. "I'll use my bare hands if I have to, I promise."

Conall sighed. "Sorry. It tried to go into the wellspring just now, but it couldn't. I haven't seen any hint that Janek's still in there, but whatever solid form it has, it got from him, so I'm guessing that's what's keeping it from going through."

"Reasonable guess. And incredibly fucking lucky for the good guys. And speaking of which, do you happen to have any idea why it hasn't come charging out of there to put an end to us?"

The ginger mage actually smiled. "I had a word or two with the air—not quite elemental magick, but pretty close. If it stays where it is, it's allowed to keep breathing. More than a step or two in any direction, though, and all the air in its lungs decides to be... somewhere else. And no living magick there for it to feed on."

"Just how sure are we of that?"

"What are you—oh, *mac'fracun*."

Son of a whore, indeed. The *Marfach* had apparently just noticed the untethered magick being spat out of the wellspring, and was trying to warp it into something it could consume. Tiny, arc-welder-bright sparks of living magick went an unhealthy, almost radioactive shade of green, then bruise-purple, then charred to black and dropped to—and through—the floor.

It was like watching an unimaginably ugly bug zapper kill fireflies.

Not all of the fireflies died, though. A few survived long enough to be consumed. Then a few more, and a few more.

"We're going to have to get it over to the nexus somehow," Cuinn murmured.

"I'm open to suggestion."

* * *

"We must have been next." Maelduin shifted Terry into a more comfortable position across his lap. He spoke slowly, weighing his words, studying the room as if the walls and the floor whispered to him. "When I arrived, the only others here were those who are already in the tale."

Kevin recognized that gaze, the measuring stare of the blade-dancer. If he'd needed any more evidence that there had been a battle here, the *scian-damhsa*'s appraisal would have provided it.

"I remember trying to draw it out, to lure it to the nexus." Maelduin frowned. "Using my sword. Which is not here. And swordplay was the last thing on my mind when I lost my memory, I promise you that."

Terry turned bright red. "I, um, might be able to fill in that piece."

* * *

"You have to Fade." Fortunately, Terry had a fairly good idea where Maelduin had thrown his jeans, and they hadn't gone far. He glanced up, leaving the delicate business of settling his half-hard cock and avoiding the zipper to his sense of touch. His eyes were needed to convince a stubborn Fae to do as he'd been told.

"Not when you cannot." Maelduin, already dressed, reached under the bed for his sword.

"They need you, not me."

"*I* need you." From the look on Maelduin's face, that obviously settled the issue.

"Point taken. But judging from what Josh said,

they need you five minutes ago. I'll follow as fast as I can, I promise."

"The subway is too slow."

Jesus, the Dimple of Obstinacy was coming out on Maelduin's chin. "Where are the keys to your bike?"

Maelduin paused in the act of buckling on his sword-belt. The sight of his own personal blade-dancer strapping on his weapon never failed to leave Terry weak in the knees, even when that blade-dancer was being a git. And was getting ready to throw himself between two worlds and the personification of hatred, pain, and death. "You hate my bike."

"Hate's too strong a word. Do I wish you'd gone for that sweet little Yamaha? Hell yes. But I can handle your Harley if I have to. And I think I have to." Terry was proud of the way his voice remained steady. Letting Maelduin know he was scared shitless for him wasn't going to make an already daunting task any easier.

Of course, he'd reckoned without the acuity of Fae hearing, and the ferocity of his particular Fae's love. Before he could move, he was being crushed against Maelduin's chest, feeling lips pressed against his close-cropped curls.

"If you're brave enough to let me go, I have to be brave enough to go without you."

"You're the brave one." Terry's voice was muffled in Maelduin's chest, but that was okay. He knew the Fae could hear him. "All I have to deal with is a chopper built for someone eight inches taller than I am."

Maelduin's finger on Terry's chin tipped his head

up, to meet a warm blue faceted gaze, a hint of a smile, a lock of long blond hair falling softly against his cheek, a gentle kiss. "Juliet's keys are in the drawer of the nightstand," he murmured. "Hurry."

Then Terry's arms were around nothing at all, as Maelduin Faded.

Terry closed his eyes, the better to stop seeing his SoulShare's image hanging in the air where it wasn't any more. When he was sure it was gone, he blinked, hard, and slid open the drawer on the front of the black lacquered table next to the bed. Yes, there were the keys to the Harley, right on top of three strands of anal beads, a battery-operated butt plug, and last month's issue of *Deadpool: Classics Killustrated.*

And something else, a faintly glowing purple stone a little smaller than the palm of Terry's hand. Maelduin's *comhrac-scatha.* He wasn't sure why he picked it up, or why he slipped it into a front pocket of his jeans.

He didn't stop to ask questions, though. When a Fae was involved, there was always a chance he might get an answer, whether or not he really wanted one.

* * *

Clearing his head of the peculiar fuzziness that came with sharing the memories of other people, not to mention Fae who didn't really think like other people, was taking Kevin longer each time it happened.

"...must have happened right before we got there. Because I can remember now, a little. Maelduin, trying to get the *Marfach*'s attention."

He became aware of his surroundings again

partway through something Garrett was saying. *God damn it.* He needed to remember, too—was just short of desperate—but there was nary a stirring in the darkness of the memories that were still his alone.

Conall nodded. "I remember that too. The nexus didn't care much for me trying to fuel a channeling from it, and the way it was acting I didn't dare draw from it much longer. You and Lochlann solved that problem nicely."

Everyone in the chamber suddenly remembered exactly how Lochlann and Garrett had solved that problem, and Garrett, at least, went red to the roots of his curly dark-blond hair. "You know, it wasn't easy just switching on the four-alarm animal magnetism. Especially when I'd been expecting to find Janek down there swinging a red-hot poker or some damn thing, not half a minute before."

"You're an artist, *grafain*." Lochlann slid his arm around Garrett's waist. "It took both of us to give Conall what he needed."

Peri struggled to sit up; Fiachra helped him prop himself against the wall, then laced an arm with his to hold him upright. "We must have followed you in, then." Strangely, his voice sounded more like Falcon's than his own, but hoarse. "We'd been on our way out for the night when Josh called—I think I lost Falcon's wig on the way over here."

Fiachra passed an open-palmed hand over Peri's bleached-blond spiky hair, drawing a smile from the bedraggled drag queen. "It's an interesting look."

"You know better than that. Falcon *never* goes out without her hair." Peri flashed a quick smiled, then sobered. "I don't think the monster paid much attention to us once we got here—it was trying to figure out if it was safe to attack Conall."

At fucking last. Kevin remembered a flutter of sea-foam green disappearing into the magickal doorway in the alley, right before the Merc's brakes squealed and caught.

And more...

* * *

"I refuse to go up against the Marfach in a fucking penguin suit." Tiernan was shedding his tuxedo almost as fast as he undressed when sex was on offer, while simultaneously channeling open the dresser drawer into which he had stuffed his jeans. "You go on down and start the car, I'll be along in a minute."

Kevin stared incredulously. "I did not hear that."

"What?" Tiernan didn't bother to look up; no innocent expression was going to make Kevin buy the notion that Tiernan was going to get into the Merc with him of his own free will.

"I'm not sure trying to save the world will be any easier after a panic attack than it would be in a penguin suit. Or have you forgotten your last ride with me?"

"Not likely." Tiernan shimmied into a pair of jeans. "Have you seen my leather jacket?"

"I'm pretty sure it's downstairs by the fireplace, where you threw it after we got home last night. Look—"

His husband wasn't in a looking mood; he was already out the bedroom door, barefoot and shirtless, and Kevin had no choice but to follow if he wanted to continue the conversation.

Or monologue, more like. "You heard Josh. The *Marfach* is already at the nexus. We don't have time for both of us to take the long way there. They need you."

"And you don't?" Tiernan took the last five stairs in a jump he made look easy, skirted Kevin's weight machine, and bent to pick up his black leather jacket.

"I..." Kevin frowned. "Of course I do. But what does that have to do with—"

Still circling his shoulders to settle the jacket, Tiernan clasped both of Kevin's hands in his. "Now it's my turn to ask you—do you remember our last ride together?"

"I'm not likely to forget it." Kevin repressed a shudder. It hadn't been long after he'd first been approached at Purgatory's bar by a Fae with fornication and not much else on his mind, not long after he'd found himself imperfectly SoulShared with that same Fae. The *Marfach* hadn't yet been freed from its prison in the ley lines, but the flaw in their Sharing had given it a way into Kevin's mind. And the hell-ride through a sleet storm to Purgatory, with Tiernan clinging desperately to the inside door handle of the Mercedes and turning several shades of green, while Kevin fought off one blinding mental attack after another by a being bent on torture, was permanently seared into Kevin's memory.

From the way Tiernan was looking at him, it almost seemed as if his Fae husband was sharing the memory with him. "Exactly." Blond hair fell over one blue topaz eye as Tiernan nodded. "If I go on ahead of you, that's all I'm going to be thinking about until you get there. I don't know how much good I'll do you if the *bodlag* does come after you... but if it wants you, it's going to have to take me first."

146

"I love you." The words were silent, Kevin's voice being caught behind the outsized lump in his throat.

Tiernan's responsive grin was pure wickedness. "I know." He channeled magick, and the keys to the Mercedes flew off their hook by the door to the garage; he snagged them in midair and handed them to Kevin. "Let's go do this."

By the time the car was backed halfway out of the garage, Tiernan was as pale as Kevin had ever seen him, and his knuckles were paler still where he clung to the inside door handle.

Kevin knew better than to ask whether his husband had changed his mind. And he hoped like hell that Lucien's odd Fae gift, protection from police scrutiny, extended to the Merc, because if his trusty old car could fly, it was going to do it tonight.

* * *

"And I remember your arrival." Rhoann was smiling—a faint smile, but still a smile. "I remember thinking that I had never heard brakes make a sound like that before."

"Me either." Kevin managed not to wince at the memory Rhoann's words called up, but a few of the Fae weren't as successful. "But it beat getting into an argument with the back wall of the bodega across the alley."

"You would've lost," Lucien deadpanned. "I used to be a mechanic. Trust me on this."

"I'll leave that assessment to the expert." Remembering that Tiernan had made it as far as the club was a relief... but Kevin's memory ended with that glimpse of

147

Falcon's gown disappearing into the hidden door. "Can anyone pick up the story from there?"

Lucien nodded, passing an open palm over the top of his bald head, wiping away sweat. "I think I can."

* * *

"What are we doing down here?"

Mac was making good time down the stairs, but Lucien was beating him handily—him and Rhoann, who was hanging back to pace Mac.

"I just need to see—*Crisse de câlice de tabarnak d'esti de sacrament!*"

Lucien took the last few stairs in a bound and raced over to the bar. They didn't have time to waste, but he couldn't just pass by the ruin someone had made of the bar. Not when it was giving him flashbacks like a son of a bitch. Shattered bottles, alcohol all over the floor—it reminded him all too much of the wreckage his fight with the *Marfach* had left behind in the old Purgatory.

"Holy shit," Mac breathed.

"Every time I think I understand a human word, I find I am wrong." Rhoann was studying the huge swimming tank, as if he expected to find it had met the same fate as the bottles. "What is holy about this shit?"

Mac smacked the Fae's arm lightly. "I can never tell when you're serious."

Lucien stirred the broken glass with the toe of his boot—stopped, staring. "Is that blood?"

"Looks too brown to me—even for dried blood." Mac scratched his head. "But in this light, who can tell?—and there are footprints of the stuff heading toward the back door." He pointed toward the service entrance, leading out to the back alley. "So you may be right."

"Maybe it's the *Marfach*'s." Lucien skirted the wreckage and made his way toward the service entrance, careful not to step in the blood, or whatever it was. "Janek always bled brown." He hawked and spat off into the shadows. Janek's name tasted worse in his mouth than the *Marfach*'s did.

"Hey?"

Josh's voice echoed down the front stairwell—if he'd called out just a few decibels louder, Lucien would have gladly traded his left hairy nut for a pair of Depends.

"Back here," Mac called, in the same tone.

The eerie green glow of the safety lights concealed Josh as much as it revealed him easing around the half-open black glass door. "What the hell happened down here?"

"I'm going to go out on a limb and guess it had something to do with the *Marfach*." Lucien thought he was doing a decent job keeping the memory of getting his skull caved in by their very own basement monster out of his voice.

Until Rhoann loomed up close behind him and Mac took his hand. *Oh, well. Things could be worse.*

"Do you want to wait here, *laród-ar*-Fuzz?" Rhoann's breath tickled Lucien's ear hairs. "Mac can help me if I need to channel—"

"*Merde de merde,*" Lucien growled. "I'm not going to scream and faint. And I need to tear off a strip of that tattooed hide as much as anyone." He squeezed Mac's hand, though, just the same.

"Let's move." Josh herded the three of them toward the back door.

The door opened onto the alley with a hydraulic-assisted hiss. Lucien had barely gotten a foot out the door when a squeal like a sow being tortured sliced into his eardrums.

"Christ, did it get out?—is it up here?" Mac shoved past Lucien, with Rhoann and Josh right behind him.

No, no flayed pig, and no murderous monster. Just an old Mercedes, the smell of scorched rubber, a white-faced Kevin and a green-faced Tiernan.

And a trail of bloody footprints, wet and brown, leading straight to the hidden door and, as soon as the keyword was spoken, down the stone steps.

* * *

By the time Kevin was sure he'd fully emerged from the shared memory, Lasair was kneeling on the floor in front of Bryce, examining the soles of his feet. Setanta was helping—or, more precisely, "helping," still holding his right front paw off the floor but eagerly sticking his cold wet nose in where it didn't belong.

It was hard to tell whether Bryce was wincing or smothering laughter. "Setanta, if you lick that, so help me God—"

"Your blood is red, *sumiúl*."

That has to be a good sign. The wall between Kevin and his memories was still bugging the hell out of him, but if Bryce's formerly polluted blood was running red again, it stood to reason there was good news on the other side of that wall.

Hopefully Tiernan was there, too.

Conall was smiling, for possibly the first time since everyone had awakened. "You have no idea how happy I was to see you come down those stairs." He was, of course, looking straight at Josh, in a way that shut out the rest of the room.

"Oh, yes, I do." Josh still looked like he'd been through the proverbial wringer, but his answering grin lit up his face. "I felt it for myself when you Faded into me."

* * *

Took you long enough.

Josh chuckled inwardly. *Noted and logged.* The glow of Conall's delight, and the rush of his relief, took any conceivable sting out of his words. *You seem to be doing just fine without me, though.*

Like hell. His SoulShare's inner voice went from light to weary in less than a breath. *Lochlann and Garrett got here just in time... but it cost me so much to keep the damned monster contained before they got here, I haven't been able to recover.*

Josh wasn't sure whether the impulse to squeeze Lochlann's hand came from him or from Conall, but he supposed it didn't really matter. Before Josh had arrived, Lochlann had been feeding Conall living magick—ley energy tapped from whatever source Lochlann had been able to call to himself and transmuted in his body into the form a Fae could use—but only at the rate Conall could take in on his own. Now, with full access to Conall's legendary channeling capacity restored, the magick rushed into their shared body as if Lochlann had turned on a pressure washer.

Scathacrú spun crazily overhead, bumping his golden head against the ceiling, giddy on the rush of power. And *Areán* perched on the head of the leather chaise at the heart of the nexus, looking for all the world like a cat stoned out of his mind on nip.

Relax, d'orant. I've got this.

Did you just actually tell me to relax? Josh felt Conall grin. *Because if you did, you realize you're in charge of my relaxation, and chances are I'm going to need some very shortly.*

Josh didn't have a lot of breath to spare for laughter, the way the magick was thundering through him, but he found enough. *You genuinely are a horndog, baby. Don't ever change.*

* * *

Everyone shared in Josh's remembered chuckle. Almost everyone—Coinneach still sat cross-legged on the floor, listening intently, roots curling out from his fingertips and trying against and again to penetrate the living Stone without success. And Setanta just looked confused, nosing gently at the palm of Bryce's hand.

Kevin's heart felt like it was trying to kick him in the ribs, as his memory yielded up to him, and to everyone else, laughter that wasn't there.

* * *

"Nice to see our *draoi ríoga*'s functioning properly."

Tiernan's soft laughter was all Fae, all wickedness, and despite their desperate situation, it jump-started a delicious heaviness in Kevin's trousers.

152

Which was all right, since Kevin was probably going to have to give Tiernan the same sort of help Garrett and—apparently—Josh were giving their *scair-anaim*, and Cuinn and Rian were starting to give each other, very shortly.

"How's your, um, functioning?"

Tiernan's arm slipped around Kevin's waist. "Do you need to ask?" He leaned in for a quick nip at Kevin's ear, but Kevin noticed his gaze never left the *Marfach*.

Maelduin was trying to lure the male form of the monster toward the nexus, or drive it there, going from leaving himself a lot more vulnerable to attack than any Fae with a sense of self preservation ever would to feinting, as quick and light as the flicker of a snake's tongue. But the *Marfach* didn't startle, and it didn't seem all that interested in scoring itself a Fae, either.

"It looks sluggish," Kevin whispered. "Bryce must have done a real number on it."

"Good eye." Tiernan, too, kept his voice low. "We'll make a Fae out of you yet."

"I'll settle for having a little Fae in me from time to time."

More of that uncanny Fae laughter drew a soft groan from Kevin, no more than a breath.

"You make my point perfectly, *lanan*." Crystal fingers worked their way up Kevin's side. "Could I persuade you to toy with me a bit? Maelduin's making a gallant effort, but it looks as if he could use some help."

Obediently, Kevin moved to shield Tiernan from view with his body—not that he'd ever minded being on display for or with his husband, but he drew the line at sharing him with the *Marfach*. All the same, a chill skittered down his spine as he tongued Tiernan's earlobe between his lips and took firm hold of his hard-muscled ass. "You do remember you're unarmed, right?" He tried to make the murmur as sexy as possible. "Let the kid handle the slicing and dicing."

Tiernan snorted softly, grinding against Kevin with a slow heat that probably would have gotten the two of them thrown out of any dance club in D.C. other than Purgatory. "I'm never unarmed. And if there's anything left of Janek in that monster, it's going to come after me a lot more readily than it will ever follow Maelduin."

You had to go and remind me of that, didn't you?

He didn't say it out loud, but he might as well have. Tiernan pulled back, just far enough to look Kevin in the eyes. He smiled, that perfect wicked smile that had snared Kevin the moment he'd laid eyes on him.

"*S'vra lom tú, elafantabod.*"

"Seriously?"

But *elephant-dick* made Kevin grin, as Tiernan had surely intended.

Something over Kevin's shoulder caught Tiernan's attention. It didn't take a genius to guess what.

"Hai, *feol'marh!*"

Something about Tiernan's challenge reminded Kevin of a fish-hook, or maybe a matador's lance. He turned, just in time to see the *Marfach* look up— slowly, as if its filthy matted head was the heaviest thing it had ever lifted.

Eyes the fitful glowing red of burning bone peered out from under wiry brows.

The monster smiled.

Kevin's mouth went dry.

"There's nothing left here of poor Meat but his meat." The *Marfach* cackled. "But we do owe him your head, I suppose. It's the least we can do to honor his memory."

Gently but firmly, Tiernan moved Kevin aside. "I specified *dead* meat." Eyes that had been warm and teasing moments before were now the eerie impossible blue of glacier ice. "And you look about as lively as carrion. But if you think you can take me, you're welcome to try."

* * *

Oh, shit. Shit. SHIT.

Kevin balled his hands into fists to stop their shaking. "You all can quit staring at me." He thought his voice was remarkably even, under the circumstances. "That's all I remember."

Fae were notoriously bad at following directions. "Tiernan's *rinc'marh* made me ashamed I ever called myself a blade-dancer." Maelduin's hand enfolded Terry's. "Even unarmed, he drove the monster where he wanted it, kept it in place, let it go when he willed."

Cuinn nodded. "He was buying us time—Conall was recovering his magick, and he and I were trying to figure out what the fuck to do with the *bodlag*."

Kevin could see it all as they spoke, the lethal grace his husband wore as naturally and as lightly as his beautiful smile. *Why did they remember that, and not me?*

Terry cleared his throat. "I think that was where I came in. And Maelduin, just for the record, I am never driving Juliet again. I will ride behind you. I will ride in front of you. I will wrap my arms around your neck and fly like a flag in the wind of your passage. But I am never driving that bike again."

Despite the growing tension in the room, Maelduin laughed softly. Kevin almost did, too—the memory of Terry's feet not quite touching the ground when he was forced to stop at a light would have been worth at least a chuckle, any other time.

"You rode her when it mattered—"

"Oh, shit." Fiachra's whisper, barely audible, was still enough to cut Maelduin off mid-reassurance. "Now *I* remember."

* * *

Not everyone looked away from the death-dance when Terry stumbled down the stairs—the *sciain-damhsa*, in particular, were laser-focused on the *Marfach*, and Fiachra suspected that not even the building coming down around them—again—would change that.

But enough were distracted to give the monster the idea that some odds, somewhere, had shifted in its favor. The space around it warped, and suddenly Tiernan faced the monster in its most nightmarish form, a thing like a scorpion with powerful jaws, dripping fangs, and a tail made of small copies of itself, arching up over its back to brush the ceiling and ending in a lethal barbed stinger.

And it laughed. The sound made Fiachra want to jam knitting needles into his ears.

"*I HAVE PLAYED WITH YOU LONG ENOUGH. I HUNGER.*"

156

Fiachra's truthsight had never been more of a curse.

The *Marfach*'s jaws extended toward Tiernan—but its tail stabbed down toward Peri.

"*Básagh gan'anma!*" No channeling Fiachra knew could save Peri. But he needed none. He leaped and caught the giant barb in his arms, knocking it aside to smash into the floor with a force that would have shattered any stone not living.

The *Marfach* didn't bother to look away from its primary prey. It didn't need to, not when its tail had a thousand times a thousand tiny minds of its own.

That tail wrapped around Fiachra. He had just enough time to feel the tiny monsters jostling for position against his skin—then the *Marfach* found its meal, the magick in every cell of a Fae's body.

Fiachra's flesh began to melt.

* * *

Fiachra's jaw was clenched against screams Kevin remembered all too well from his own experience with the *Marfach*; Peri's arms were tight around him, a living reminder that the melting the dark Fae remembered—that they all remembered, now—had never happened.

Or it had been healed, somehow.

"Yes..."

The breeze, the whispering of leaves spoke for the first time since the sharing of memories had started. Coinneach wasn't staring at the floor any more; he locked gazes with Fiachra, a new light in his eyes.

"Yes. I heard you cry out, even over the thunder of the magick through the wellsprings. Blood calling to blood. And I came."

Kevin remembered the moment now, though he hadn't realized right away that the creature in the wellspring was Coinneach. He'd heard stories—the *Gille Dubh* weren't called the "Dark Men" solely for the color of their skin. They had another form, one they rarely took.

One that the *Marfach* itself should have had screaming nightmares about finding in its closet, or under its bed at night.

Dark Coinneach roared, a lightning-shot gale.

And with that roar, it was as if a dam burst. No— as if a tsunami came ashore, a horrible unstoppable force, like last year's horror in Japan, driving everything before it.

Everything. Everyone's memories, all at once.

Kevin remembered...

Chapter Sixteen

Kevin remembered...

Peri, terrified, resolute, stepped forward and willed the *Marfach* to turn and look at him. It had grown, it glowed with a darkness that pulsed around it. But Falcon was wrapped around Peri like armor, like a cloak, her ferocious determination and refusal to be touched. *She's my Fae gift*, he realized, stunned. *My magick.*

The monster swiveled an eye toward him.

"Let him go," Falcon snapped.

To everyone's astonishment but Falcon's, it did.

Kevin remembered...

THE MONSTER CANNOT TOUCH THE MAGICK OF MOTHER MOON.

The *darag*'s gentle voice cut through Dark Coinneach's rage like one of the silver sickles of the *draoidhean*.

Her magick... is gentle. Thinking was hard. Fury was much easier. *Too gentle for this.* Fiachra—his blood kin—lay on the floor, the flesh of his torso twisted and melted into a parody of Fae shape. Coinneach's feet ached with the need to grow tendrils through the *Marfach*'s obscene body and rend it the way roots shattered stone.

159

ITS TOUCH WILL DESTROY YOU. DESTROY US.

The sent-image of his *darag*'s death, the vivid reality and the certainty of it, brought Coinneach up short. *Not that. Never that. But what can we do?*

ENVELOP IT IN SLOW-TIME.

Yes.

Dark Coinneach started receding into the *Gille Dubh*'s heart. Rage was a devourer of energy, and slow-time required a massive outpouring of magick for very little visible result. He could not maintain both.

And short of a time-slip, for which he and his *darag* would have to call on every other *darag* and *Gille Dubh* awake in the human world, slow-time was the only chance he could give Fiachra. Or any of them.

Kevin remembered...

Rhoann tore himself from the restraining arms of his husbands and dropped to his knees beside Fiachra. The dark Fae's face was like a candle left too long by the fireside, his body warped in ways impossible for living flesh.

"I can heal you, *dre'thair*." His words were as much for the trembling Peri as for the terrified Fiachra. "This was done by magick alone. I can undo it. But I need water."

As well ask for the sun on a strand of stars. There was no water in sight, only the hurricane swirl of ley energy around the nexus and the razor-sharp glint of unbound magick over the wellspring.

And the *Marfach*, rising up over them all, jaws opening wide with a creaking, deafening groan like the sound of bones taxed to their utmost and snapping under unbearable weight.

Mac and Lucien knelt on either side of Rhoann; he put an arm around each, hoping they could feel his gratitude for their presence.

Wind rose around the monster, at once a zephyr and a whirlwind, chill air spilling off a glacier and a desert blast. The dreadful roar faded to a whisper, the dully glowing red eyes stared straight ahead.

Slowly, the *Marfach* blinked.

"Hurry."

Rhoann turned with everyone else, at the voice like the creaking of branches under the weight of snow. Coinneach, like the *Marfach*, was nearly motionless, his hands stretched out in front of him and his fingers interlaced in what was obviously a warding gesture. Unlike the *Marfach*, though, he trembled under some terrible unseen strain. And in the sudden silence, a soft rustling seemed loud—the *Gille Dubh*'s toes, growing, receding, trying vainly to root him in the living Stone.

"Hurry," Coinneach repeated. "I cannot hold it this way for long."

"Let me help." Tiernan skirted the edge of the nexus cloud and knelt beside Coinneach, touching the floor next to the *Gille Dubh*'s restless feet.

A shimmer of crystal, elemental Earth magick, rose from the Stone. Coinneach's roots instantly sank deep, and the strain in his stance gave way to relief.

Lucien leaned in, his lips brushing Rhoann's ear. "Now that Bryce has broken the ward and Tiernan's breached the protection of the Stone—can you talk to the water in the tank upstairs?"

Rhoann's eyes went wide. "You are my wisdom, *laród-ar*-Fuzz."

"If we weren't in trouble before, we sure as hell are now." Lucien nipped at Rhoann's ear in the way he knew Rhoann loved. "Get busy, *amant*."

Kevin remembered...

Agony sleeted along every twisted, tortured nerve in Fiachra's twisted, tortured body, agony so consuming it brought back his body's memories of the Pattern-passage. Nothing existed—nothing had ever existed—but a universe of pain.

Except Peri's hand in his. Peri's lips on his forehead. Peri's voice in his ear.

"Hold on, *aisuruhito*. Hold on. Help's coming."

Fiachra tried to tell Peri that he would hold as long as Peri needed him to. That he loved him. But he was fairly sure he no longer had a mouth. All he could do was try to squeeze Peri's hand.

Peri stroked the back of Fiachra's hand. *I love you, too,* the touch said.

How had he forgotten their language?

Water. There was water rising all around him. And where it touched him, he had flesh again, flesh free of pain.

Hands splashed water over his body. Cupped hands poured water over his face. He blinked open eyes that hadn't been there a minute ago and looked up into faces—Peri's, Mac's, Lucien's, Rhoann's. Rhoann's eyes were closed, and Fiachra could sense magick flowing from him into the water.

"Thank you," he whispered, to each of them, and to all of them.

Kevin remembered...

Water charged with the healing magick of the Fae welled up swiftly around Coinneach's roots, bracing and soothing all at once. The relief was indescribable. Even the strain of maintaining the slow-time skin around the *Marfach* was eased as the water rose.

And his cousin, his kin-Fae, was whole again, unmarked—

A low sound, a tremor in the air and in Coinneach's core, intruded on the healing flow.

Louder, and higher. Coinneach's ears hurt. So did everyone else's, if hands or paws clapped over ears were any indication. And to a man and to a Fae and to a blind puppy, they were all staring at the *Marfach*.

The *Marfach* was staring as well... staring at the rising water. And screaming.

Coinneach's pain slid into agony as easily and as painfully as a rusty razor slicing into flesh as the monster's scream scaled up. He dropped into a crouch and wrapped his arms around his knees, trying to curl into a ball, trying to shut out the sound of the *Marfach*'s terror.

Kevin remembered...

Fuck.

Josh wasn't sure how he heard Conall's whisper inside his head, when the *Marfach*'s scream was like a living thing trying to crawl into his brain and his body.

What is it?

Can't focus... to channel...

Josh staggered, and Conall with him, battered by the hellish screeching.

And then the force of the monster's panic snapped the time-channeling Coinneach had put on it, and hell truly broke loose.

The next shriek was almost too high to hear. It knocked Josh off his feet, sending him stumbling over

Bryce's outstretched legs to land face-first in the water. Everyone else was down, too—except for Coinneach, who had the advantage of being literally rooted to the floor.

"Oh, fuck, no," someone moaned. Josh thought it was Kevin; the trail of blood on the wall behind him suggested he'd hit the stone hard and slid all the way down. Now he struggled to sit up, his hands scrabbling and splashing, as he watched...

We're dead. Slowly.

Josh wasn't sure if the words were his or Conall's. They made sense, though. The *Marfach* was shedding tiny ravenous monsters from its tail, shaking them loose. They fell into the water like a horrible rain.

Unlike their terrified parent, they could swim.

And exactly like their parent, they were hungry.

Kevin remembered...

Kevin's eyes kept drifting in and out of focus. Maybe it was the blow to his head. Maybe it was sheer blind panic at the thought of being devoured—for real, this time, not just trapped in his own mind and forced to imagine being eaten alive for the *Marfach*'s amusement.

"I'm not going to let it get you, *lanan*." Tiernan's voice was firm, but just a little too loud, the way someone might talk who had spent the last couple of hours in front of the speakers at a doom metal concert. "No fucking way."

Kevin managed a nod. Tiernan had killed to protect him before—right here, in fact, in the previous incarnation of Purgatory's basement. It hadn't been Tiernan's fault that Janek hadn't stayed dead.

But at the moment, Tiernan couldn't quite pull himself together enough to stand. And the water was full of chitin-toothed horrors.

Another shriek came from overhead—a lullaby compared to the last one. *Areán*, the black-headed hawk normally tattooed on Josh's chest, dove and snatched a tiny monster from the water—no, two, one in its claws and one in its beak. Two sharp snaps, and the creatures fell lifeless into the water as the bird wheeled in the tight space and dove a second time. And a third.

Scathacrú, Josh's gold-winged dragonet, quickly picked up on the new game. Its flame was less effective in the water than *Areán*'s beak, but its claws were just as deadly as the bird's.

"Jesus," Kevin whispered reverently. The little monsters were schooling, dodging to avoid death from the air, ignoring the humans and the Fae except when trying to hide behind and under them.

Dripping jaws shot out, almost too fast to see, and snapped around *Areán*, plucking the hawk from the air and snapping its body nearly in half. The severed tip of one wing splashed into the water as the rest of the bird disappeared into the *Marfach*'s gaping maw.

"*Scathacrú!*" Josh shouted, holding up his arm; the dragon dove and coiled around it, its head still raised and spitting defiant flame.

Kevin remembered...

#burning feather smell# #tear-scent# #fear-scent# #strange magick#

why does human-who-flies smell like magick?

"Hey, pup, what are you... oh, fuck, Terry brought my *comhrac-scatha*..."

165

swordfae knows what the stone in human-who-flies' pocket is! #tail wagging# #splash into the water# #stone still in my mouth# #goodpuppy#

"Take it to Conall—hurry!"

#stop# #think#

"conall" is the magefae. and i can smell him. i could smell that much magick without a nose. but his scent is wrapped up in inkscent and fire—

"Hurry!"

monster smell is closer, rotting meat, acid, nose burning. i fade to magefae and inkscent—

flyingfire spitting at me! #growl# #yelp#

"*Scathacrú*, goddamn it!—hey, what's this?"

#wagging#

"It's my *comhrac-scatha!*" *swordfae's voice is hoarse and raw, and hard to hear after monster-screams.*

"Sweet bleeding Jesus."

what did magefae just do? magick scent is so strong—can't breathe—i hope firstmaster doesn't set me to hunt this mage till i'm grown—

inkscent strokes me, gently, no fear-scent on him. but magefae is near, and nervous. i lick my fangs and try to look fierce.

inkscent puts the stone back in my mouth. it tastes different. i try to bite it. #whine#

"It's not a treat, pupper."

pupper?

"I think you have to drop it on the *Marfach*." *inkscent whispers in my ear. it tickles. but he is so serious, i hold still and don't shake my head.* "Can you do that, *tréan-cú?*"

#tail wagging# but only firstmaster can set me to hunt. i turn toward his scent, and i know when he

closes his eyes because i can see. see firstmaster, newmaster, inkscent, water everywhere—

deadmeat acid monster walking slowly through the water, all jaws and armor and burning eyes and a giant tail. and the stench of magick gone dark.

#snarl#

#sit#

was that sound me?

no time to be frightened of my own growl! i pick my spot, low on its back, right before the tail, a crack in its armor, like the curl-up-smell-bad bugs in our basement. i fade.

it knows i'm here, tries to stab me with its tail—i drop the stone—

hard thing on the end of its tail hits me—

paw stuck #yelp#

#flying#

#splash#

Kevin remembered...

What's wrong, baby?

Josh's inner voice, for all its arid humor, was remarkably soothing under the circumstances. Not that any amount of soothing was going to do Conall any good. *Apart from the imminent end of two worlds, you mean? That dog was bred to send Fae like me mad with growls just like that—oh,* spiraod n'Draoctagh...

Setanta went flying through the air, flicked off the scorpion-thing's back like a fly whisked off a horse's back with a lashing tail. And before the pup could hit the water, everything blinked.

And now there were two *Marfachs.*

The fact that Conall had known this was going to happen didn't make the sight any easier to deal with.

The two monsters glared at one another, unmoving except for tails twitching like thousands of tiny lethal creatures having simultaneous seizures.

Conall would have held his breath if he'd been breathing. *If I got that channeling wrong, and they both turn on us...*

One *Marfach* lunged at the other, knocking it off its clawed feet and into the water. A shriek almost as eardrum-piercing as the first one followed, a barbed tail elongating to wrap around the attacker.

One less thing to worry about.

"Twinklebritches!"

Cuinn and Rian were kneeling in the middle of the wellspring next to Coinneach, nearly invisible in the whirl of untethered magick. They weren't inaudible, though, and Cuinn was beckoning with the hand on the far side of the war zone the nexus had become. As if the *Marfachs* were going to notice anything but each other right now.

Which, Conall suspected, was a large part of the irritating Loremaster's reason for summoning him.

Crossing the room was interesting. Josh had to duck a sweeping tail twice, and stopped briefly to scoop Setanta out of the water and gently toss the pup to Lasair and Bryce.

"You bellowed?" Josh's throat was still raw, Conall noticed, from his call to *Scathacrú*, and probably from holding back cries at *Areán*'s fate. One more debt to be paid out of the *Marfach*'s chitinous hide.

"I did, because I have an idea."

Kevin remembered...

Cuinn had learned a channeling once that let him tune out sounds selectively, such as the hellish cacophony of two nightmares dry-fucking one another with barbed tails. Unfortunately, he needed said hellish cacophony to stop long enough for him to collect his thoughts and remember the channeling.

Oh, well.

"Listen, Twinklebritches, Coinneach, I think I know how we can trap the *Marfach*. But it's going to take both of you. Maybe all three of us, I don't know."

Rian shook his head. "Not you, consort mine. You're going to be needing to hold open the way back to the Realm—"

"Back to the Realm?" The voice was Josh's, but the *you-are-out-of-your*-bod-snadhm'e-*mind* was all Conall. "Pardon me, but wasn't that what this was all intended to avoid?"

"Ideally, yes. Things stopped being ideal when the monster stole a march on us. Now, listen."

Remarkably, Conall shut up.

Cuinn hoped the twisting feeling in his guts meant there were a few more miracles lined up waiting to be pulled out of his ass, because they were all going to need them.

"Coinneach. So far as we know, you have the only magick the *Marfach* can't turn."

"Time-magick, moon-magick. Yes."

"What about the—" Conall shut up again, but not without a pointed glance at the spare *Marfach*, or maybe the original, presently trying to figure out how to get its narrow inner set of jaws around its opponent's armored throat.

Cuinn shrugged. "It could probably snack on the *comhrac-scatha*, if it realized it was there, and if the extra *Marfach* were inclined to let it. I think all it noticed

169

on its back was Setanta, though, and now it has other things to worry about. Like we do. May I go on?"

"*Do dalat-serbhisach.*"

"If we live through this and I ever need a saddle-servant, you'll be the first one I call."

"GentleFae," Rian chided softly. "Focus, if you please."

Cuinn felt Rian's hand slip into his, and relaxed—not much, but enough. *Get me through this,* dhó-súil.

I will.

"Right, then. Twinklebritches, can you hook up with Coinneach, use his time magick to craft a *laród-scatha* around the *Marfach*? One it can't break down or break through? One that's safe for us to send back to the Realm so the Loremasters can take their time, so to speak, figuring out what to do with it?"

If Josh's expression was anything to go by, Conall's first reaction to his suggestion had something to do with figuring out which combination of animals to tell him to go fuck. But Cuinn, like everyone else, knew the ginger mage couldn't resist a good magickal conundrum, not even with untethered magick sleeting around him and death times two duking it out a few feet away.

"Maybe with Lochlann's help... no, he'd only turn moon-magick into living magick, that's no good..."

"What is a *laród-scatha*?" There was movement under the water—Coinneach's roots retracting from the floor and becoming toes again.

The Frown Line of Extreme Pensiveness had appeared between Josh/Conall's brows, so Cuinn took the question, not wanting to interrupt anything important. "It's a sphere made of magic, and it only has an inside, no outside. We used one to send the *Marfach* to Antarctica and to keep it trapped there under the ice."

"And you want to craft one from a timeslip?"

Cuinn couldn't tell if the *Gille Dubh* was impressed, amused, or appalled—his wide-eyed stare could have been any of the three, and it was hard to tease emotional inflections out of the sound of a gale-force wind. "That was the general idea, yes."

The sound of creaking wood came up through the floor, muffled slightly by the water. A TIMESLIP CANNOT CLOSE ON ITSELF AS A SPHERE DOES. TIME DOES NOT ALLOW IT.

The voice of Coinneach's *darag*, or maybe of all the *daragin*.

And of course, one of the fucking monsters had to choose exactly that moment to scream at the other. Cuinn thought he could feel his ears bleeding.

Rian squeezed Cuinn's hand. *It was a good notion, any road—*

"Wait." Josh held up a hand, and Cuinn thought he could see the excited gleam of Conall's apple-green eyes in Josh's. "That's perfect. A folded flat mirror can do the same thing, and use less magick."

"You're thinking of the mirror you were trapped in. Right after we met." It was still Josh speaking, but now the voice was all his.

"I am." Now the voice, a light tenor, quivered slightly. "And it's going to be a pleasure you cannot even imagine to turn that channeling back on this *tón-grabrog*."

171

Kevin remembered...

Coinneach half-listened to the plans being hastily made around him. He was ready to rejoin the conversation when he was needed, but for the moment most of his attention was devoted to his *darag*'s calm, and calming, presence.

I have never tried a channeling this great alone.

YOU ARE NOT ALONE. The gleam of moonlight in the *darag*'s voice was kind. BUT CARE MUST BE TAKEN.

Care with the trapping?

CARE WITH THE CHANNELING. FORCE THE MOTHERS' MAGICK TOO MUCH, AND TIME ITSELF WILL SNAP BACK, ERASING MEMORIES OF WHAT HAS BEEN.

Coinneach managed a smile. *Then I will have to count on you to keep my memories safe for me, as you have always done.*

Silence, broken only by the rasping of the *Marfachs*' dead shells as they circled one another, so different from the gentle creaking of the *darag*'s branches.

THIS MOMENT, I WILL FORGET. AM FORGETTING. FORGOT.

But you never forget anything!

"Coinneach?"

The Fae princeling called the *Gille Dubh* out of his communion; both Cuinn and Josh, or Conall, had fallen silent.

"Yes?"

"We'll need to be about this soon, if it's to be done at all. Time magick doesn't sit well in this place, there's been too much of it used here in the past. And there's no telling how long our monster's twin can keep it occupied."

Rian ducked as he spoke, and Coinneach flinched back, both to avoid a lashing tail.

"I'd better get my pert round ass over to the nexus, then." Cuinn's smirk was as insouciant as it ever was, but he had gone pale as birch bark beneath his tan. "Somebody has to open the door."

Coinneach watched the Loremaster circle around the edge of the maelstrom of ley energy that was the great nexus, keeping a wary eye on both combatants as he looked for a clear path to the center. There was a slight possibility that one of the *Marfachs* might ignore him, but Cuinn seemed unready to chance it.

Coinneach didn't blame him.

"Do you think you can feed me your magick? Or will you have to be the one to channel the *laród-scatha*?"

A soft rustle of reassurance came through the wellspring. "My *darag* says I can gift you our magick."

Conall's quick smile transformed Josh's face—and somehow, Coinneach found the observation not the slightest bit confusing.

"Then let's—"

"Fuck. Me. With. A. Pneumatic. Pile-driver."

All eyes—except those of the *Marfachs*—turned to Cuinn, crouched in the center of the nexus.

"What is it?" Rian crouched slightly, ready to throw himself between his consort and obscene death.

Cuinn looked up, his pale jade eyes unnervingly wide. "The other Loremasters have sealed the portal with a timestop—Fae time magick, pretty much the only time magick we've got. I can't get through to them. Twinklebritches, you're the only one with the wattage to break through this."

Josh/Conall shook his head. "I can't. Not and build the *laród-draoctagh* at the same time."

Lochlann helped Garrett up from where they had both fallen. "Let us see what we can do to help."

Kevin remembered...

Terry was glad he had Maelduin's arm to hold him up. "Any chance the mirror *Marfach* might kill the real one?"

Maelduin's gaze never left the horrifying combatants, but something in his touch told Terry his *scair-anam* was well aware of the fear he thought he'd managed to hide. "Yes, that possibility is always there. The *comhrac-scatha* would be a poor teacher, else."

"I guess that makes sense."

Maelduin drew him back a few steps, carefully keeping him out of the arc a tail might pass through. Space was scarce; Cuinn was crouched in the middle of the nexus next to the black leather chaise, one hand on the floor under the water and the other hand holding Lochlann's, and even though Terry couldn't see the magick they were channeling, there was a wavering around them like the air over an arc welder.

Every so often, one *Marfach* or the other spared a hungry glance at what had to be a magickal feast for the ages, but whatever Josh and Conall and Coinneach were up to was starting to take shape right behind the eye of the nexus, the hazy outline of a mirror, and fortunately for Cuinn and Lochlann, the monsters didn't want anything to do with it.

Unfortunately for everyone else, the magickal

work meant the rest of the basement was getting considerably more crowded. Tiernan had recovered from the godawful scream more quickly than most, and was doing his best to keep one step ahead of the clashing *Marfachs*, distracting them where he could and helping others stay out of their way when he couldn't.

"How much longer, Twinklebritches?" Cuinn's shout rose above the monsters' hisses.

"Couple of minutes." Josh/Conall's voice was even, but Josh and Coinneach were both sweating, and their clasped hands trembled.

"Take your time," Cuinn rasped. "So to speak. This timestop isn't budging. What the fuck are the Loremasters in the Pattern thinking?"

"Probably that they don't want us to do exactly what we're trying to do. Imagine that."

No matter how many times he saw and heard it happen, Terry didn't think he was ever going to get used to the way sarcastic repartee was an integral part of any battle to the death involving a Fae.

"I'm a little busy for daydreaming—"

One moment, Terry was craning his neck, trying to see the nexus through the water and the billows of almost-but-not-quite-invisible ley energy. The next, he screamed as a barbed tail cut between him and Maelduin like a whip cracking, coiled around his waist, and lifted him clear of the floor.

Kevin remembered...

Maelduin's breath hissed through his clenched teeth. One of the *Marfachs* was bringing Terry up to use him as a shield against the other. Or, more likely, as bait, hoping to provoke a strike.

How the fuck *did I let that happen?*

Terry, after his first terrified scream, had gone silent. He was trying to force the monster to let go of him, but pushing at the tiny creatures that made up its tail did no good—they just moved out of the way and re-formed where Terry's clawing hands weren't.

Maelduin forced himself to loosen his death-grip on his sword, to let the sword become part of him instead of a thing he wielded.

The *Marfach* holding Terry feinted toward its opponent, dangling Terry off to one side like a bull-dancer's banner.

The other monster hesitated.

Terry's captor shook him teasingly, jarring a cry from him.

The other *Marfach* took the bait, lunging.

Maelduin pivoted and struck, severing the tail that held Terry, catching Terry in his free arm, and continuing the pivot until they both slammed against the far wall.

"Are you all right?"

"Yeah, I'm—oh, son of a *bitch*."

The sudden silence told Maelduin what he would see, even before he turned—his *comhrac-scatha* gleaming a sullen violet through the water, and a host of tiny scuttling monsters re-forming the tail of the sole remaining *Marfach*.

Kevin remembered...

Tiernan moved into position to distract the monster even before Maelduin had finished severing its tail. He would have cursed the water, sloshing around his shins and slowing him down, but he had better things to curse.

"Hey, *feol'marh!*"

The insect-like head turned slowly toward him, jaws agape. Tiernan thought he could see two more sets of jaws working inside the first, at right angles to one another, dripping something that made the water smoke. Several plates of its armor were missing or broken, too, and whatever was oozing from underneath made a Fae's sensitive nose want to curl up and hide.

Tiernan didn't give a fraction of a fuck what the *Marfach* looked or smelled like. No matter what face it wore, to him it was always going to be the monster that had chained and tortured and raped his *lanan*. The monster he was personally going to kill.

From the look of things, he didn't have much time. Conall needed him to keep the *Marfach* busy, that much was obvious. But the trap was growing quickly, which meant he needed to haul ass if he wanted to be the one to make the monster pay.

If?

The sideways set of jaws poked out of the *Marfach*'s maw, tasting the air. "*YOUR GRACE.*"

Apparently it didn't need the inside jaws to talk. If talking was the right way to describe what it was doing—it sounded like a meat grinder, caught on a chunk of bone.

"You must have missed the memo, *lofa'bod*. That stopped bothering me years ago——oh, no you fucking don't." Keeping his tone light and sarcastic was an effort, because the monster had started to turn toward Kevin. And his *lanan*'s face was nearly as pale as his dress shirt, his expression a window onto memories no human should ever have.

Most definitely not Tiernan Guaire's SoulShare.

Circling around to head the monster off, Tiernan

177

held out his hand as he passed Maelduin. His nephew didn't have to be told what Tiernan needed; the silk-wrapped hilt of his lovely and lethal sword slipped into Tiernan's hand as if it came of its own accord.

"Tiernan..." Kevin's voice was hoarse, but the tightness around his eyes was gone, now that he was looking at his husband and not at his worst nightmare.

Yet there was something haunted in those dark brown eyes just the same—something Tiernan only caught a glimpse of before he had to turn back to the horror picking its way spider-like through the water.

"You don't have to watch, *lanan*. I've got this."

"Wouldn't miss this for the world."

Kevin's determined enthusiasm brought a lump to Tiernan's throat.

A cold, cutting wind whirled around the nexus chamber, stirring the water and Tiernan's hair, stinging bare flesh with invisible sleet. "Buy us another minute, blade-master, no more. The trap is nearly set."

A strangled sound drew Tiernan's attention to the center of the nexus. Cuinn was down on one knee, one hand on the floor and the other reaching back toward Lochlann. Lochlann, in turn, was calling up a torrent of ley energy fierce enough to make Tiernan glad he was comparatively blind to the stuff.

"I hope you can... feed the meter for... longer than a minute," Cuinn gasped. "This... *bod-snadhm*... of a timestop... isn't budging."

"We cannot wait." It was easy to see why Coinneach was doing the talking; Josh's face was set in lines of concentration so acute Tiernan suspected he and Conall would barely notice if the building came down around them again. "Time resists being bound this way. Much longer, and the backlash may kill us all."

The Marfach laughed. At least, Tiernan thought that's what the sound was. "*I TIRE OF LISTENING TO YOU TALK TO THE WIND.*" A clawed appendage reached for the mage and the *Gille Dubh*. "*A MAGE'S AGONY WILL BE A DELICACY.*"

Shifting the sword to his right hand, Tiernan produced a crystal blade from the living Stone of his left and hurled it at the monster's right eye. It sunk in and vanished, slicing through the thick membrane protecting the eye, releasing a viscous greenish-yellow fluid.

And another eardrum-shattering shriek, as the massive head swung back toward him.

"Now that I have your attention, don't you and I have some unfinished business?"

The *Marfach* lurched toward him, thrown off balance by its attempt to claw at its eye.

Tiernan lunged, dodging the claw and flaying seeping flesh left bare by a broken plate. There were times the art of the *scian-damhsa* and that of the bull-dancer had a great deal in common, and this was definitely one of them.

The wind howled. "Now, Loremaster, *now!*"

Out of the corner of his eye, Tiernan saw the eerie glow of the mirror-trap. He also saw Cuinn's sheer desperation.

"I fucking can't!"

"Then you have to unmake the Pattern."

Lochlann's voice was strangely distorted by the power passing through him, but there could be no doubt as to the source. All Tiernan could make out clearly was the corona of the other Fae's dark hair, crackling with ley energy. Even Garrett was hard to see, though Tiernan knew he was there, wrapped around his SoulShare, acting as his anchor.

"You knew you might have to—the Loremasters told you themselves, the Pattern was proof against anything but one of their own, wielding the power of a whole world."

"Fuck," Cuinn replied, with the perfect simplicity of a prayer.

Oh, no, you don't. Not before I kill it.

Getting close was easier than he'd thought it would be. The monster's front appendages were good for grabbing and lacerating things at a middle distance, but they sucked for close-in work. His only real worries as he sought a vulnerable spot were its movable jaws and the acidic ichor dripping from its wounds.

And the smell. Sweet Nefertem, the smell.

"*IMPATIENT TO DIE?*" Those jaws couldn't possibly be smiling, but Tiernan thought they would be if they could. "*FOOL. NONE OF YOU WILL HAVE QUICK DEATHS.*"

"I thought you were going to cut off my head." Tiernan smashed the hilt of the sword down on the inner sets of jaws where they protruded a few inches. "Seems pretty quick to me."

Tiernan thought he heard a low roaring sound from behind the *Marfach*, like a blowtorch being gradually turned up. Or a flamethrower.

The *Marfach* didn't seem to notice, or if it did, it didn't care. "*YOU HAVE NO IDEA HOW LONG I CAN KEEP YOU ALIVE AFTER I TAKE YOUR HEAD.*"

180

Oh, fuck me.

The roar escalated. Even a Noble like Tiernan could see the torrent of Cuinn's magick now, like an aura around the *Marfach*, fed by Lochlann and reflected and amplified by the mirror-trap.

"Now, damn it, *Mastragna*, now!" Josh shouted, in Conall's voice.

Not yet, Tiernan wanted to yell. Not before he found a way to kill the unkillable.

Although he thought he understood the mage's near-panic. His vision was blurring—as if he saw the cracked, oozing face as it had been an instant ago, as it was now, and as it would be a moment from now, all at once. And his body was—disconcertingly—out of his control, in the same way, moving before he willed it, when he willed it, and lagging behind.

"*Elirei!*" Cuinn screamed.

And the Prince Royal answered. Tiernan was nearly blinded by the freeing of the elemental magick of the *ceangail* bond of the Prince and his consort. Every color of elemental magick, and a few Tiernan suspected were being invented just for the occasion, joined the hellish flamethrower.

All the magick of a world. All of it. Living, elemental, ley and lunar. Fae magick, the magick of the *daragin*... and the human magick of love.

Taking advantage of Tiernan's distraction, the *Marfach* opened all three sets of jaws at once—

"*Bi'scaol'e.*"

No one should have been able to hear Cuinn's quiet "be unbound." But everyone did.

And the Stone groaned under their feet, as a space that was nothing at all irised open.

With Conall's cry of pure relief, Josh made a sharp cutting gesture. The time distortion caught hold of the *Marfach*, dragging the monster toward the trap.

The monster's rear claws and barbed tail raked frantically across the floor, straining to slow its backward progress. Unfortunately for Tiernan, its front appendages were otherwise occupied, lashing out and crushing him to its jointed torso.

Fuck me senseless.

If he could just move an arm—either arm, he didn't care which—and somehow get the sword free—

A hand caught Tiernan's arm in a grip as unyielding as iron.

"I've got you, *lanan.*" Kevin's voice, breathless yet calming. "It's not going to have you."

"*I ALREADY DO.*" The *Marfach* glared at them both, one eye still dripping gore, its claws raking against the floor like fingernails down Satan's chalkboard, clearly audible even under water. "*AND YOUR TRAP WILL NOT HAVE ME, NOT AGAIN.*" It shuddered.

Tiernan hoped it was enjoying the memory of being locked under an Antarctic iceberg.

And his husband was mad. Certifiable. Offering himself up to a monster that had fucking near destroyed the Fae race single-handed, a monster no magick or blade-skill could best. And himself armed only with decade-old wrestling skills... and his purely human magick.

Tiernan had never been so glad of anything, or anyone, in his life.

The time distortion was worse now, stronger, dragging all three of them inexorably toward the mirror gaping wide to receive the *Marfach*. Tiernan did his best to dig in his bare heels, but a more futile gesture would have been hard to imagine. Kevin seemed to be having better luck, though, shifting his grip to get a better purchase and making some headway against the *Marfach*'s embrace, especially with the monster still shivering—

The *Marfach*'s head blurred again.

"Oh, Jesus," Kevin breathed.

The face looking back at them now was human, mostly. Alive, mostly. Bald, tattooed, one brown-bloodshot eye staring wildly, most of a mouth grinning and showing the stumps of rotted teeth. And a sickly glowing red crystal where a good-sized chunk of his head should be.

"Let's go to hell together, Guaire."

Janek stopped fighting the pull of the trap.

The mirror-trap and Janek, together, ripped Tiernan from Kevin's grip, taking most of a fingernail with them.

"*NO!*"

"*S'vra lom tú g'deo—*"

The trap closed.

The Patternless void closed.

And past rejoined present, in utter, shocked silence.

Chapter Seventeen

Blankness. Gray blankness. And silence.

Is this all that's left of me?

No. The gray was the Stone floor under Kevin's hands, in front of his nose. And the silence was a ring made up of the surviving members of the Demesne of Purgatory, standing around him at a careful distance.

There was more to the silence than that, though. It was a listening silence, the thunderous nothing of his straining to hear an answer to the cry that was still burning raw in his throat.

Someone broke the circle and knelt beside Kevin, staring at the same spot on the floor. Maelduin, Tiernan's nephew—and his *geal'le'mac*, his almost-son.

His image, too. Kevin couldn't bear the sight. He flinched away—only slightly, but more than enough for a Fae to notice.

"I should have gone." The words stuck in Maelduin's throat.

He's mourning too. Even the thought was flat and dull.

Kevin didn't answer, because what could he have said?

Slowly he sat back on his heels. He still couldn't make himself look up—couldn't meet the eyes surrounding him, all the paired sets of eyes. And he couldn't look away from the place where the world had opened and yanked his husband in.

As long as he didn't look away, it wasn't over.

"Conall. Cuinn." The sound of his own voice startled him. "Can you open it back up? Long enough for me to get through?"

"No." The mage and the Loremaster answered together, but it was Conall who went on. "There's nothing there to open anymore. Without the Pattern on the other side, the nexus isn't a portal."

"Then he's gone."

No one said anything.

Kevin staggered as he stood up. Maelduin sprang to his own feet and caught his elbow, but dropped it like it was hot when Kevin tensed.

"I have to get out of here."

"Kevin—"

Josh stepped into Kevin's field of view, hand outstretched, finally forcing him to look up. The bare patch on the tattoo artist's colorful chest where *Areán* had been was a vivid reminder of his own loss, the other piece sacrificed in the *Marfach*'s endgame.

Kevin couldn't make himself take the outstretched hand. "I'm not going to do anything stupid, don't worry. But I—I can't stay here."

Again, silence greeted him. Kevin thought he understood. No doubt relief and horrified fascination were the order of the day, gratitude at having been spared Kevin's fate, or Tiernan's, coupled with a hefty dose of *so that's what half a soul walking looks like*. Not even a Fae was likely to have words appropriate to that situation.

185

A breeze rose, heard but unfelt; unseen moonlight trickled through branches like rain. Like tears.

"I, too, have a heart buried among my roots."

"These aren't—"

Yes. These *were* his roots, the roots of the man he'd become in response to the love of a Fae.

But that didn't mean he could stay where his husband—his heart—was buried.

* * *

Step. Step. Step.

One step after another, his body on auto-pilot at least keeping a straight enough line that he didn't walk out into traffic. More than once, anyway.

He wasn't sure how long he had been walking, but he was pretty sure it hadn't been long enough yet.

Once I stop listening for footsteps behind me...

Like that was going to happen.

Step. Step. Step.

It's like walking the labyrinth.

He'd done that a couple of times—the National Cathedral had a replica of the Chartres Labyrinth—it was a kind of walking meditation. The second time he'd walked it, the thought had come to him, out of the still place the walking had brought him to, that *sometimes what feels like an incredibly twisted path is actually a straight line, it's just the world twisting around us that makes us think otherwise.*

Which was either one of the deepest thoughts he'd ever had, or utter bullshit, because right now a straight line wasn't getting him anywhere.

Not even out of his own head.

Step. Step. Step.

After another while, he thought he'd finally figured out where his feet were taking him. It was as good a place as any, he supposed. And it had been a long time since he'd talked to Tanner.

* * *

Bryce snuggled Setanta close, burying his nose in the Fade-hound puppy's wiry fur. It was good to have a distraction from Lasair's probing, gentle though it was—anything that sent his thoughts somewhere else was a good thing, when he was being reminded of the taint the *Marfach* had left in him.

Then there was that other thing he needed to forget.

No one's life had mattered to him before Lasair. Not even his own. But then his Fae had brought him half of his soul, and now...

That's idiotic. It wasn't the first time Bryce had entertained that particular notion, but it was hitting him over the head now with more than its usual force. *It's not half a soul, not if we share it.* As if you could divide a soul, anyway.

What did that mean for Kevin, then? Had he just lost half his soul? Or all of it?

Bryce was pretty sure he knew how he'd answer that question, if he were in the lawyer's shoes.

Lasair made a soft, soothing, wordless sound; his palm opened over the old ache in Bryce's side. "Almost finished, *sumiúl*."

The nexus chamber sounded, and looked, a lot like a funeral parlor.

Terry and Maelduin were sitting on the black leather chaise, Maelduin leaning heavily on his much shorter partner. Bryce had wondered why Maelduin didn't seem to be crying, despite his obvious heartbreak at the loss of blood kin—until he'd seen the diamonds falling from the Fae's blue topaz eyes.

Lochlann and Rhoann were still tending to the evening's surviving casualties—pretty much everyone, one way or another—with their separate forms of healing magick. At the moment, they were both crouched beside Fiachra, checking him out yet again.

Bryce shuddered at the memory of what they were checking for. If what the *Marfach* had done, had tried to do, to Fiachra was any indication of what it had intended for the Realm, maybe even for the whole human world... losing one of their own was a ridiculously small price to pay to put a stop to it.

Except that it wasn't.

Long blond hair fell along the side of Bryce's face, and lips brushed his cheek. "We would have lost this battle, if not for you."

"Seriously?" Bryce turned to give his *scair-anam* all the side-eye he could manage. "I was about as useful as testicles on a tennis racquet—"

"You were the only one who could drain the *Marfach*'s magick. And you kept it from the nexus until Conall could... what in the name of...?"

Bryce never got the chance to find out what name a Fae might have chosen to invoke in bewilderment; Lasair, along with everyone else in the room, lapsed into stunned silence as the nexus chamber was filled with a tree.

Once he'd blinked a few times, Bryce was

considerably less sure about what he was seeing. A tree, yes. Maybe. It was several stories tall, easily, even though the ceiling of the nexus chamber topped out at around nine feet. Except that it was also the kind of stunted, wind-gnarled oak he'd seen in pictures of the Scottish Highlands. And then there was the way it wasn't really there at all—half the room was just occupied by a kind of tree selfness.

Great. He'd kept his sanity through a pitched battle with one of Satan's fever dreams and the death of someone he'd actually hoped to expiate his past with and maybe someday earn the right to call a friend, only to lose it to a tree.

Coinneach's sudden burst of pure joy, though, was enough to make Bryce doubt his doubts as to his soundness of mind—anything that could make someone that happy *had* to be real. The *Gille Dubh* jumped up and flung himself at the tree.

And that was when Bryce's eyes more or less gave up trying to account for what was going on. Coinneach was still there, still in the room with them, still himself, but his form changed, merging with the tree. With all three ways the tree was real—the impossibly tall forest giant, the twisted mountain oak, and the idea of treeness.

"My brain hurts," he murmured.

Someone laughed. Bryce wasn't sure if it was Coinneach or the tree.

COME HOME. Bryce recognized the leaf-rustling voice, and it sure as hell wasn't talking to him. THE WAY IS REMEMBERED. COME HOME.

As quickly as it had come, the tree—the treeness, the *darag*— was gone, and Coinneach with it.

Conall looked like he was trying to stare a hole through the floor where the *darag* had appeared and disappeared. "That's not possible," he muttered at last.

Peri looked up from where he held Fiachra cradled in his lap. The dark Fae didn't look as if he still needed to be cradled, but Peri's expression still had enough of Falcon in it to daunt even a Fae. "I challenge you to name me one thing that's happened in the last few hours that a sane person would call possible."

"Point."

"And game, and set, and fucking match." Terry's voice was unsteady, and thick, and half-muffled in Maelduin's hair. "I'm sorry... I don't know what more we can do tonight, and I—I have to get Maelduin home."

The Fae blade-master pushed himself upright, brushing tiny diamonds from his cheeks with a shaking hand. "I can stay, if we're needed."

One by one, everyone turned to look at Rian, leaning against the wall, his fingers interlaced with Cuinn's, as if that was the natural thing to do under the circumstances.

Bryce did it, too. Because it *was* the natural thing to do. The Belfast street kid who always seemed to smell faintly of smoke was also a prince of the blood royal. Their Prince.

Slowly, Rian shook his head. "We'll stick around a bit longer, clean up here and upstairs. But you needn't stay."

He pushed off the wall—Prince or no, elemental or no, the kid was clearly running on fumes, as they all were—and crossed to Terry and Maelduin, who rose to meet him. Without a word, he wrapped Maelduin in an embrace.

Bryce thought he saw Maelduin's shoulders start shaking again. Rian held on until the shaking stopped, and then a while longer. And when he let go, it was to offer Terry the same.

"*Slán abhaile*," he murmured at last, in what Bryce was finally learning to recognize as Irish rather than Faen. Safe home. "*Agus Dia a bheith in éineacht bheirt agaibh.*" Something about God, and with both of you.

No one said anything, or moved, as Terry and Maelduin made their way up the stairs. Even Setanta sat still and left off licking his sore paw, watching them go as if he could see.

Once the door at the top of the stairs had opened and closed, though, Rian turned on a heel, surveying those who remained. "We do need to get this shit cleared away, and I'm thinking our mage and our Loremaster might like some time to work out what's happened. But..." The Royal brow creased in a frown. "We need to find Kevin. He shouldn't be alone."

"Agreed." Josh didn't even seem to notice how his hand played over the newly-bare hawk-shaped patch on his chest, the way a pregnant woman ran her hand over her baby bump, only Josh was trying to get used to a new absence, not a new presence. "But how are we going to do that, with the head start he has on us?"

Setanta surged to a standing position, tail wagging madly. He barked, startled a fart from himself, and sat back down hard.

Bryce waved a hand in front of his nose. "Gentlemen, gentleFae, I think we have a volunteer."

* * *

The little pools of light at the base of the Wall always startled Kevin when he visited at night, peering up out of the darkness as if they were trying to give light without being noticed.

They didn't startle him this time, though.

I'm pretty sure that's not a good sign.

To hell with signs.

There were only a couple of visitors at the Wall this late on a December night; Kevin hung back in the shadows until they'd finished their own personal memorial, then let his feet carry him over to the familiar section, the one where his dad's buddies' names were carved into the stone.

Tanner's name wasn't here, of course—his brother's war was still too new, too raw to have its own place on the National Mall. But this was as close as Kevin had to a place he could connect with his only sibling; Tanner had wanted to be cremated, maybe more so after he'd been trapped under a burning Humvee than he had before.

Kevin hadn't understood that kind of anger then. He might, now. Once this numbness wore off.

Hey, Tanner, what's doin'?

His brother didn't answer, of course. He'd been that way when he was alive, too, if he was absorbed in something. And that was cool—Kevin didn't need him to answer, anyway. He just needed someone to listen to what he couldn't tell anyone else.

He's gone... he's really gone, Tanner.

He'd spent most of the walk from Purgatory trying to bury that knowledge, pretend he didn't know what he knew. His SoulSharing with Tiernan hadn't made him half of a whole—it had made him part of everything that was Tiernan-and-Kevin. And it was that sharing, that two-become-one, that was gone now. Gone without leaving behind so much as an echo.

At least you'll get to meet him now—you'll see him before I do.

No, he wouldn't. Not Tanner, not Kevin. Garrett had brought a story back with him from the other side after Janek had killed him. A story of a place where humans went after they died, but Fae didn't.

Something moved, out where the light met the December darkness. Probably a Park Patrol officer, giving an anonymous visitor respectful space.

Kevin's memory filled in something else entirely. Just a wash of color, at first, slowly taking the form of a blond man, one who wasn't really a man. One who had lashed out in the throes of a nightmare, a Pattern-dream, and given Kevin a shiner to remember.

One who had tracked him down, after he'd come here to pour his heart out to his memory of Tanner, and pushed past his own fear to take one more step toward the intimacy of a real SoulShare.

But Tiernan wasn't there. Not this time.

The ground tilted under Kevin's feet. He turned, his back slamming against the Wall in time to turn a fall into a slide down the cold stone to the ground.

He crossed his arms over his drawn-up knees, put his head down, and sobbed.

* * *

Kevin's chest ached with every uneven breath as if someone had punched him in it. At some point, he'd wrapped his arms around his legs to ward off the worsening chill and rested his forehead on his knees. And he didn't want to open his eyes, because he knew that when he did, they were going to feel exactly like someone had poured steel shavings into them.

But he was going to have to open his eyes, because there were paws on his leg and there was a cold nose in his ear.

"Aw, hell," he croaked.

A tail swished through the scattering of fallen leaves at the base of the Wall.

Sighing, Kevin let his legs slide out and gathered the squirming Fade-hound pup into his lap. He was rewarded with an uncharacteristically gentle face-washing, licking the salt from his reddened cheeks and rasping against his day's growth of beard.

Setanta's eyes glowed in swirling opal shades, which meant one of the pup's masters was loaning out his sight.

Which, in turn, meant that Kevin was busted.

I wonder who they're going to send after me...

* * *

By the time Kevin heard footsteps approaching, Setanta had settled down in his lap. His eyes were dull and blind again, but his tail hadn't stopped wagging since his arrival, and he nosed insistently at Kevin's hand every time Kevin stopped rubbing the good spot behind his ears.

Kevin didn't need to look up to know who had been sent to collect him. "Hey, Mac."

The footsteps stopped. "How'd you know it was me?"

Setanta rolled to show his belly, begging for a good rubbing. Kevin obliged, not yet ready to make eye contact with a human being.

"You were complaining the other day about the noise from the hydraulics in your knee... it's quiet enough out here that I could hear it."

"We'll make a Fae out of you yet," Tiernan whispered in his memory.

No, you won't. Kevin's throat closed up like a fist.

"Hey." Before Kevin could protest, Mac slid down the wall to sit next to him. "Sorry. Didn't mean to make it worse."

"It doesn't get worse." The words came out choked, but still recognizable.

"You have a point."

In the silence that followed, Mac patted the pockets of a coat Kevin was pretty sure he hadn't been wearing in Purgatory; digging in one, he pulled out a stainless steel flask with the seal of the Marine Corps on one flat side.

"Careful." Kevin coughed. "The Park Police don't care for that kind of thing."

"Screw the Park Police. We're under Lucien's protection."

The unscrewed top of the flask became a passable shot glass. It was going to be a while before Kevin's sense of smell would tell him anything useful, after a few hours of sobbing and choking back sobs and giving up trying to hold back and starting all over again, so the clear liquid Mac was pouring could be vodka, or gin, or even Sambuca—no, Mac would never do that to him.

At least it wasn't Tennessee Honey. Thank God.

Mac offered Kevin the makeshift glass, and kept on holding it out even after Kevin shook his head. Setanta yipped, nosing Mac's hand closer to Kevin.

Sighing, Kevin took the metal cap and tossed back the contents, coughing as the alcohol seared his raw throat. "Holy shit," he breathed, when he could breathe again.

Mac nodded, took the cap back, refilled it, and copied Kevin's gesture, leaving out the choking and gasping. "I was going to bring Jack and Coke, but have you ever seen what Coke does to stainless steel?"

"Don't make me laugh, it hurts." Kevin's diaphragm was fighting it out with his nose for the title of Most Useless Organ. *How long have I been crying?*

No time at all, he had a feeling, compared to how long he was going to be.

The two men passed the cup and flask back and forth a few more times in silence. It was a hollow silence on Kevin's part, fragile. He needed it...but it was poised and waiting to be broken.

Mac broke it. "Everyone wanted to come after you. All the *Tirr Brai*, anyway."

That meant all the Fae, plus Coinneach. "That's kind of weird." Kevin reached for the flask again. At least when his throat was burning there was part of him that wasn't numb. "How did you end up with the duty?"

The ex-Marine shook the flask, nodded, and handed it over. "This isn't a duty, you know that. But the humans had the good sense to realize the last thing you needed was to be surrounded out of nowhere by a Demesne's worth of freaked-out Fae."

"Now I know you're bullshitting me." Kevin's hand shook as he poured, splashing a few drops of liquid over his fingers. Setanta nosed at the scent, curious, but Kevin nudged the pup away. "Fae don't freak out over death. Unless it's blood kin, or maybe their own SoulShare."

Kevin knocked back the shot in a hurry, to keep from choking on his own words. Better to let Mac think he was choking on the alcohol.

He wasn't fooling Mac, needless to say. "Yeah, Maelduin's taking it hard—Terry took him home right before Lucien and I left. But the others... I don't know." Mac settled back against the Wall, tipping his head back to stare up at the waxing moon, veiled in clouds. "Frankly, I don't think they get it either."

"What do you mean?"

"You really want to know?"

"Wouldn't ask if I didn't." And at least for the moment, considering a roomful of Fae Acting Strangely beat the hell out of the other thoughts chasing themselves fruitlessly around the inside of Kevin's head.

Mac shrugged. "If I were to go all armchair shrink on you, I'd say they're realizing they're able to feel empathy, after what, a couple of thousand years of thinking they couldn't? Or convincing themselves they couldn't?"

"They're probably just thinking it could just as easily have been any of them."

Mac's eyes narrowed. "That sounds like relief. I promise you, they're anything but relieved."

Kevin let out a long, unsteady sigh. Setting the flask and glass on the cold marble at the base of the Wall, he ground the heels of his hands against his closed eyes.

And instantly regretted it. *Christ, my eyeballs have been sandpapered.*

"No, not relieved. Just... hell, I don't know. I'm not thinking straight right now." Suddenly, all Kevin wanted was sleep, even though he knew with a bone-deep certainty that sleep wasn't going to be coming anywhere near him for a very long time. "It just takes a hell of a lot to make a Fae conscious of mortality. And I think tonight qualifies as a hell of a lot."

"Sorry." Kevin could almost hear Mac wince.

"Nothing to be sorry for."

The ex-Marine's laugh was short and harsh. "You're kidding, right?"

"I promise, kidding is the last thing on my mind right now."

Mac's head dropped back against the Wall. "Fuck it. Can we just start this conversation over? Maybe the whole night?"

"Please."

Kevin had never meant a word more in his life. Except the *I love you, too* he hadn't had time to say.

Footsteps approached, somewhere outside the glow of the lights. Kevin shoved the flask under his legs, in case the even tread betokened the Park Police.

As the sound moved off, he cautiously shook the flask. Almost empty. Which meant he was probably going to have to get off his ass and do something.

"They aren't expecting me to come back to Purgatory, are they?"

"Not really." Mac took the flask back and screwed on the cap. "But if you want to, they'll be there."

"No." Kevin's jaw clenched involuntarily. "No. I just... want to go home." He had no idea how he was going to get there, but that was the least of his problems.

"Yeah." Mac tucked the flask back into his

pocket, then rubbed Setanta gently behind one ear with a knuckle. "Hey, pup. *Téighras.*"

Setanta twisted to lick Mac's finger, then cocked his head, looking uncertainly up at Kevin with eyes now dim and clouded, whining softly.

I'm going to be doing that myself in a couple of minutes if I don't get the hell out of here. "Go on. Go home."

Instead of obeying either of them, Setanta braced his good paw on Kevin's chest, rose up, and started washing his face, his tongue rasping against Kevin's rough cheeks.

Mac grunted. "Well, they warned me."

Kevin was too preoccupied with the squirming bundle of increasingly frantic consolation in his lap to pay much attention to what Mac was doing. *Maybe we should have gotten a dog.* Coming home to an empty house was going to be a whole new circle of hell.

"Yeah, Bryce? It's Mac. You were right, he's not listening. Here, let me put you on speaker." Mac pushed his phone up next to Setanta, where the puppy could presumably smell it. "Go ahead."

"Setanta, *come.*"

Mac snatched the phone back in time to spare it most of a tongue-bath. "Well, at least he knows it's you."

Bryce's sigh came through loud and clear. "Let me call in the big guns."

A pause, then Lasair's clear, stern baritone. "Setanta. *Téighras, tréan-cú.*"

Setanta whined, swiped his tongue up Kevin's cheek one more time, and disappeared.

"Got him," Lasair announced a second later. "Bryce, could you put his collar on him just in case he tries to—thank you, *sumiúl.*"

199

"Sorry, Lasair." Mac wiped the phone's screen carefully with a sleeve. "Maybe I pronounced the recall command wrong."

"I doubt it. I believe he wanted to stay." Another pause. "Is... Kevin there?"

A leaden certainty in the pit of Kevin's stomach told him he was going to have to get used to the pauses, the searching for words, his friends not knowing what to say to him. "Right here, Lasair."

"Even a small Fade-hound follows its own will over any other, except the order of a Master of Hounds. I could order Setanta to find you, but once he did, it was his choice to stay." Kevin thought he heard a soft chuckle, one that only sounded slightly forced. "I say this to warn you, in case you wake up some morning soon with a mildly flatulent puppy drooling on your pillow."

Kevin wanted to smile, but wanting was going to have to stand in for the real thing. "I'll give you a call if he wanders."

"Sleep well, when sleep finds you, *Ngarradh*."

Kevin frowned as Mac put the phone back in his pocket. "That was one of the words the Loremasters sent through the Pattern, wasn't it?" The memory of the ultimately useless strategy session, Conall and the others trying to decipher the strange message from the Realm, might as well have been part of another life.

Mac grimaced. "Yeah. It means 'The Sundered One.'"

"Shit." There didn't seem to be much more to say than that.

There was an awkward-as-fuck silence, one Mac finally broke. "Hey, could you give me a hand up?"

"Sure."

Kevin lurched to his feet, his every muscle protesting hours of motionless tension in the cold. He ignored them. "What do you need me to do?"

"Just brace my C-leg with your foot so it doesn't skid and give me an arm, and I should be fine."

It took a while, and both of Kevin's arms, but they managed to get Mac upright without attracting the attention of the Park Police, or anyone else.

"How are you getting home?" Kevin's mouth felt like it was on autopilot—as if he were sending his dad's oldest friend home after nothing more consequential than an all-night BBQ-and-B.S. session at Chez Almstead/Guaire.

Chez Almstead, now.

"I'll be fine on the Metro, don't worry about me. Lucien left your car over on 21st Street, right across Constitution, outside the National Academy of Sciences. Closest he could find parking on the street."

"Is that even legal?—Wait, did you say *my* car?" Kevin patted his trouser pocket, and was rewarded with the familiar jingle of the Merc's keys, right where he'd put them.

"Legal? This is Lucien we're talking about, remember?" Normal humans tended to forget strangenesses associated with Fae or their human SoulShares eventually, and Lucien's odd Fae gift accelerated the forgetting. "And it turns out that a fire elemental may not be able to stomach riding in a car, but he can hot-wire one just fine."

"Why does that not surprise me?"

The silence that followed was finally broken by the Dopplered horn of a car speeding down Constitution. Kevin blinked, wondering how long he'd been staring at the pavement.

"Are you..."

"Good to drive? Hell yes." There wasn't enough vodka in the world to make a dent in Kevin's numb sobriety.

"Actually, I was going to ask if you were going to be all right alone." Mac shrugged, visibly uncomfortable for the first time since he'd showed up.

"Damned if I know. But I have to start sometime."

Chapter Eighteen

By the time the darkness lifted, he had forgotten there had ever been anything other than darkness.

Holding his head with both hands, he groaned with the agony of light returning. Even light filtered through his thick, swollen fingers was too much.

He groaned again, in wordless confusion. There was something wrong with his head. On one side, he could feel his fingers touching flesh, feeling bone. On the other, he felt nothing at all, from fingers or face. And when he lowered his hands and blinked into the light, only one eye teared, only one eye saw.

He was pretty sure he was supposed to have two of those.

One was enough, though, to show him what was around him. And he began to be afraid, because he recognized none of it. The light arched over his head, brighter to one side of him. A pale circle floated where it was darker, far out of his reach. Tall things stood around him, dark and solid where they touched the ground, breaking up into small things that whispered as the air made them move. Brightly colored things sat in them, making sounds that he didn't think meant anything. Somewhere behind him, he heard another sound, soft, liquid, flowing.

Water.

The voice was in his head. It wasn't his. It sounded as confused as he felt.

It also sounded afraid. He liked that, for some reason.

Water, it repeated, less urgently than before. Maybe it was losing interest.

"Fuck it," he mumbled. He had no idea what the words meant, but they sounded familiar.

"Wha'...?

He wasn't alone.

Bracing himself, he lurched to his feet—at least he seemed to have the right number of those. A figure lay sprawled on his back on the ground in front of him, slowly raising an arm to cover his eyes with a forearm, trying in vain to shut out the light. Pale hair was tumbled around his face, and his free hand clutched...

A sword.

He remembered.

Tiernan Guaire.

He remembered.

Hate.

Looking down, he saw the knife tucked into his own boot.

He remembered.

Death.

* * *

Even through closed eyelids, light dazzled.

And then it didn't.

Instinct sent him rolling to one side, though his muscles protested. Something struck the ground near his head, something that smelled of metal and rotting meat and hate.

Though how he recognized any of those smells, he wasn't sure.

He came out of his roll in a low crouch, fighting dizziness to stay on his feet.

"Guaire!"

Was the thick, slurred sound his name? A warning? Someone vomiting? All three, possibly.

He opened his eyes just in time to see the source of the noise lurching back to his feet—and felt like vomiting, himself. He faced a putrefying giant, dripping body fluids and thick brown blood, with a mass of dull red crystal taking up a little less than half his head. Its head.

Either would do just fine, for all he cared. He wanted nothing to do with the thing.

"Tiernan Guaire." The giant had a knife in his hand. His swollen, cracked, suppurating hand was too big for the hilt. He seemed just fine with grabbing the blade along with the hilt, though, and didn't appear to notice his blood slicking both hand and metal.

He—Tiernan Guaire, he supposed—didn't give a fuck. About any of it. He was just starting to notice that part of him was missing.

Not his left hand, though it did look strange, transparent and gleaming in the light, holding a metal thing that whispered *sword*.

Something else. Something at his core. His heart, maybe.

It hurt.

It hurt more with every breath. Every heartbeat.

"Guaire!" the giant bellowed.

205

"Fuck off."

What had he lost?

"You did this to me." The giant was having trouble talking around his slack and swollen tongue. Unfortunately, he wasn't letting that discourage him. "I cut your boy toy, and you sent me to hell for it."

Tiernan was inclined to ignore him, were it not for the spark of recognition the monster's reference to a "boy toy" woke in him. "You what?"

"Cut. Him." The monster beckoned him closer with the knife. "And you fucked up my head and left me to die. So now I get *your* head."

He remembered, now. A little. A cold gray room. Pain. The giant, except there was no glowing mass in his head, just inked designs—a skull, symbols that meant *danger* and *warning* and *poison*.

And someone else was there. Memory showed him dark hair, compelling dark eyes, pale skin. Fear, imperfectly concealed. A knife, the same knife the giant held now, and blood trickling from the male's throat.

Love, shaped like the hollow ache at Tiernan's core.

In the here and now, the giant stumbled forward, roaring, knife upraised.

Maybe he was supposed to be afraid.

Fuck that.

Tiernan stepped to one side, raised his sword, brought it down.

Blood, thick and brown, gouted from the stump of the giant's neck.

The misshapen head rolled in the grass. It was smiling.

It looked fucking relieved.

Off to one side, the giant's body slowly toppled, still clutching the knife. Or maybe the blade was embedded in the fingers that gripped it.

A spark flared in the crystal half of the giant's head, the sharp hot red of pain.

The head snarled, but its one flesh-and-blood eye was wide, panicked. Its lips moved in a silent scream, with no breath to form words.

"Kill it. Kill us."

Tiernan stared. Not giving a fuck was apparently a luxury he didn't have at the moment. Beheading was supposed to be fatal.

The head gurgled, blood draining from its mouth.

"Meat," it grunted, somehow forcing air through the grayish-pink gristle of its ruined larynx. The red flared brighter.

Just as his body had known what to do with the sword he held, it knew what to do to the obscenity on the ground. All he had to do was touch it—a groping touch, because his own face was turned away to spare his stomach, and the tip of his finger punctured... something. An eye, maybe.

Power welled up in him, staggered him, flowed through him, flowed out of him.

And the head turned to sand, sand that held the shape of the severed meat-and-crystal head for an instant and then collapsed.

Tiernan overbalanced, stumbled and fell face-first into the grass.

Somewhere behind him, a headless body was still bleeding out. The stench was indescribable.

He ignored it, preoccupied with holding on to the one memory the giant had given him, the dark-eyed face seen through a haze of his own fury and panic.

Kevin.

He didn't recognize the voice echoing in his head. But he did recognize the truth of what it said.

Your SoulShare.

Just for an instant, he caught another glimpse. Kevin sat somewhere dimly-lit, flashes of white and colored light playing over him. There was music, an insistent beat resonating with a sweet heavy throbbing in his own groin. He was short of breath, dizzy with need.

Then—silence, as grass and sunlight and the corpse behind him reclaimed his senses.

But there was no reclaiming the hole in his heart.

Chapter Nineteen

Long hot showers were a blessing Thomas Almstead was never going to get tired of, no matter how many years or decades separated him from barracks living. Secretly, he didn't mind the VA doc's admonition to get more exercise, especially not when he had hiking trails so close to home and a new Nikon D7100 to get to know, but the billowing clouds of steam and the decadent adjustable shower head his son-in-law had installed for him were the icing on the cake.

The phone was ringing as he turned off the water in the shower. Kevin's ringtone. Cursing, he lunged for the trousers he'd left in a crumpled pile on the bathroom floor, digging his phone out of the pocket just as the last bar of a sweet Hendrix riff started to fade. "Sorry, son, you caught me at an awkward moment. What's up?"

Silence. Then, "Dad?"

Thomas froze. He remembered that tone. Hadn't heard it in nearly half a century, but he wasn't ever going to forget it. He'd heard it in country, too many times, from kids—only a few years younger than he'd been himself, back then, but lacking his experience in the Vietnamese jungle. Kids who had seen too much, and done too much, and were one step from shattering. "What is it? What's wrong?"

Kevin cleared his throat. "Um... are you busy? Can you come down to Purgatory?"

From the sound, his son had taken a step back from whatever ledge he was on, but Thomas found no comfort in that assessment. "Sure. Just give me a few minutes to dry off and get dressed. I'll be there in..." He thought quickly, as he reached for a towel and wrapped it around himself as best he could one-handed. "Let's say an hour. Maybe less, depending on the traffic."

"Right. See you then."

Son of a bitch. Thomas wished he could fly.

* * *

Kevin set his phone down with excruciating care on the thick glass top of the bar. Not that he thought the phone was in any danger of breaking. Or the bar, for that matter.

Which left him.

All the lights were on, making the underground club almost obscenely cheery. Once it was open for business, of course, it would be plunged into properly decadent shadow. But no amount of light was ever going to chase away the darkness of—last night? No, night before last.

A faint electrical hum called his attention to the door; the black slab swung inward, letting in a hint of the afternoon light from the street above, along with Josh and Conall.

"You're early," Kevin croaked.

"I don't think so." Josh was the one who answered, but Conall nodded as if he'd been the one to speak. And they hesitated together, as if unsure how to approach.

Two bodies, one soul.

Jesus.

He didn't realize the door had shut behind them, didn't even hear them cross the floor, didn't notice anything until Josh's arms were around him and Conall's hand was on his shoulder.

Damn. I thought I was done crying. Josh's soaked shirt told him otherwise, though.

"I wish you'd called one of us last night." From the feel of things, Josh wasn't planning on letting go of Kevin any time soon.

Kevin didn't give a fuck about Josh's plans; the former college wrestler shrugged out of the embrace and walked off, down the length of the bar. "There's no such thing as just one of you. The rest of you come in pairs."

God, or karma, or someone still had it in for Kevin, because Rhoann Faded in just in time to cock his head in that adorable puzzled way he had, hearing his last utterance.

"If you say 'or threes,' Rhoann, so help me Christ I'm going to..." Of course, Kevin had no idea what he was going to do. He hadn't had any idea since his world had disappeared forever, something like 36 hours ago.

"I would never." Rhoann took an uneasy step back, his hands slightly raised.

Fuck. If they don't make me a pariah, I'm going to end up making myself one. No Fae he'd ever known was the slightest bit squeamish about death—any of them would laugh at the thought, he was sure. But he himself was something new to them: half a SoulShare. Yes, Lochlann had almost found himself in Kevin's

211

situation once, and he'd followed Garrett into death to bring him back rather than face living without him.

Kevin hadn't had that option.

I should have done it anyway.

No. Digging himself out of that hole had been hard enough once; he wasn't going to do it again. And that was a promise he was bound to break, he knew. Just... not yet.

"Sorry, Rhoann." Kevin cleared his throat, eyeing the tall Fae sidelong. "I'm not contagious, don't worry."

He regretted the bitterness as soon as it was out, for all the good regret did. Strangely, though, no one seemed to notice—or at least, no one minded, if they did. In fact, everyone seemed to relax a little.

Now that I'm acting the way they expect?

God, this had been a bad idea. He was in no shape to deal with anyone. Not the room full of Fae and their *scair-anaim* who were going to be congregating here, and most definitely not his father.

But it had to be done. Kevin had to tell his father that his son-in-law was dead. And Thomas wasn't going to understand, he wasn't going to believe the story Kevin had to tell, unless he heard the *whole* story. And believing his son was crazy was going to be a hell of a lot easier than believing the truth, unless Kevin had some help in the telling.

That was the glib explanation, and it was even partly true. But Kevin knew the whole truth, as he looked from Rhoann to Josh to Conall, and up as the door opened to admit Lasair, Bryce, and a limping but enthusiastically wagging Setanta.

His dad was going to need the whole story, but Kevin couldn't tell it. Couldn't even think about it. He was probably just going to have to crumple into a chair and let other people do the talking.

Does that make me a coward? Or fundamentally broken?

* * *

Thomas jogged down the last half-dozen steps to the doors of Purgatory, to hell with what his knees thought of the idea. Good thing the traffic into the city had been light... though he couldn't shake the feeling that he'd been needed here a long time ago.

The lack of any knob or handle on the featureless black glass at the bottom of the stairs stymied him for a second. But the doors swung inward as he reached for them, with a soft electric hum.

He wasn't sure what he'd been expecting. Definitely not the crowd waiting for him in what his son had told him was called the 'cock pit.' He recognized a few of them, Mac and Lucien and the tattoo artist who had the studio up at street level next to the club. He thought he recognized a few others from Mac and Lucien's wedding. But a few of them were strangers—including one who looked enough like his son-in-law that Thomas had to give him a good hard look to be sure he wasn't.

But... Tiernan wasn't there. And where was Kevin?

Almost on cue, his son made his way through the cock pit, out into the light. And Thomas' heart nearly stopped. Kevin looked like a shell of himself, pale, his eyes red-rimmed, his broad shoulders hunched around a great hollow space.

Thomas knew that space. He'd been introduced to it in Vietnam, and he'd lived in it after Tanner's death, and then Louise's.

"Jesus, son," he whispered.

Kevin stumbled, and Thomas opened his arms to catch him, braced himself to catch his weight.

"He's dead, Dad." Kevin's voice caught hard, and Thomas felt it in his own chest. "Tiernan. He's gone."

Numb, Thomas wrapped his arms around his son and braced him—Kevin hadn't fallen, but the former sergeant knew a man near collapse when he was holding one up.

What the hell do I say?

He'd never expected to have a son-in-law, and when he'd first met Tiernan, the young man's impossible good looks had, for just a second, whispered "gold-digger."

But that first meeting was ancient history, now. Tiernan was—had been—everything his son had ever wanted.

Which meant he'd been everything Thomas had ever wanted for his son.

He didn't have words for that. He just held Kevin tighter, and stifled a groan when he felt his son's body start to shake with sobs.

More than one pair of hands gently urged Thomas to step backward; he realized with a start that he and Kevin were surrounded, and being guided toward a black leather loveseat.

Thomas needed to know who they were. What they were doing here. But Kevin was all that mattered to him right now. The rest could wait as long as it had to. He waved the circle back as he drew Kevin down to sit beside him.

"It's okay, Dad," Kevin choked. "I asked them to come. There's... a lot you need to understand, and I'm not in any shape to explain any of it."

"Tiernan's dead—I need to understand more than that?"

Ever since Vietnam, Thomas had raised his voice when he was confused, as if he could shout sense into a world that didn't make any. He felt Kevin flinch, and cursed himself. "Sorry—"

There was a dog between him and his son. Front legs on Thomas' thigh, back legs on Kevin's. Growling, the tips of what sure as hell looked like fangs showing.

It hadn't climbed up. It had just appeared.

"Setanta! *Cu droc!*" someone snapped.

The dog—no, the puppy—instantly dropped down, ears wilting. And the air was filled with a brimstone stench that would have made a rotten egg gag.

Someone stepped up to claim the pup—another blond, this one with hair that fell in waves halfway down his back. "My apologies, sir, for his poor training."

Kevin, miraculously, looked like he might remember how to smile someday as he watched the puppy being gathered up and moved firmly to the floor. "It's okay, Lasair. He'll figure out I don't need protecting from Dad eventually."

The silence stretched out, broken only by the thumping of a tail against the floor.

"Son..." Thomas gestured helplessly. "Talk to me. What's happened?"

Kevin's sigh seemed to empty him; he sagged back against the back of the loveseat, grinding the

215

heels of his hands into his eyes. Finally, his hands dropped, as if they were too heavy for him to hold up. "I don't know if I can do it, Dad. I'm tapped out." His arm twitched, echoing the gesture of a defeated wrestler.

"No, you aren't." The speaker was another man Thomas recognized, the owner of the massage parlor upstairs. Lochlann something. "If you were, I'd know it."

"Fucking empath," Kevin muttered.

"Guilty. And you need to talk."

I would give my left ball to understand what's going on here. And his right one to pull his only surviving son out of the deep pit he was falling into right in front of him.

Kevin looked slowly around the circle. One by one, the men shook their heads. Even the puppy whined.

"God damn it." Kevin dragged himself to a more upright position. "All right. I'll try."

Thomas took a deep breath and willed himself to relax, to open himself up, even though he knew he was about to follow his son into hell. He'd learned how to help carry other men's pain from a Marine chaplain, decades ago in Vietnam. He'd owed it to his men then, and he sure as hell owed it to his son now.

"I can't tell you all of it. Not now." Kevin laced his fingers together, so tightly the knuckles were white. He'd done that ever since he was a kid, when things were too much for him. "And the part I have to tell you—you're going to think I'm crazy."

"I would never—"

"Tiernan's not human. *Wasn't* human."

And what do I say to that?

216

Kevin nodded as if Thomas had spoken. "He was a Fae. So are half the people in this room."

No one protested. In fact, some of them were nodding. Lochlann, the big blond standing between Mac and Lucien, a redhead who looked several years too young to be in a club like Purgatory, the puppy's owner, Tiernan's almost-twin, a dark-skinned man who might have been Spanish or Portuguese, a young man with blond hair curling over one eye and an arresting set of eyebrow piercings, and the man hovering protectively at his side, his peculiar pale-green eyes missing nothing.

"I ought to be asking you—all of you—a lot of questions." Thomas chose his words carefully. "But that's not what you're here for." And, frankly, he didn't have it in him to interrogate anyone right now. Even polite questions would be a stretch.

"You're right." Kevin's voice sounded like his throat ached. "But I know you. The questions are still there. And it's important that you believe me about this, or you sure as hell aren't going to believe what happened. Conall?"

The red-haired kid—well, not exactly a kid, Thomas supposed, he'd fought next to men his age, a long time ago—almost flinched. But not quite. "What do you need from me?"

"Magick. Something Dad will have to believe."

"I thought you were going to say that." Conall sighed. "Here's hoping this channeling turns out better than my last one."

He glanced around the room, and for the first time Thomas noticed the bright, almost unnatural green of his eyes. Tiernan had eyes like that, except his were a startling blue.

217

Had had eyes like that.

"*Draoi rioga*?" This from the other youngster in the room, the one with the pierced eyebrows.

A corner of Conall's mouth twitched up. "Sorry, Highness, but most of my channelings of late have happened in the middle of combat or while I've been helping Josh practice *M ji kaikyaku tsuri,* and I don't think Kevin is looking for either of those."

Highness? Thomas was having a hard time keeping his resolve not to ask questions.

Conall laid a hand on Josh's arm. "*Dar'cion*, would you mind rolling up your sleeve?"

Josh nodded and unbuttoned his left shirt sleeve. As he tugged and rolled it up, a vivid tattoo slowly became visible—a gold dragon, mouth opened as if it was getting ready to breathe fire.

One look at his son's haggard face was enough to make Thomas think about breathing some fire of his own. "What the hell are you—"

Conall held up a hand and closed his eyes. He didn't move, but something around him was moving in a way that made Thomas want to rub his eyes, except he didn't want to look away from whatever was happening.

The dragon lifted its head from Josh's arm, craned its neck, and spat blue-white flame.

"Jesus Christ," Thomas whispered.

And then the rest of the dragon started peeling away from Josh's arm, golden wings beating the air even before its tail came free.

"Hold out your hand," Josh said softly.

Thomas did as he was told.

The dragon hovered in front of Josh, staring at him with bright black unblinking eyes.

And then those eyes were looking at him.

The dragon hissed. Grabbing air, it swooped up and around behind Josh's head, then arrowed straight for Thomas, bating its wings at the last possible second and grabbing the base of his thumb with talons like Satan's tailor's needles.

Thomas jerked his arm back, choking back most of a shout. The dragon clung tightly, flapping its wings to stay balanced.

"*Scathacrú!*" Josh snapped.

The dragon arched its wings, hissing.

"Let go!"

It hissed again, then launched itself from Thomas' hand. Thomas watched it take wing, his pain already forgotten... stared as it settled on Kevin's shoulder, as gently as a falling leaf, and butted its head up against the roughness of his unshaven cheek.

Kevin didn't seem to see anything out of the ordinary. He reached up and stroked under the dragon's chin with a fingertip. "Sorry, Dad. He's not really tame."

"Kind of like Tiernan." The words were out before Thomas had a chance to think about them. But he couldn't call them back... and didn't really want to. "I think I always knew there was something different about him. But he was right for you. And that was all I ever gave a damn about."

Tears welled up in Kevin's already red-rimmed eyes. "He was the other half of my soul. That's how Fae cross over from their world to ours. Half of his soul gets torn away, and comes to our world, and is born in a human."

Thomas didn't answer. In fact, he held his breath. *Talk, son. Let it out.*

219

Kevin drew a deep, shuddering breath. "An enemy of the Fae was locked away in the human world, thousands of years ago. It should have been safe—it couldn't do harm here. But Tiernan accidentally set it free, when Art O'Halloran's nephew tried to kill me."

"I remember that. Some of it, anyway." O'Halloran, a partner at Kevin's law firm, had been trying to blackmail Kevin, courtesy of an extremely compromising picture taken by O'Halloran's nephew Janek.

Kevin nodded. "It went into Janek O'Halloran. I guess you could say it possessed him. Saved his life, mostly, but there wasn't much of him left except his hate. For Tiernan—he blamed him for turning him into a rotting meat wagon for a monster. And for the *Marfach*."

"That's the monster?"

"It was." Another silence. "It turns out some of the Fae had known all along that the *Marfach* would get out eventually. They made sure there would be Fae over here to stop it when it did."

"And Tiernan was one of them?"

"Yes." Kevin swallowed hard. "I'll tell you the whole story some other time, as much of it as I know. But two nights ago... it came for us. For the last time."

Kevin closed his eyes, breathing deeply.

Thomas thought he recognized the way Kevin was sitting, the strange depth of his silence. There were mornings seared into his memory, too many mornings getting ready to move out into the jungle by the ghost light of false dawn, not knowing what was going to come at him.

You could be as prepared as you could possibly be, but you still knew your preparation might not matter a damn.

But he'd never watched his son pick up that burden before. And he would have given anything to be the one shouldering it now.

"It was trying to get home, to the Fae Realm. To destroy it. And it would have been happy to destroy this world, too, for being its prison for a couple of thousand years. The easiest way back to the Realm was here, in Purgatory's basement."

"And you had to stop it."

"We had to kill it. Except, it couldn't die." Kevin stared at the floor between his feet.

Thomas wondered what he was seeing.

"We trapped it. All of us. Everyone had a job to do, a part to play—as if it had been planned that way. Maybe it was."

This silence was different. It was strained, taut, dangerous. The others sensed it, too; they moved closer, tense and wary.

"Everyone." Kevin spoke through a tightness in his throat. "Even me. My job was to—hold Tiernan. Keep him here, keep the *Marfach* from taking him. My only job. And I—I *failed*—"

Kevin's voice broke, raw and anguished. He doubled over, sending the dragon flapping off in a panic.

Thomas didn't stop to think. He grabbed Kevin and pulled him close.

Kevin fought him, but only for a second. Only until the sobs started to tear their way out of him. "It's my fault." Thomas' jacket muffled Kevin's hoarse keening.

If I could carry this for you... Thomas ducked his head, clenched his jaw tightly against cries of his own. He couldn't cry, not now. He had to hold Kevin together.

"Jesus, I didn't think anything could hurt worse than just losing him, losing him that way, but I let it happen, I *failed him*—"

"You didn't." Conall's soft voice cut through Kevin's cries.

"I did—"

"You didn't. Listen to me, *Ngarradh*."

Whatever that word meant, it made Kevin tremble, but it also made him go silent.

Conall rested a hand on Kevin's shoulder. "You didn't fail. I've been thinking about that fight, what I sensed toward the end of it. The *Marfach* assumed Janek was really dead. Which means he must have been buried so deep in the monster, he almost didn't make it out, in the end. But he wanted the *Marfach* dead, just as much as he..."

"Wanted Tiernan dead." Kevin's voice sounded like a dull knife. He wasn't looking up. But at least he was talking.

"Yes. And he saw his chance to have both, I think. He managed to take over their shared body, at least enough to make it stop fighting my channeling. And you kept Tiernan here, kept the *Marfach* from finishing him, long enough for that to happen. I don't think anyone else could have done that."

Thomas wasn't sure how he'd ever thought of Conall as a kid. The solemn red-haired Fae looked centuries old. Maybe he was.

Kevin raised his head slowly, as if it weighed

more than he could normally lift. His eyes were reddened and red-rimmed, staring unseeing at nothing in particular, as if the man behind them was weighing the likely cost of the climb out of hell, trying to decide if it was worth it.

Thomas tightened his grip on Kevin. *You bet your ass it's worth it. I've lost one son already—no, two—and I'll be damned if I'm losing a third.*

Kevin's sigh was more like a groan. "So my job was to hold on to him long enough to let him die at the right time."

Conall nodded. "The right time to save two worlds."

"Maybe someday that will be a comfort."

Chapter Twenty

I promised.

Cuinn stared at the ceiling, arms crossed behind his head. He was acutely aware of Rian, asleep beside him—finally asleep. Cuinn's cock and ass were both still singing in chords, after what it had taken to get his *scair-anam* to the place where he could fall asleep.

The moon was riding high tonight. Cuinn could feel it. Feel her. Every Fae who had ever come through the Pattern and survived the experience could feel her, thanks to him.

I promised I'd set her free. Cuinn closed his eyes—not that that mattered, he could still feel her. *There's no Pattern left for her to guard. No reason to keep holding her prisoner.*

If only it was as easy to confront an angry goddess as it was to come up with reasons to do it.

Maybe if I lie here long enough contemplating my trora, *the moon will set.*

Stifling a sigh, Cuinn Faded up to the roof. As good a place as any for what he had to do; the moon was the same in all places, and all times. If she weren't, "Cuinn an Dearmad" would quickly have become a curse in at least two worlds, a long time ago.

When Cuinn took form again, he was lying in the same position he'd been in, only now he was up on the roof of the brownstone. And he was staring straight at the moon, a sight he normally avoided as assiduously as any other Fae in the human world. He'd never felt so naked.

Of course, he was naked. Sweaty, too. He'd gotten a workout in the hours just past—Rian had needed more than a little of his old favored consolation. And the wind was brisk, raising prickles everywhere he had hair.

Pants wouldn't hurt, I suppose, if I'm going to be having an audience with a goddess. And it was simple enough to channel his favorite leathers, now that no Fae had to worry about how much magick he channeled any more. So what if they were assless?— this was going to be a face-to-face conversation.

Assuming it happened at all.

Concentrate, amad'n.

Concentrate. Pfft. Call down the moon. Easy enough, right?

How had he done it the first time? Desperation had probably had a lot to do with it, the need to slam the door to the Realm shut in the *Marfach*'s face.

For some reason, he found himself remembering a cartoon he'd seen years ago, back when human newspapers still held news and were still printed on paper. There had been a kid—probably a Fae changeling, if his temperament was any indication—trying to figure out which muscle to flex to make his ass light up like a lightning bug's.

Cuinn could empathize.

He didn't want to look at her, which meant he probably should. Wronging others was a Fae art form; the desire to acknowledge a past wrong and repent was unheard of, and even the concept bordered on mental illness. Not a lot of precedent for him to follow, in other words. But facing what he'd done seemed like a reasonable start.

Slowly, he got to his feet. And it looked as if the moon grew larger. Cuinn was sure his imagination was to blame. Fairly sure.

She won't crash herself into the earth just to get her karmic justice, will she?

Maybe I should have thought of that sooner.

"Will you come down and speak with me, Lady?"

Silence.

"Will you speak with me at all?"

More silence. Or maybe it was just the same silence.

Cuinn guessed he understood. If someone had enslaved him, then waited a couple of thousand years before coming back to find out what he thought about the situation, he would probably flip them the Great Cosmic Bird by way of reply, too.

Empathy was something Cuinn had learned from his SoulShare—something pretty, something nice, but he wasn't about to let it come between himself and what he needed to do. The prospect that the goddess in the moon might be as obstinate as a Fae wasn't exactly attractive, but at least he had a few ideas as to what to do about it.

The channeling he'd used to bind the moon in the first place had mostly been improvised, and he wasn't sure he remembered all of it. He remembered enough, though, to channel a temporary binding, enough to draw her down for a proper conversation. He hoped.

Closing his eyes, he reached for the living magick now woven back into the fabric of the human world. It came slowly, almost by osmosis, but it came. And when it started to overflow, he spun it into silver-blue cords, and cast the cords upward.

Fishing.

Cuinn hated fishing. He'd been tricked by a salmon, once, in the Realm, and being laughed at by a smart-assed fish was an experience no Fae would ever want to repeat.

The cords caught, tightened.

Here goes nothing. Cuinn wasn't sure turning his back on the moon was a good idea, especially in assless chaps, but it was going to be fucking hard to haul her down while facing her. He turned, and he planted his feet in the cool concrete and he squared his shoulders and he pulled.

Absofuckinglutely nothing happened. He might as well have anchored the cords in the ground three stories below and tried to drag the earth around with them.

Which made a certain amount of sense, he supposed. Since this was the moon he was messing with.

Sense had stopped mattering a long time ago, though. A couple of thousand years ago, give or take a few centuries. Cuinn wanted to give his *scair-anam* the moonlight, and that was all that mattered.

Swiftly drawing in a fresh supply of living magick, Cuinn sent a blast along the magickal cords. Not a blast, really—just an attention-getter. A knock at the door.

The jolt traveling back down the cords staggered him, nearly dropping him to his knees, scattering tiny bursts of light behind his closed eyelids.

"Fuck!"

That does seem to be your solution to almost everything.

The voice in his head sounded coolly amused. Cuinn hoped that was a good sign.

227

Slowly he turned to face the moon. It was still an orb in the night sky, rather than a woman, but he thought the dark patches he'd always seen as a woman combing her hair in front of a mirror looked more womanly than usual. "I'm a reformed Fae, your Worshipfulness. I'm only interested in that kind of solution if it involves my mate."

I... think I am relieved.

Cuinn tried very hard not to sigh. "Will you come down, Lady? I would like to talk with you, and this way of doing it is very hard on my neck."

I suggest you learn to deal with it—is that the phrase? The smile in the voice was still there, but Cuinn thought he detected more than a little smirk. *I am a prisoner, and cannot come down.*

Cuinn clamped his jaws shut on what would undoubtedly have been a very unfortunate retort. *There are times when social skills other than seduction would be nice things to have.*

When he thought he could probably reply without finding himself on the receiving end of a lightning bolt, or whatever goddesses did when they were pissed off, he took a deep breath and tried again. "I was actually hoping to talk with you about that. I'd like to try to set you free. Now that the Pattern and the *Marfach* are both gone, and there's no need to guard the way between the worlds any more..." His voice trailed off. "You're laughing at me."

Not really.

Yes, that woman in the moon was looking at him. And settling her skirts more comfortably as she did so, as if readying herself for an audience.

She nodded, as if she could see him looking at her

from a few hundred thousand miles away. *The magick I share with my Bride is the stuff of time. Do you think a time-bound creature such as yourself could have bound me had we not allowed it?*

Cuinn gaped. He couldn't help it.

The laughter in his mind was cool, but not unkind. *You were not meant to know. Your pride need not suffer.*

"It's not my pride I'm worried about, for a change."

What is your concern, then?

"I admit, I wish there had been a way to handle everything, back in the day, that didn't involve imprisoning a goddess and essentially killing off two races of the Tirr Brai. But wishes are a spectacular waste of time." Suddenly tired, a couple of thousand years' worth of tired, Cuinn sat down heavily on the cement ledge running around the roof of the brownstone. "I just want to give my *scair-anam* back the enjoyment of moonlight."

I... do not understand.

"No, I don't suppose you do." Cuinn's pale jade gaze wandered out over the lights of Greenwich Village, the high-rises of lower Manhattan and midtown peeking up over the nearer buildings. He'd come to love this place, once his almost-human Prince had reminded him what love was.

And taking in midnight Manhattan beat the shit out of trying to convince himself that what he was feeling every time he looked at the moon wasn't guilt. Fae barely had a passing acquaintance with the concept—even the word had been borrowed from ancient humans.

Confession was almost as rarely encountered a

concept. *With this kind of luck, I should be playing the lottery.*

"When a Fae left the Realm, through the Pattern, you were the last thing he saw before the most excruciating pain he'd ever known or would ever know." Cuinn started to take a deep breath, but sighed it out before he finished. "The only channeling I could figure out how to craft that would trigger a transition without using living magick—which we knew was going to run out sooner or later—was one that automatically released the barrier keeping the worlds apart when you appeared through a window in the Pattern-tower."

The silence that followed stretched out for so long, Cuinn started to think he'd been forgotten. *I wondered why your kind avoid me now, in the human world*, the moon whispered at last. *In the Realms, they dance in my light.*

"Realms?" The woman in the moon had Cuinn's full attention once again.

Yes. The end of the Marfach gave birth to a Realm that has never known it.

Conversing with deities, Cuinn noted, was not unlike being repeatedly upended with two-by-fours to the head. He was beginning to understand why Fae had apparently decided the practice wasn't worth the headaches. "You're telling me there's another Realm."

Yes. But only as long as I watch over it, to connect it to the Realm-that-Was. If you unbind me, it will cease to exist.

"You mean I'd end up destroying an entire world. A hell of a lot more efficiently than the *Marfach* ever could have."

I'm afraid so. And your conscience has carried

enough; it does not need this burden as well. The cool voice seemed just a little warmer than it had been.

Cuinn tried not to roll his eyes—a quarter of a million miles away the moon might be, but he was sure she'd see it. "I left my conscience sound asleep downstairs, rolled up in all our blankets."

You will tell yourself that, until you do not need to believe it any longer.

"You sound awfully sure of that."

I told you, my magick is that of time. I am *sure.*

Even the cool breeze winding lazily between the rooftops wasn't going to stave off Cuinn's incipient headache much longer. But he wasn't going to let go of this conversation until hc had at lcast somc of what he'd come up here for.

"Lady, I've watched Fae suffer through transitions for the last couple of thousand years. One of them means more to me than my own life. Rian was raised as human—he has a human's love of you, a poet's soul." A poet of suffering. Most Fae would find the concept exquisite, would give anything to witness it, savor it.

Cuinn, though, didn't have the luxury of being 'most Fae' any more. "But he can't bear the sight of you, love or no love. I would change that, if I could. But freeing you was the only way I could think of to do it. And if that's impossible..."

She was smiling. Cuinn knew she was.

Luckily, you *need to do nothing. Except ask.*

Cuinn was getting tired of staring with his mouth open. "That's all? Ask?"

How often does one Fae care enough for another one to ask a goddess for his healing?

"Can't think of the last time, since Fae don't have

gods." Though maybe the middle of a conversation with one wasn't the best time to bring that up.

Cuinn could still sense her smile, but he hoped he was only imagining the slight edge it seemed to have taken on. *You believed in me enough to bind me, yes? But that was my doing, and my Bride's, as much as yours, so no matter.* The woman in the moon slowly waved a hand, sketching a tiny, perfect silver crescent. *By my light, and the light of my Bride the Sun, may the memory of past pain fade like the echo of moonset. And from this day forward, may moonlight ever be a joy and a blessing to every Fae soul, and moondark a cloak to wrap your hearts and hold them safe.*

For the third time in his very long life, Cuinn an Dearmad knew himself to be the recipient of a gift completely undeserved—Lochlann's friendship, Rian's love, and now this... forgiveness? Blessing?

They are all one, Loremaster.

"What th' feck are ye doin' up here when there's a perfectly good bed and your Prince downstairs?" Rian's voice was blurred with sleep. He stood in the open doorway of the stairwell leading back down into the brownstone; his luscious forelock looked like it had been combed with an eggbeater, and he hadn't bothered to belt his thick terrycloth robe.

The moon was silent, and whether she was watchful was her own affair at this point. Cuinn took a deep breath, and beckoned to his Prince. "Come here, *dhó-suil*. Let me show you something."

Chapter Twenty-One

"Kevin."

Tiernan spoke the name aloud. A lot. It was one of the few words that meant anything to him. He only knew his own name because the fucking homicidal monstrosity had given it to him. He had no real need of it; names were only necessary when two things needed to be told apart.

He had no such need.

Kevin's name, the memory of his face, were hooks sunk deep into Tiernan's heart.

* * *

Tiernan lay on his back, arms crossed behind his head, his gaze fixed on the silver crescent rising over the trees up the hill from his makeshift bower. He'd figured out how to make a bed of branches or reeds or whatever presented itself after his first night on bare ground, years or centuries ago, but the moon—he was convinced—was the one who had showed him how to channel magick to make, not only clothes for himself once he'd worn the set he'd arrived in to rags, but a cover for the bracken he'd been using for a bed on one particular night.

Soft laughter sounded in his mind. *I tried to get your attention before then, if you'll recall. You claimed to be more comfortable naked.*

Tiernan squinted up at the crescent. He was fairly sure it had been waxing for the last week or so, but it seemed more slender tonight than it had been. Which made perfect sense, really. Time was a capricious *mac'fracun* in this place; seasons depended as much on where he was as on the passage of time, and this was far from the first time the moon had danced in the sky.

"What I claimed was that there was something I needed a hell of a lot more than clothes or fancy bed-coverings." Tiernan's eyes narrowed; this was an old argument, one he'd lost 10,000 times already, and would no doubt lose 10,000 times 10,000 more.

Unless his heart found its way home on its own before then.

The other half of your soul is not a thing you, or I, can create. You must find it. Find him.

She'd planted that seed, too. She'd given him Kevin's name, and his name had been enough to pry loose the tiny fragment of memory Tiernan still carried like a precious jewel.

At least the moon had the good grace to sound sad.

* * *

Where are you, lanan?

Tiernan hated fog-dreams like this one. He could hear Kevin's voice, catch a glimpse of a figure moving through the mist, but could never see him properly, or get any closer to him.

He hated the dreams, but when they came, he never wanted them to end. *I'm trying to find you. I'm not giving up. I fucking won't.* His throat closed hard and tight around the words, even though they were only in his mind.

He didn't think Kevin had heard him. *I've lost you, haven't I?*

No—I'm right here, I'm—

Something heavy jumped onto Tiernan's abdomen, jolting him out of restless sleep. He manifested a knife from his crystal hand even before he was fully awake; he'd had to kill too many nocturnal predators to count during his wanderings. Waiting, even waiting for his eyes to open, was a luxury he rarely had under those circumstances.

Nothing was trying to kill him yet, though. And whatever was crouched on his bladder was too damned small to feel so heavy. Small, and sleek, with claws like ivory versions of his own blades.

"Are you going to extend those hind claws until I bleed out through a femoral artery, or just wait where you are until I piss myself?"

A slow golden blink was all the answer he got. That and a leisurely lick of whiskers as long as Tiernan's hand, a slight flexing of claws. The creature perched warily on his abs had enormous pointed ears, tufted at their tips, and fur dusted with starlight.

Cat, the moon whispered.

Fucking inconsiderate of a male's morning bladder, Tiernan whispered back.

Cats don't care.

Now that he had been helped to remember what cats were, Tiernan thought he remembered them

235

having gotten accustomed to being worshiped, once upon a time. He'd given up trying to figure out which memories were legitimately his a long time ago. The moon occasionally filled in the blanks, but not nearly enough of them.

So what do I do? Worship it?

The cat started cleaning a paw, totally ignoring Tiernan. Though he thought the flexing of tiny scimitars in the course of the tongue-bath was a reasonably direct message.

"Get off."

One ear twitched. The cat started on its other front paw.

"I said, get off."

The cat flopped over on its side and started to purr.

"I'm getting up."

The purr was louder; the cat arched its back to look at Tiernan, its golden eyes closing and opening in a slow, mesmerizing blink.

It has eyelashes. Fuck.

"I told you, I'm getting up. You've been warned."

Cats didn't care about warnings, either.

* * *

"Seriously? You think you have to feed me?"

Cat looked up at Tiernan over a mouth full of rabbit. The rabbit was easily half Cat's size. Cat was nothing if not determined. Actually, Tiernan suspected his companion was simply contemptuous of his hunting ability. It was hard to be sure, though.

"I got along fine for a few hundred years before you showed up, you know."

Cat purred. Tiernan was fairly sure the purr was sarcastic.

"All right, drop it. I'll skin it and cook it and you can have half. Deal?"

Tiernan enjoyed his conversations with Cat, though he'd surely never tell Cat. Cat was full enough of himself as it was. But Cat's presence was the first thing he'd found to take the edge off the constant hollow ache in his chest, the ache that came from missing Kevin.

But only the edge was gone. The ache itself wasn't going anywhere. It was part of him.

* * *

Tiernan pulled his cloak more tightly around himself, more to keep it from flapping in the gale roaring down from the mountain pass to the Hidden Sea than out of any real need to be warmer. It took more than wind from above the snow line to discommode a Fae.

Or a cat. He'd thought Cat was a creature of the temperate climate in which they'd found each other, but snowshoe hares and ermine and ice-doves were apparently just as easy to hunt, and just as tasty, as anything the two of them had found in the primeval forest of the Summerland.

The view of the Sea below was somewhat more discommoding, though. Tiernan grabbed his hair in his crystal hand to keep it from blowing in his face as he studied a view very different from the one he'd seen the last time he'd been this way.

Weather in the Realm—and sometimes geography —was anything but predictable. Tiernan had a vague memory of remembering a time when it hadn't been, but the skies and the land varied at magick's whim in the ever-changing here and eternal now.

Still, even for magick, this was one hell of a caprice. Mountains ringed the Hidden Sea, and only a few passes gave access to the water. That was as he remembered it.

But the wind was something new. It had driven back the shoreline of the Sea a league or more, if the naked appearance of the rocks and sand below the vegetation line was anything to go by. And what he could make out of the new shoreline was anything but the calm waterfront he recalled; he could hear the thunder of the waves from where he stood, a constant presence under the roar of the wind.

Might as well go down where it's warmer, find some shelter.

And once he was out of the wind, he could try to figure out what to do next, since a leisurely sail to the far shore of the Sea probably wasn't on offer.

* * *

The skiff was a pretty little thing, all curves and gilding and unicorn-ivory oar fittings. And someone had taken care to tuck it into the one sheltered spot along what had once been the shoreline of the Sea— either that, or the waves had thrown it here when the deep went dancing.

Tiernan couldn't see how it was going to do him any good, though, as delicate as it was. Cat had found a use for it immediately, of course; its elegant prow was sheltered from the wind, in among the roots of the stand of huge, ancient oaks where water and wind had eroded the soil away. And it caught the rays of the early afternoon sun, which made it the perfect spot for a nap.

Thoughtful of someone.

He rested a hand on the oar-lock—glanced down, already grimacing, as the wood flaked and crumbled under his touch. A closer look revealed spots of dry rot, a few cracks... a spot in the bottom where the boards were pushed out of true, betraying the probable presence of a rock or a root under the hull.

So much for that idea.

Dusting his hands together to rid them of clinging paint-flakes, he took a few steps back into the shelter of the bank and looked out over the barren stretch between the old shoreline and the new one.

It was asking too much, probably, to expect this kind of terrain to continue all around the shore of the Sea. And if it didn't, he was going to have to give some serious consideration to turning around and chancing the trip through the mountain pass again. The mountains held the Hidden Sea like a cupped hand, and the steep slopes ran all the way down to the water in most places. Not exactly a hospitable landscape for hiking.

On the other hand, he wasn't in any hurry—

Allow me to restore something you have lost.

Tiernan's first impulse was to roll his eyes, and Fae were, by and large, ruled by impulse. "Did you happen to find that self-piloting personal barge that fell out of my rucksack somewhere between here and the Summerlands? Much obliged."

He thought he heard the moon sigh. *Your magick can return the boat you have to a useable condition, if you wish.*

239

Tiernan's snort woke a ruffled and vaguely indignant Cat, just long enough to lick a paw and turn to present his other flank to the sunshine. "My magick is barely enough to let me create clothes, and food when my personal hunter takes the day off."

Living magick, yes. But you possess another magick, one you have forgotten: the elemental magick of earth.

One thing Tiernan had learned from Cat was the wisdom of not seeming too interested in something interesting. "You mean what you showed me when I first woke up." Turning the still-living head of an undead monster to sand wasn't a thing a Fae forgot quickly. Or ever. Though he'd tried.

Yes.

"I'm not sure I'd be any better off with a boat made of sand."

You are being purposefully obtuse, I think.

"I'm a Fae."

True. Perhaps I should temper my expectations. Yes, that was a sigh. *You have the ability to turn anything that once lived to stone. Not only sand, but any kind of stone you wish—even stone light as air and strong as truesilver.*

Maybe slightly less snark was called for. "Go on."

Silence.

"Please."

Cat opened one golden eye and stared at him.

You two are well suited for one another. There was a faint breath of laughter in his mind. *Close your eyes, and reach out, as if to touch and channel living magick.*

Tiernan did as he was told. The magick was elusive, as it always was, skittering away from him, dancing through the trees and the sky and even the sandy soil under his boots—every now and then, he got the impression it was snickering at him. Which was not outside the realm of possibility—magick was alive, magick was a Fae thing, so it was undoubtedly snide.

Let the living magick be. This time, you are going deeper.

He arched a brow, without opening his eyes. "Deeper how?" He scuffed the dirt with a toe.

Not deeper down. Deeper within. Toward the heart of the Realm, the lines that bind it that bind it together.

She'd been about to say something else, he was sure. But he could feel something calling him, sweet as a song, urgent as a cry, deep as a buried memory, and everything else faded away.

Yes. Follow.

Living magick stirred all around him, restless, teasing. He ignored it, intent on whatever lay beyond it.

He was not prepared for his first inner sight of elemental magick—a line of pure dazzling power, a barely tamed lightning-bolt humming with energy. Something in him hummed the same toneless music, sending shivers of recognition down his spine. Slowly he reached out—

Wait.

The moon's voice, normally soft and cool, grated when it interfered with the siren call of the light. "What?" he snapped.

Before you touch it... before you came to the Realm, Kevin's love, the joy he gave you, is what kept you from harm when you tapped directly into elemental magick. The energy may be different now, in a Realm that has never known the Marfach's blight...

"But it may not be." Not reaching out for the energy left Tiernan aching. Yet his forgotten past resonated to the moon's words, confirming their truth. "So what do I do?"

She took longer to answer than he liked. *Hopefully memories of your* lanan *will suffice.*

"I don't even have those, unless you count the memory of how I felt. How Kevin made me feel—how I still feel." Tiernan's fists clenched, flesh and crystal. "Every time I try to remember him, something happens—I get distracted, or I get attacked. The time I fell sound asleep crossing the Cloud Bridge in *Tiar'na'Slevte* and didn't wake up until after moonset was more entertainment than I needed, by half."

This silence was even longer. *You are already in pain. I would not increase it.*

"You were the one who told me how to fix the *folabod'ne* boat. And if you've been able to give me back my memories of him all along, and haven't—"

I cannot. Each word sounded heavy, a stone dropped into still water. *But my children can.*

"What do you—"

The wind in the few leaves clinging to the branches over Tiernan's head, the creaking of the old oaks, formed words.

ONE ONLY. LEST YOU BREAK UNDER THE WEIGHT OF MORE.

* * *

So good of you to strengthen me, your Grace.
Dank steam wafted under—or maybe through—
the heavy door, the creation of Kevin's mind yet also
solid wood now edged with crystalline Stone. Tiernan
found the smell of the steam almost as noxious as he
had ever found the *Marfach*. "I'd tell you to go fuck
yourself, but there's a slight chance you might enjoy it
if you did." Steeling himself against the rising heat, he
pushed more power into the magick.

***I live in the lines, amad'n — when you use their
power, you strengthen me***. The laughter Tiernan
sensed was somehow very female, and the essence of
evil. ***And yet you need that power to defeat me. Shall
we race, warrior? With the swiftest to enjoy the
delights of your plaything?***

In the fucking lines? Tiernan's jaw clenched, and
his arm tightened around Kevin. The Stone crept
inward from the edges of the door. The heat increased.

Kevin groaned softly, his head falling forward.
"Tiernan..."

"Almost there." The door was Stone, save for a
shrinking circle maybe half a yard across. "Almost... oh,
fuck me blind." The wood within the circle was glowing.
Like a coal. And Kevin's whole body stiffened, in the
circle of Tiernan's arms.

A red haze settled over his vision. "Just another
minute, *lanan*—"

"Tiernan." The whisper was soft, yet there was
steel behind it.

Startled, Tiernan turned, and had time to catch a
glimpse of his lover's face, pale and drawn and framed

with hair plastered to his temples by sweat, before Kevin shook his head.

"No—the door—fight it—but if you can't hold it..."

Tiernan growled, blasting more power through the conduit his body had become, shrinking the circle still more. But that circle was glowing, a sinister flickering orange-red. "I'll hold it."

"If you can't... you have to kill me."

"You are out of your fucking mind."

"Actually, we're both *in* my fucking mind." The thin skein of quiet humor gleaming through the pain in Kevin's soft voice staggered Tiernan. "But if you can't stop this thing, then you have to get out of it. And you have to kill me." The words were coming between gasps, now, as the glow from the door brightened. "I took your knife, as we were leaving—it's in the pocket of my duster. Thought it might come to this."

"No fucking way. Not negotiable."

"It's you that it wants. And it can't have you." Tiernan felt Kevin's head come to rest on his shoulder, whether deliberately or because the human could no longer hold it up, he had no idea. "I'm not letting it have you. I... love you."

Everything stopped. Breath, heart, thought. Even the *Marfach*'s laughter couldn't reach him. "You what?"

"I love you. You idiot." Just a hint of breathless laughter, a brush of parched and chapped lips against Tiernan's ear. "I think I always have. And it doesn't matter whether you ever love me in return. I can feel whatever the fuck I want."

He knows Fae don't love. I told him so.

"I'll never love you in return." Tiernan brushed

244

his lips across Kevin's unshaven cheek, held him against his sudden trembling. "Never 'in return.'" Deep, unsteady breath. "I just love you." The second kiss was a real one, all too brief. "And that thing will have you over my three-days-cold ashes."

"You—"

The cell was filled with a blinding light. Or at least, that's what Tiernan had to assume it was, because he couldn't bear to look at it. It was coming from the door.

"We are so fucked," Kevin breathed.

"What is it?"

"There's a hole. In the damned door."

The laughter came clearly now, and the stench in the air threatened to turn Tiernan's stomach inside out. *You make matters difficult, your Grace, but not impossible.*

Shielding his eyes with one hand, Tiernan tried to peer at the door between his fingers. The Stone had stopped short of the center of the door, leaving a hole with charred edges, not even two inches across. There the Stone stopped, for there was no magick of Earth that would form Stone out of air.

"Oh, sweet bleeding Christ." Kevin's voice was nearly inaudible. "Not them. Kill me. Right fucking now."

"Them?" Even as he asked, Tiernan knew, with a sickening certainty, what his lover meant. "You don't have to say it —"

He was cut off by a burst of laughter that made the walls shake around them. *Say it, or not, it doesn't matter, your Grace. My little pets are real enough, on this level of your beloved's mind. You cannot keep*

245

them out forever. And long before they have finished eating him, enough of my substance will be within him to begin on you. And then I will take you. From within.

"Tiernan. You have to—"

"No." Tiernan turned to face Kevin squarely. "There's another way." Gently, he kissed his human, stroked his cheek.

He staggered a little as he got to his feet, his legs not anxious to obey him after so long kneeling on stone. He drew a deep breath, ignoring the laughter in front of him. Ignoring everything but his awareness of the male who knelt on the floor behind him. His *scairanam*, his SoulShare.

Calmly, he reached out and placed his hand over the hole in the stone.

"NO!" Kevin lurched to his feet.

Softly, Tiernan spoke the forbidden word of Royal magick that turned his living hand to living Stone. And then the second word, that shattered it at the wrist.

The cell quaked around him, pitching him to the floor. Somehow, he was in Kevin's arms, doubled over, his left forearm clutched against his stomach, and his lover wrapped around him. "Jesus, Tiernan... oh, Jesus. No. No." He was being rocked, held.

There were tears falling in his hair, he could feel them trickling over his temple, down his cheek. How strange, to feel tears. Earth Fae wept diamonds.

When they wept.

Which they didn't do.

"Stop, Kevin. Please... stop." The pain left him breathless, but it would pass. "I'll be all right. And it can't get at you any more. A small enough price."

"Your opinion." Kevin continued to rock Tiernan, stroking his sweat-soaked golden hair, comforting the Fae as if he were a small child.

And as if it were the most natural and normal thing in the world, Tiernan closed his eyes, and let himself be held. "Fuck, yeah, it is."

* * *

The gentle pricking of daggers brought Tiernan back to himself. No, not daggers. Cat's claws. He was lying on his back among tree roots, in near darkness, with Cat hunkered in on his chest, purring madly and kneading as if he thought Tiernan was hiding a working nipple somewhere under his shirt.

Or as if he was trying to knit Tiernan's heart back together before it broke.

I told him Fae didn't love. And he loved me anyway.

If he closed his eyes, he could bring back the sensation of lying in Kevin's arms.

Earth Fae did, in fact, weep.

And the sandy soil was dusted with diamonds before Tiernan fell asleep, exhausted, boat and moon forgotten.

* * *

Something soft struck Tiernan on the shoulder.

"Cat, fuck off," he mumbled. There was light beyond his closed eyelids, the light of a morning whose acquaintance he had no desire to make just yet.

Something harder hit him in the same spot. A rock.

Quicker than thought, he rolled to get his feet under himself and manifested a blade from his hand.

And found himself quite startled to have done no such thing, having been brought up short by a gossamer silver web that tightened in anticipation of his every move, and opened a loop to encircle his crystal wrist, causing the hand to lose all feeling.

"Good morning, prey!"

A young female's indecently cheerful voice came from somewhere out of sight—up among the oaks, probably.

Neither youth nor gender was any reason for one Fae to let down his guard against another, of that Tiernan was sure. Not that he had much guard to put up at the moment. "Good for one of us, but I don't think it's the one who was just called prey."

Light laughter and a fall of sand and tufted grass preceded his captor's leap from the stand of oaks into his field of view. A girl, yes, whip-slender and graceful, her red hair bound back from her face, great gray-blue eyes dancing with a dangerous sort of good humor.

"You make an excellent point, prey." She dropped to her knees beside him, close enough for Tiernan to make out the fine stitching on her leather leggings and the golden animals intricately embroidered around the neckline of her tunic.

Then the point of the wickedest knife Tiernan had ever seen was under his chin, tilting his head up, and he stopped giving a damn about what his captor was wearing.

The girl studied him intently, her knife-tip digging just a little deeper every time Tiernan so much as thought about moving.

248

Carefully, Tiernan schooled himself to stillness.

Moon?

No answer.

Fuck.

Finally, the girl sighed. "You look so sad, and so beautiful. Just like the stories."

Stories? "*Maighd'n*, I—"

The knife-point twitched, but the redhead's wistful expression never changed. "I almost wish I had chosen a different *tástimhór*."

The girl's accent was strange to begin with, and her last word escaped Tiernan entirely. "Could you stay your hand, at least long enough to tell me what a *tástimhór* is?"

Her laugh was merry, but there was a hint of wildness to it that made the hairs on the back of Tiernan's neck stand up. "I am not as easily fooled as all that. You could not have become a *scian-damhsa* without facing your own *tástimhór*."

Now he understood, or thought he probably did. "If you think you can become a blade-dancer by binding and killing a helpless male—"

Another burst of laughter interrupted him. "Me, a *scian-damhsa?*" The girl held her knife up between them. "Does this look like a *damhsai'sciana?*"

Tiernan guessed this other unfamiliar word meant 'dancing-blade,' and no, it most certainly did not. The pointed blade was wider than a dagger, almost triangular, sharpened along one edge and a few inches back from the point on the other. And there was a wicked curved notch carved out of the sharpened edge of the blade, forming a hook or barb pointed back down the length of the blade. "I can't see you dancing with that, no."

"Of course not." She shook her head. "This is both finishing-blade and skinning-blade." She spoke now as if to a young child, one who required a good deal of patience. "And I am Aine, bound to Niall Master-Hunter, on my *tástitór* to earn my own blade and my freedom. Do you understand now, prey?"

"Possibly more than I want to." Cautiously, so as not to brush against earth or fabric or net and make any betraying noise, Tiernan flexed his hands behind his back. Only his right hand obeyed his instructions—the net still rendered his hand of living Stone as unresponsive as the unliving variety—and he could feel the fine chain of the net bite into the skin of his wrist as soon as he made a deliberate move.

Aine shook her head. "That is most unlike a *scian-damhsa*, not wanting to know."

That'll teach me to run my mouth while my brain is busy somewhere else. "Point taken. But it's also most unlike a hunter, to hunt other Fae."

Gray eyes narrowed. "Now you try to convince me you are a Fae?"

Moon! What the everlasting fuck?

Still nothing.

No sign of Cat, either. Tiernan was on his own for this one.

"What else am I supposed to be?—and before you say anything or decide to take my hide and be done with it, I'm not in the habit of asking rhetorical questions."

The girl rocked back on her heels and stood, all in one flowing motion. She was wary, now, in a way she hadn't been before, holding her blade in a guard position and checking her net as if to be sure it still secured him.

"None of the tales have ever called you trickster," she murmured. "And even if you were such, the *grasán* should bind you to truth, as it binds you from fighting or Fading."

Tiernan tried to calculate how many orders of magnitude more capricious than a run-of-the-mill Fae one would have to be in order to be considered a trickster by other Fae. His preoccupation with the knife in Aine's steady hand left him little attention or inclination to play with large numbers, though.

"Trust your net, then, if you don't trust me." If he could keep her talking, keep her listening—keep her interested—he ought to be able to keep himself clear of the business edge of her blade, long enough for the moon to rise. Or Cat to come back. Or for some better idea to present itself.

Though being bound to tell only the truth was going to be a serious handicap.

Slowly she nodded. "No harm in that, I suppose. For a little while." Without needing to look, she backed up a pace and sat down on the edge of the skiff. The ancient wood barely creaked under her weight. "You believe you're nothing more than a Fae?"

"I suppose that's one way to put it." Tiernan put up an eyebrow. "Since that's what I am—though I take it you disagree."

Aine laughed. "I believe that you believe it. But my test of mastery requires me to study, and track, and kill, a creature out of myth, and so I have done and mean to do."

This does not augur well.

"And tell me," she went on, "what mere Fae—

even a blade-dancer—could wander the world for the entire history of our race, without falling afoul of some wild beast, or angering another Fae enough to earn himself *cairtas-óntais?*"

"When you put it that way, I suppose it does sound unlikely." *Surprising justice* struck him as a fine euphemism *as'Faen* for revenge. "But I heal from any wound that isn't immediately mortal, and I seem to have a knack for avoiding decapitation."

"So far," the girl deadpanned, turning her knife just enough to let the sun glint off the blade.

"So far. And as for other Fae..." Tiernan's voice trailed off.

"Yes?" she prompted.

It took him a while to find his voice, plunged as he was into the memory of a memory, lying in Kevin's arms. "Other Fae have nothing I want."

Aine leaned closer, studying him curiously. "There are diamonds falling from your eyes," she observed.

"Tears."

She sat back, startled. "Tears are a human thing."

"You know of humans?" Tiernan cursed, silently, at the way his voice caught. *Never let a Fae know what you need,* the moon had whispered to him once. *Your people have a saying,* An'Faei a ngaill, ta'Fhaei an tráll.

The Fae who needs, that Fae is a slave.

Aine did not seem to have noticed his lapse, but seeming meant nothing when it came to a Fae. "Humans wander into the Realm from time to time." She shrugged. "Their minds are fragile, I think. They break if they stay here too long without proper tending, or if adults play too much with them."

Tiernan fought to slow the racing of his heart. What if Kevin was trying to find him? If he found his way into the Realm, by accident or by sheer force of will... but in the wrong place, or the wrong time...

The moon would tell me. She would.

"What do you have to do with a human?" Aine's keen gray-blue gaze had missed nothing, of course. "Humans are like day-flies, and Fae are the flames around which they dance until their wings scorch."

Tiernan shook his head, scattering diamonds to fall among the ones already littering the ground. "No. I seek... a human I lost. My lover. My *scair-anam*." The word came back from his memory of battle, and threatened to bring more diamonds with it. "My SoulShare."

If she laughs...

Aine didn't laugh. She frowned, a thoughtful expression older than her years. "I... probably don't understand."

"Probably?"

"When I was young, my mother found a human, one of the lost ones. I thought her very beautiful, even though her eyes were strange. Mother must have thought so too—I never saw them at play, of course, but my uncles teased her all the time about having *cúpál-macnas* for her pet." The way Aine's head tilted reminded Tiernan of a curious bird. "She told me, though, that no Fae could have mate-lust for a human."

Cúpál-macnas. Another word he didn't remember ever hearing before, though it perfectly described the only thing he'd ever believed himself capable of giving Kevin. And how deeply had he wounded Kevin by telling him so?

"She was wrong."

Aine's eyes seemed to grow darker, like the ocean under storm-clouds. "Even my uncles tread lightly when they challenge their sister. Who are you—an ordinary Fae, no kin of ours and claiming to be no creature out of legend—to do so?"

It occurred to Tiernan that it would probably be prudent for him to pay attention to the barely leashed anger in the voice of the knife-wielding girl who had him trussed like a boar ready for the spit.

Fuck prudence.

If someone had tried to tell him, before he'd met Kevin, how much love would change his life, would change *him*...

...would he have listened?

Could he have spared Kevin the wounds he'd inflicted?

"She was wrong twice over." Inwardly, he shrugged. *What the hell, it's not going to make her any more likely to kill me than she already is.*

"I have studied you, and the stories of you, since I was old enough to apprentice-bond." Aine checked the sharpness of her blade against the ball of her thumb, and shook off drops of blood onto the sandy soil. "I do not think you would throw your life away on a whim." Her grip on the leather-wrapped hilt of her knife tightened. "So tell me. How was my mother wrong?"

Could a nameless human woman have found love with a Fae, and the Fae with a human, if the Fae had been less blind?

"What you call *cúpál-macnas* is possible between a Fae and a human. I can testify to that. But there can be more than that, if the Fae opens himself up. Or herself. More than I could, when I met Kevin."

"You are describing vulnerability."

Tiernan couldn't tell whether Aine had any experience of the word she tossed off so easily. The Fae adolescents he vaguely remembered had no experience of sex, or of interest in sex for that matter. That awakening came with full adulthood. And Fae of all ages usually avoided emotional intimacy the way one would give a wide berth to a colony of starving swarm-voles.

Yet she was listening. She seemed genuinely curious. And marginally less likely to kill him.

"Yes. And next you're going to tell me that vulnerability is an unnatural state for a Fae."

"I was going to say 'impossible,' actually." The flash of her smile surprised him. "But I think I believe you. You wear my *grasán*, after all. And you must understand vulnerability—since you let me sneak up on you."

Sweet shimmering fuck, he was blushing. "Can we let that be our little secret?"

"For now." A hint of a mischievous smile lingered. "Go on."

Tiernan took a deep, slow breath... let it out, and took another. "I wasn't left any choice about opening up to Kevin. I still don't completely understand why—or I don't remember. And I fought it."

"Understandable."

"But stupid." Another diamond dropped to join its fellows on the ground. "I hurt him. More than once, I think."

Aine leaned in and picked up the diamond he had wept. Resting it on a fingertip, she studied it. "So you think my mother was wrong. That she hurt a pet." Her eyes narrowed—or did he imagine it?

"If she saw her human as no more than a plaything, yes. And she denied herself a chance at something sweeter than mate-lust."

"Love?"

Somehow, Aine managed to speak with no inflection at all, nothing to indicate whether she believed him, or disbelieved, or was wondering if taking his head would spoil his pelt.

"Yes. Letting someone see the truth of what you are. Trusting them to touch that truth, to hold it, as close as you hold it yourself." He wasn't sure where the words were coming from—maybe they'd been slowly accumulating in him, since he'd come to the Realm, the way water filtered through sand and stone and soil to fill deep underground pools. Surely he was no poet.

"What would a Fae want with love?" Aine shook the diamond off her fingertip. "What do you gain?"

There it was, the eternal Fae question. And a sudden sparkle in Aine's blue-gray eyes, Fae curiosity winning out over feigned disinterest.

Just for a heartbeat, everything stopped.

Every once in a great while, a handful of times in all the centuries of his wandering, Tiernan had felt a strange clarity, as if things never disordered were falling into order, as if a fog that had never really been there was lifting to make a pattern clear.

As if maybe there was some fucking reason he'd been torn from the male he loved, some condition he could fulfill to earn safe passage home.

And as long as I'm wishing, I'd like a saddle-broken pegasus and the sun on a chain of stars.

He got neither, of course. He got nothing at all, except that odd sense of clarity and a curious Fae girl.

What do you gain?

Naturally, she wanted to know. No Fae ever gave anything away, except for a guarantee of something greater, sweeter, more valuable, more beautiful. Tiernan was sure of that, down to the marrow of his bones.

At least, no Fae would make such a gift who hadn't been forced into a reckoning with his own nature.

"I'm not sure. Maybe joy. Maybe your soul."

The wind filled the silence, stirring loose wisps of Aine's copper hair. The girl's fixed gaze reminded him of Cat's.

"And you have lost both joy and soul. Am I right, prey?"

Tiernan didn't need to answer. There was nothing he could have said that the empty whistle of the wind wasn't saying better.

Aine leaned forward. Before Tiernan could do more than flinch back from the bright flicker of a blade under his nose, she had snagged the metal cobweb of the *grasán* in the hook of the skinning-barb and drawn the net off him.

Reflex powered Tiernan to his feet and brought a knife of Stone from his crystal hand.

Aine blinked calmly up at him, her slight smile unchanged. "A *scian-damhsa* knows grace, and the elegant kill. But not mercy."

Her words had the sound of a proverb. "But a hunter knows her prey. And I don't see you rushing to defend yourself."

Aine's edged yet merry laughter was caught up by a swirl of wind. She shook out her net, folded it impossibly small, and eased it into a silk pouch hanging from her belt. "I bid you farewell, prey—I have messages to carry, now."

"Oh?" There was something about being dismissed so casually by the slender girl who had taken him captive that didn't sit well with Tiernan.

One ginger brow quirked up, and Tiernan got the impression he was being seen through. "I need to return to Master Niall, and tell him my *tástitór* is complete. "

"Is it? Without my skin, I mean?" *Am I seriously trying to get myself killed?*

From the way Aine was eyeing him, she was probably asking herself a closely related question. "Knowing one's prey is the greater part of the *tástitór*. A master's skill is not needed to kill prey bound by the *grasán*."

There didn't seem to be much for Tiernan to add to that.

Aine nodded, as if he'd spoken. "And I have learned what the stories and the legends could never teach me." She slipped her knife into its boot-sheath. "Sometimes killing the prey is the wrong thing to do."

"The prey has a name, you know." Tiernan let the Stone knife absorb back into his left hand, while casually resting his right on the hilt of the blade he'd been mostly lying on. "Tiernan Guaire."

"You have another name among my folk." If Aine noticed the sword—and it was inconceivable that she didn't—she didn't seem worried by it. "But Tiernan *Fánadh* suits you as well as *Fánadh* alone."

The name chimed like struck crystal in Tiernan's heart. *I've been called the Wanderer before.* "I suppose that will do as well. Anything that isn't 'mythical being' or 'prey' is an improvement."

Aine's eyes glinted blue-grey as facets caught the sunlight. "I'm afraid you can't wish away your mythical status so easily. Mother will probably find it funny, if a male who has been alive—and alone—for longer than any Fae's memory runs has given her the way to win her Suan."

"Win her—what? Who?"

The girl hopped down from the side of the boat. "Suan is my mother's human."

Tiernan closed his mouth firmly, just in time to keep his jaw from dropping. The only thing more embarrassing than being taken in by another Fae's half-truths would be seeming to be surprised by them. "You were no child when you saw this happen, then."

"Actually, I was, when she first came." Slowly, Aine wrapped a loose lock of hair around one finger, her gaze fixed on the ground—though Tiernan was sure that it would be a huge mistake to take up a blade, thinking she didn't see. "Suan... drifts. Some humans lose their grip on time when they come to the Realm. Or time loses its grip on them."

"I'm not sure I understand."

The girl's slender shoulders lifted, as if to shrug, then subsided with a sigh. "Each day she wakes with no memory of Mother, or of how she came to share a Fae's bed, or even how she came to the Realm. And each day, Mother charms her, woos her, all over again."

Would I do that for Kevin, if I had to? Hells yes.

"I'm not sure how much you're actually going to have to teach your mother about love."

259

His words startled a little laugh from Aine. "No Fae would ever abandon a pet so fair—"

As if on cue, a strange sound was suddenly audible over the whistle of the wind, equal parts dragging over sand and stone and wet flapping. Tiernan and Aine turned, looking out past the boat toward the sea.

Beside him, Tiernan heard Aine gasp at the sight of Cat, wet and bedraggled and triumphant, hauling a rainbow-scaled fish nearly as large as he was and most definitely not dead yet. Every few steps, he had to stop and put it down, letting it flop around while he licked his whiskers and paws and tried in vain to groom himself.

"I should have known," Tiernan muttered.

"You... tamed a *karakul*?" Aine looked from Cat to Tiernan and back again. Cat responded to the attention with another round of preening.

"I think you have that backwards." Tiernan debated telling her the story of his first encounter with Cat, but decided against it. "I'm fairly sure he assumes I'd starve to death without him."

"Whoever heard of a *karakul* sharing its kill?" Aine's laugh was merry. "I should be on my way, before I forget you are no creature out of legend." She sketched a quick bow. "*Slán'abhonn, slán'aslán, slán'abhal*, Tiernan *Fánadh.*"

Before he could respond, Aine rested a hand on an exposed oak root and vaulted up, out of the shelter of the tangled roots and eroded bank, and out of sight.

Safe met, safe parted, safe home.

260

Chapter Twenty-Two

The black glass doors to Purgatory swung open at Conall's touch. Josh crowded close behind him, no doubt anxious to give his eyes a chance to adjust to the faint light of the safety telltales.

Conall enjoyed the crowding, enough that he waited a few seconds longer than he needed to before whispering the word that channeled magick to bring the house lights up.

Much to his delight, Josh didn't step back when the lights came on. Instead, his *scair-anam* wrapped beautifully-inked arms around him from behind and rested his chin on Conall's shoulder.

"This looks a little... off," Josh murmured, nipping gently at the curve of Conall's ear as a kind of punctuation and waving a hand in the general direction of the decorations hanging from the ceiling over the dance floor.

Conall grinned. "I'll take your word for it. I have a hard time telling human holidays apart."

He was teasing, of course. Even if he'd been inclined to mistake "Happy 2014" and "New Year's Resolutions Broken Here" for Christmas decorations— which, given Josh's passion for filling their apartment with season-appropriate pine boughs, angels, tiny lights

and popcorn garlands, was completely impossible—
Cuinn had been after him for at least the last week to
commit to attending Purgatory's grand re-opening
dressed as Baby New Year. In a twinkling diaper, no
less.

So far, he'd managed to keep from breaking out
the invisible ball gag. He was proud of himself.

"Are you going to tell me what we're doing down
here?" Josh let Conall go, but slid a hand down his
arm and laced his fingers through the mage's. "Or is it
a surprise?"

"No surprises yet, your Christmas present is still
under the tree." Conall didn't bother to hide his shiver
of delight; he'd caught Josh shaking the wrapped
cylinder, and even human hearing couldn't have
missed the clanking of chains and the heavy shifting of
the suspension bar.

If he'd needed any confirmation of his suspicions,
Josh's smile gave it to him. "Okay, so what *are* we
doing down here?"

Conall tugged gently at his SoulShare's hand and
led him over to the bar. "I want to give this one more
try."

He rested his free hand on the bar's thick glass
surface. They'd found a specialist in effects lighting—
probably the closest D.C. had to an actual wizard, apart
from Conall himself—but even the justly renowned
Helmut Lustig hadn't been able to re-create the
spectacularly hellish lights of the old Purgatory's bar.

Josh leaned over, peering down into the bar. It
was a hollow shell now—Lustig's mechanism was
sitting on the floor behind the bar, having been
removed to await some fine-tuning from the master in

a couple of days—but they'd both seen it in operation. Strategically placed mirrors did a reasonably good job of hiding the lights, and when the display was switched on, it was hard to see the hardware unless you knew what you were looking for.

But that wasn't good enough. Not for Conall, and not for anyone who remembered the old Purgatory.

"If it's fire you're looking for, wouldn't it make more sense to ask our Prince?"

"I talked with Rian about it a couple of days ago, actually. He's not comfortable with setting up a permanent cold-fire channeling—his control is getting better, he says, but he's sure that sooner or later, it would go hot. And he really doesn't want to burn the place down, even accidentally."

"Is that what they call *noblesse oblige*?"

Conall couldn't help laughing. If there had ever been a Royal less concerned with the privileges and perquisites of royalty than Rian Sheridan, that individual had been blotted out of Fae memory long ago. Although, now that he thought about it, the young Prince Royal had looked a bit wistfully at Mac, Lucien and Rhoann, the one time the subject of human *droit du seigneur* had come up.

Josh squeezed Conall's hand gently. "So you're going to give it a try, I take it?"

Conall nodded. "It's about time I tried to figure out what happened to living magick in the human world when we... um, when the Pattern unraveled and the wellsprings went away." *When we sent the Marfach wherever it was we sent it. When we lost Tiernan.*

When he, Conall Dary, specifically and personally, had done all that.

263

He'd thought about reminding Kevin of that simple fact—that regardless of what the human had or hadn't done during that last battle, it had been Conall's hand and Conall's magick that had sealed Tiernan into a reflective coffin with every Fae's nightmare and a bloodthirsty zombie—but it probably wouldn't have helped.

Josh's arm slid warm around Conall's shoulders as his kiss nuzzled its way into his thick, wavy red hair. His partner knew exactly where his thoughts had gone—and, probably, why he hadn't tried a single channeling since his reluctant demonstration for Thomas Almstead.

"Let me know what you need." Josh's voice was soft, low—the intimate tone that reached straight into their shared soul and touched Conall where no one else ever had or could.

"Just you."

"Always."

Conall closed his eyes, sighing unsteadily as Josh kissed his neck. Gentle warmth, and the promise of more, brought his own magick to surging life within him—he could feel it, hurling itself against the walls of his flesh, stubbornly willing to be free.

I can't.

He couldn't let go, any more than he'd been able to for all the centuries he'd lived in the Realm. He didn't trust the magick, of course—but that wasn't the problem. No mage in his right mind ever trusted the wild caprice of living magick, any more than he would trust a tornado.

Conall didn't trust himself.

How could he?

"You're shaking, baby." Josh closed his arms around Conall from behind, enveloping him in sweet strength. "Need to come inside?"

"I... I think so. Yes."

Normally, the moment Conall let go of corporeality to Fadewalk was tense. A normal Fae wouldn't even attempt it unless he or she was in extremis and had no other choice, and even Conall had a healthy respect for the risks involved. Most Fae never returned from their first Fadewalks—Fiachra had found that out the hard way.

Right now, though, letting go and stepping back into Josh was pure relief. Safety was Josh's gift to him, whether it was the safety of ropes and chains keeping Conall's power in check or the comfort of his human's body sheltering his own.

"Better?" Josh murmured.

"Much. *G'ra ma agadh.*" Conall didn't speak aloud, of course—they'd tried that a few times, sharing control of Josh's mouth, but the resulting confusion had been epic.

"At your service." The truesilver chain tattooed around Josh's wrist responded to the presence of Conall's magick, becoming solid and real and jingling as Josh reached down to adjust his already semi-hard cock.

Conall allowed himself a faint groan at the shared sensation. Arousal was going to make this much easier—assuming what he wanted to do could be done at all, he reminded himself.

Again the magick rose up in him, stronger than before, wilder. But Conall was more than he had been. He feared nothing—not even himself—with Josh's strength around him.

He knew what he wanted the channeling to look like, the mesmerizing swirling flames of the old Purgatory's bar, deep red shot through with occasional flares of orange and rare, eye-searing bursts of blue-white.

The knowledge alone would be enough to shape a one-time channeling, but Conall needed more to make the flames self-sustaining. He had to tie them into a local magick source.

And that was going to be, as they said, the rub. He couldn't link directly to the raw ley energy under their feet the way Lochlann could. He could have linked the channeling to a wellspring, but the wellsprings were gone.

And while there was apparently enough background magick in this reboot of the human world to satisfy the resupply needs of the less magickally gifted members of the Demesne, Conall had his own peculiar issues. Once he'd spent his own internal store of living magick, he was tapped out until he took a ridiculously long time to restore himself or got help from Lochlann.

"Need a hand?"

Conall could feel the wickedness of Josh's smile from the inside, as his *scair-anam* unzipped his jeans and freed his cock. His breath caught sharply at the doubled sensation, Josh's arousal added to his own, as Josh started a slow, firm stroking. "Um... I'm not going to be doing a major channeling... what are you... oh, fuck..."

Josh laughed. "I'm priming the pump, *d'orant*."

"You," Conall pronounced as clearly and precisely as he could, "are a fucking genius. Literally."

The magick was awake. And not only the magick

within Conall—Josh's touch was an invitation, and the living magick all around them couldn't resist such a perfect enticement. Any more than Conall himself could.

It was easy, now. Easy and delicious and decadent. Conall closed his eyes, focusing on the touch of his lover's hand, Josh's low groans, the heat and heaviness... the sweet tension that held his magick in check as the trickle of power flowing into him grew to a stream, and then a flood.

"Say 'when,' baby." Without slowing his strokes, Josh used his other hand to run a fingernail lightly over one hard-puckered nipple through his shirt, grinning as Conall swore. "Better make it soon, though."

"If you'd just let a Fae think..."

Fire. He needed fire. Cold fire. Flames twisting like a drumbeat, a heartbeat, the pulse that was going to be flooding from him any second now if he didn't get a grip on himself. The fires of the humans' Hell, but holding a promise of heaven.

The image began as the ghost of a thought behind his closed eyelids, gradually taking form the way a Fading Fae did, more vivid with every pull and twist of Josh's busy hand.

At last, he could see it in his mind, whole and entire. He could almost touch the flames, almost hear a soft siren call that twined around the flames the way the flames twined around his arousal. All he needed now was a word, to name and catch and bind the living magick in the form he'd created for it.

"*Ca'ain*," he whispered. *When.*

Josh heard. And the magick heard.

Josh staggered with the force of doubled orgasm,

barely catching himself with a hand on the bar. Conall released his new-fledged channeling, letting the magick flow out of him, through Josh, down into the empty space under the glass top of the bar.

The fire flared—the exact same dazzling white flare that was all but blinding Josh as his cock and hand became slick, as wet as that first time in the shower with Conall on his knees and—

"Jesus, are you trying to kill me?" Josh groaned as their shared memory came into sharp relief—seen from both of their perspectives at once. By now, this was a familiar strangeness, given how much they both loved to remember that moment.

"I don't think so. But you might want to consider breathing."

Josh opened his eyes. There was still a white heart to the fire in the bar, but it was shrinking, cooling to blue and then orange.

"Problem solved—"

A wind whirled around them, heard but not felt.

The wind formed words.

What am I doing here?

* * *

What am I doing here?

The *darag*'s answer was a few moments in coming. *YOU SHOULD BE AT THE FAR END OF THE LOCH, NEAR THE RIVER MOUTH.* The *daragin* had few words to describe a thing that was not as it was expected to be, mostly because *daragin* had few, if any, expectations of reality. Reality was what was, and expectations changed almost nothing about it. *ARE YOU NOT?*

Not exactly. Josh was putting his trousers to

268

rights, and blushing. His astonished expression sat oddly with the blush, but Coinneach suspected the astonishment was Conall's. *I am in Purgatory*.

The *darag*'s silence spoke louder than any rush of wind or creak of branch.

Conall was taking form beside Josh—more quickly than was his wont, Coinneach thought. And it seemed he spoke even before he was fully corporeal. "How did you get here?"

Coinneach forgave the abruptness. He was feeling more than a little abrupt himself. *We have discovered that I can travel outside the circle of my* darag's *roots without need of a wellspring. I sought only to cross the loch on the far side of our grove, to test the limits of this new thing.*

"You've discovered..." Conall blinked. "Seriously?"

The Fae's incredulity gave Coinneach no choice but to laugh. *Seriously. Although I am unclear as to how I came here. Neither I nor my* darag *intended to... interrupt anything.*

Conall's brilliant green gaze went, not to his lover, but to the bar, where white fire was slowly fading to orange and a deep red that even a creature of wood found sensual.

"I might understand."

Chapter Twenty-Three

The Moon didn't return until Cat's trophy was scaled and filleted and steaming over a fire Tiernan had coaxed to life at the edge of the shelter created by the trees and the eroded bank.

You survived. I am pleased.

Tiernan arched a brow. Carefully lifting one of the leaves covering the fish with a stick and peering underneath, he ignored the orb edging over the horizon.

I am not sure whether Cat taught you manners, or you taught Cat.

The Moon sounded amused, rather than put out. Tiernan wasn't sure how he felt about that.

A sigh was barely audible over the crackling of the fire and the constant sweep of the wind. *You wonder why I left you at the girl's mercy.*

"You were taking a big risk, if you were assuming she had any mercy to leave me at."

Cat stretched and yawned, ivory claws raking the sandy soil beside the fire and scattering tiny diamonds. His long whiskers twitched interestedly at the scent rising from the leaf-wrapped bundle.

"Looking for a reward? I didn't notice you being much help either."

Cat didn't so much as blink.

I could not interfere—too much was at stake.

"That's convenient." Tiernan carefully kept his voice disinterested, his stance relaxed. Resentment had simmered quietly in the back of his mind for a handful of centuries, as far as he could tell, and after the events of the last few hours, it wanted out. But a *scian-damhsa* would never betray himself or his motives to a target so quickly.

I daresay it seems so. If the Moon noticed anything was amiss, she wasn't letting on. *But I am not as powerful as you seem to think I am. I rule time, but I cannot change its nature. When it has been disturbed, as the great Fae mages did, or will do, it refuses to behave as it should until the ripples of the disturbance settle.*

"Awfully oracular of you."

If I tell you too much, I will create turbulence of my own. Your time of exile has finally served to balance the damage your Loremasters did; I would not prolong it further.

"You're talking as if you're finally ready to send me home." Tiernan measured his words carefully. This was far from the first time he'd dared to hope, and he wasn't sure he could handle having hope shattered again.

I cannot do that.

So much for being careful. She had never spoken his doom so plainly before. "Then why the *fuck* did you just say—"

My children can.

The Moon's calm cut into Tiernan's nascent rant as efficiently as Aine's knife in his throat would have. With an effort, he closed his mouth. "Your children?" he croaked.

271

Words formed from the rustling of oak leaves over his head, the creak of branches, the changing patterns of sunlight. *WOMB-CHILDREN AND CRADLE-CHILDREN OF THE MOON AND THE SUN, OUR MOTHERS.*

He'd heard that voice before. Yesterday, before he'd been dropped headlong into a memory of Kevin so vivid he'd expected to smell the smoke of the *Marfach*'s burning on coming back to himself.

This is a darag. *My cradle-child.*

Tiernan pictured the Moon smiling, a fond parent. It was a strange picture, given the level of snark that usually accompanied his own interactions with her.

Time is the darag's *treasure, each moment separate from all others, to be lived when it pleases. It can place you in the time from whence you came.*

"Right now?"

Cat looked as uneasy as Tiernan suddenly felt. The big-eared feline was crouched in something like his usual attack posture, tail twitching, hindquarters shifting. But instead of fixing his prey with an intent stare, he was looking around nervously, pupils dilated, apparently wondering where the hell his prey was.

The Moon laughed. *No, not now. You will need the help of my womb-child, the* Gille Dubh *who lives within the* darag. *But he cannot come out until sunset. Wait. Feed your cat—he has been more than patient.*

* * *

The fire's embers still glowed fitfully in the new evening, stirred by the never-ending wind, when the wind once again formed words.

You seem overdressed for an adventure.

Cocking a brow, Tiernan turned and looked up the bank. A male figure stood beside the largest oak, hands on hips, grinning, dark skin gleaming in starlight and ember-light.

And naked. Very naked.

"Oh, I don't know," Tiernan replied evenly. "I prefer to keep something between me and the kind of adventures I've been having lately."

Fair enough. I saw your encounter with the charming young huntress. Laughter was apparently the same *as 'Faen* and in whatever language the dark male spoke—"male," not "man," since there was little that was human about the being other than his outer form.

Especially certain insistently erect details of his outer form.

Tiernan cleared his throat. "If you were watching, you know my name. Which means you have the advantage of me."

And no Fae could possibly allow such a state of affairs to continue. The smile faded to a wicked gleam in eyes that seemed to flash brown and green by turns, depending on the light. *I am Nycholl. And I am a* Gille Dubh, *paired with my* darag. He laid a hand on the trunk of the oak, as if that explained something, and just for an instant Tiernan thought he saw hand and bark become one.

Maybe it did explain something, at that.

"I take it you and your *darag* are our way home?"

"Our" way? Nycholl's head tilted to one side, like a bird's. Or a cat's. *Accommodating you will be something of an inconvenience, but one I will gladly endure for the sake of your close company—*

273

"Don't get your hopes up. You're returning me to my own close company, or you'd better be."

You are a most unusual Fae. The tree spirit shrugged. *The addition of your cat may prove more than our close quarters can bear. You will have to hold it, and cats of my acquaintance are not overfond of that.*

"Which is one reason I overdress for adventures."

Cat stropped himself against Tiernan's shins, purring. But not, he noticed, retracting his claws.

"What do we need to do?"

Our Mother says you need to Fade without traveling, and come into the darag *with me. From there, the* darag *will choose to live in the future-moment She has given it for this purpose, and you and I—and your cat—will simply live along with it.*

"Nothing much, then." Tiernan didn't even bother trying not to sound sarcastic. Fading was a thing he'd discovered fairly recently and didn't entirely understand; it seemed to involve letting go of the part of himself that was physical in one place and willing that part to be reconstructed around the living magick of another place. Each time he did it, it felt a little like stepping off a cliff—somehow, the knowledge that he'd survive if it didn't kill him immediately wasn't any comfort in either case.

And doing it without traveling anywhere, just deciding to become un-physical, sounded remarkably like stark raving lunacy.

But if that was what he had to do to get back to Kevin?

Tiernan glanced down at Cat, and braced himself, recognizing his feline companion's *I'm-about-to-*

pounce ass-wriggle. He managed not to yelp as claws sank into his leggings and vest and linen shirt; gritting his teeth, he plucked a hind-claw out of his navel with one hand while supporting Cat's weight with his other arm. "You're going to have to hold still and *not* do that again—I've never tried Fading both of us before, and I'm going to need all the non-hindrance I can get."

Cat licked his whiskers.

You talk to cats?

"Not cats in general. Just Cat." Tiernan drew a deep breath and turned to Nycholl. "Are you ready to do this? If I can even manage this kind of Fade, I don't think I can hold it for long."

Define "ready."

"I think I hate you."

Nycholl laughed, wind and starlight. *We are at your service.*

And with that, there was nothing for it but to try.

Taking a deep breath and doing his damnedest to relax, Tiernan imagined himself and Cat dissolving in a perfectly still pool of light, clear as crystal but touched with silver-blue.

He'd had enough practice to make the transition fairly simple, even with the addition of a passenger— the trick was to keep from reaching immediately for some other place in that pool of magick to anchor his physicality and start building it back up again.

Hm. Perhaps you should have stopped while I could still see you.

"If I'd done that, I could hardly walk into a tree, now, could I?"

Nycholl gave no sign that he'd heard.

"Fuck."

Tiernan shrugged shoulders that didn't technically exist at the moment, and climbed up the eroded face of the bank to stand beside Nycholl.

Or he tried to. Telling his legs to move produced something like a ripple in the pool of magick he was part of, and moved him not quite a finger's-breadth toward the bank.

He tried again, harder. Two fingers.

At this rate, he wouldn't have to move through time inside the *darag*, because he wasn't going to get anywhere near the *darag* for a few centuries.

Are you ready?

Tiernan's reply was brief, colorful, probably anatomically impossible, and largely automatic, preoccupied as he was with figuring out how to get up to the tree.

In the end, of course, it was—as so much else was—a simple matter of breaking the rules. He'd been told to Fade without traveling, but that was going to leave him stuck in his own world's past, with no chance of seeing Kevin again.

So Tiernan Faded into the trunk of the tree.

Cat's yowling, and the bizarre burning stiffening pain wracking his body, stopped him from rebuilding his body around the *darag*'s magick before he'd done much more than think about it.

COME, NYCHOLL. IT IS TIME.

Suddenly there was someone else in the tree with Tiernan and Cat. Someone occupying exactly the same space. Not that Tiernan could see anything

I did warn you about the close company. Nycholl chuckled. *Are you sure you have no wish to—*

"I wish to get the hell out of here before I lose

control of my Fade or my cat." Tiernan wasn't sure how he was speaking; he was just grateful that he could.

There is wisdom in your counsel.

* * *

Wake up.
WAKE UP.

How the fuck wind was blowing inside a tree was a mystery Tiernan couldn't fathom. Although, truthfully, he wasn't all that interested in fathoming it, at least not until the top of his head stopped trying to come off.

You must leave us now.

The amusement in the voice tipped Tiernan off. "Nycholl." Well, that explained the wind. "Am I supposed to have a hangover that would kill a large farm animal?"

Somewhere around his feet, Cat meowed pathetically.

"Or a smallish non-farm animal."

"Supposed to" is a difficult concept, when no Fae or smallish non-farm animal has ever done this before. Nycholl sounded somewhat discombobulated himself. *But it seems appropriate.*

"I don't suppose you have a cure handy?"

Leaving the darag *would be a good first step.* Nycholl sighed dramatically. *A shame. But the mage our Mother warned of your coming is here, and anxious for your arrival.*

Tiernan closed his presently-imaginary eyes against the pounding behind them. "He can't be half as anxious for my arrival as I am to get out of here. No offense to present company intended."

Politeness? The breeze sounded shocked.

"Gratitude for service rendered. Please don't make me regret it."

Nycholl laughed. *Perhaps we shall meet again someday, Wanderer. And the mage is preparing a channeling not far from here. If you can sense the magick of it, that direction is safe to Fade in.*

Gathering his awareness of Cat close as best he could, Tiernan Faded.

When he took form again, the drumbeat in his head was gone, vanished like the light of a snuffed candle.

He and Cat stood in a small clearing in thick woods, where minutes ago they had been finishing a fish dinner on a low-tide beach. A slender auburn-haired female in elegant robes stood on the far edge of the clearing, tracing a finger in an intricate pattern over the surface of what looked like a large mirror; another female, dark hair caught up in a scarf of the same finely-woven blue linen as her dress, tended a fire in a stone pit. Both turned toward him, startled—

A wave of pure vertigo dropped Tiernan to his knees. Cat screeched, getting out of the way just in time.

Tiernan pressed his forehead into the cool grass, hoping it would make the Realm stop spinning around him. *What the pernicious fuck? Where did* this *come from?*

Even thought was difficult. He couldn't shake a bone-deep sense of *agór*, wrongness. He'd gone into the tree in one place, and had come out somewhere else, and his body and hindbrain had some very definite opinions on the impossibility of such a thing.

Can I have the hangover back?

"Suan!" The voice was coming from the far side of the clearing, where the taller female had been tending the mirror. "I dare not leave this channeling until I can stabilize it—"

"I will help him, Lady."

A hand under Tiernan's elbow urged him to stand, took his weight when he staggered.

"Easy," he muttered.

Light laughter greeted his grumbling, as if he had said something clever. "You act like you just got out of a covered litter."

"I beg your pardon?"

The female eased her shoulder under Tiernan's arm, the better to hold him up. "You know."

"I've never even seen a covered litter, never mind been in one."

As parsing the difference between up and down preoccupied him less and less, a murmuring in the back of his mind became louder—and louder still when he looked at the mirror the mage was preparing.

His memories. However many centuries' worth of them there had been before he'd been hurled backward in time to slay a monster and midwife a world. They were chaotic, indistinct—but a few were trying to get his attention. The emergent few had one thing in common: being closed inside some kind of metal moving conveyance about the size of a coffin, from which he had emerged almost exactly the same shade of green he could feel himself turning now.

Wonderful. I'm almost close enough to my memories

to touch them, and instead of finally remembering Kevin, I relive being locked in an iron vomit wagon.

"See? You know." The female blushed as she looked up at him, trying and failing to suppress a smile, the attempt bringing out several very fetching dimples and setting the light of the fire dancing in her eyes.

Her unfaceted, brown, human eyes.

Suan. How had he forgotten that name?

Well, he hadn't exactly forgotten it—remembering it had just been forced to wait its turn behind keeping his fish dinner where he'd put it.

"You're Aine's mother's—" Tiernan barely managed not to blurt something unfortunate like *pet* or *plaything.*

"*Cheanglá.*" Suan nodded, the smile she'd kept back now blossoming.

Tiernan heard the echo of a word that had been familiar once—*ceangal*, a binding. A tricky word, one that could mean captivity or betrothal or marriage, depending on the context.

"The channeling is nearly ready, *sule-speír.*" The mage still didn't look away from her working, but her smile showed she'd been listening, and made Tiernan glad he hadn't been unnecessarily rude to her human mate. If *never piss off a mage* wasn't a Fae saying in this Realm, he was willing to wager it ought to be. "Is our guest well enough to travel?"

Before either Suan or Tiernan could answer, Cat let out one of his overlook-me-at-peril-of-your-clothing yowls.

Both females laughed. Suan looked down at Cat, who was arching against her shins; that being all the invitation Cat needed, he swarmed up her skirt-swathed legs and settled himself with the very tips of his hind-claws digging into the generous curve of her right hip and his fore-paws kneading at either side of her throat.

Tiernan arched a brow. "I've never seen him do that before—when he wants to get my attention, he usually sits on my bladder."

Suan giggled, curving her free arm under Cat to take some of his weight off his hind-claws. "That must be—*au!*—uncomfortable."

The mage left off her preparations, gliding across the grass and slipping her arm through Suan's. "Please forgive my manners; I should have noticed you came with a companion."

Tiernan didn't bother to comment on the rarity of a Fae apology, since it was obvious the auburn-haired mage was looking at Cat. Cat, for his part, purred like the low rumble of thunder accompanying the constant flicker of summer-lightning, and leaned into the mage's caressing fingertips so hard he nearly unbalanced himself and had to clutch at Suan with all four pointy ends to keep his perch.

"Maybe I'll be traveling alone," Tiernan muttered.

Three heads turned toward him; three pairs of eyes blinked slowly. Two pairs, at least, seemed amused.

"I daresay our novelty would wear off in time." Dropping a half-wink to her human, the mage extended her free hand to Tiernan, open palm up to show she bore no weapon. "I am Méalla, and you were my daughter's master-hunt and teacher."

Tiernan returned the gesture with the hand of living Stone that was all the weapon he needed. "Is that why the Moon chose you to send me home?"

"It might well be, though that Lady keeps her own counsel." Méalla took Tiernan's outstretched hand and led him toward the mirror. "I would enjoy keeping you here a while—long enough at least to tell you what you wrought when you spoiled Aine's hunt—"

Tiernan cleared his throat. Neither Méalla nor Suan seemed to notice.

"—but you have waited long enough to go home, I think."

He shook off Suan's support, dropped Méalla's hand, and hurried the last few paces, stepping around the mirror and coming face to face with—

Himself. And Cat, and the clearing behind him, and trees behind trees behind trees fading off into a hazy golden afternoon.

He rested a hand on the hilt of the sword belted at his waist, relaxing into a balanced stance, shaking off the last of his gryphon's pellet of a hangover to open his senses up to his surroundings. Aine had caught him unawares; her mother would have a much harder time doing the same.

"*S'ocan.*" Méalla's tone was gentle, but firm. "This is no trap, *scian-damhsa*. The channeling is prepared, and waits only on a summoning from the other side."

"Forgive me if I keep my guard up while I wait." Cat, picking up on Tiernan's tone, wove a quick set of arcs around his feet before crouching between them. "It seems I've been dancing someone else's figures for a very long time now, and I've had enough of it."

"Any Fae would say the same in your place."

"I seriously doubt any Fae has ever been in my place."

His memories grew steadily louder. They were

like the roar of a waterfall, now—but he was in a cave behind the fall, near deafened but untouched. Faces jostled one another just out of sight; voices murmured, shouted, laughed, wept, all unintelligible.

So close.

Méalla said something. Or he assumed she did—hers was simply one more voice in the chorus at this point. "Try that again?"

"When you feel the call, step through." The mage spoke slowly, enunciating carefully. "Do not Fade—the mirror will trap your soul if you do."

"Fuck me backwards."

"An interesting concept." Méalla raised one perfect brow; Suan blushed.

Cat arched and hissed at the mirror.

Music swelled within the roar of Tiernan's memories, music with a driving beat, an insistence. Music that was itself a memory.

"I hear it." He wasn't sure if he whispered, or shouted, or even spoke aloud at all. "The call."

Cat swarmed up into Tiernan's arms, claws digging deep into chest and arms and abs, furry chin tucked firmly under Tiernan's scruffy jaw.

"Go!" Méalla raised her hands, feeding living magick to the channeling.

Tiernan hesitated in front of the entirely solid-looking mirror.

"Trust my Lady! Go!" Suan's hand between Tiernan's shoulder blades pushed him forward.

The beat called him, the pulse of memory.

Tiernan stepped into the mirror.

* * *

A giant scorpion with a face out of nightmare and pincers by Ginsu yanked Tiernan out of Kevin's grasp—

Only for Kevin would he even consider an entire evening in a tuxedo—

"Gan cé g'vratheann m'croí," he whispered, straddling his lover's thighs—

"Enjoying the show?"

"The kinslayer's awake."

Fuck me if I am entering yet another world on my fucking face. Tiernan would have loved to collapse on the grass and cover his head with his arms as Bastet alone knew how many years' worth of memories descended on him like a barrel full of building-bricks. But a Fae had his limits, and his pride.

Prudently, Cat leaped free of his arms and raced off, yowling as if someone had knotted his tail around a burning branch. Hopefully he wouldn't run out of earshot before the cacophony in Tiernan's head settled down—at the moment, adding visual input to his internal chaos seemed like overkill.

Someone—several someones—caught him by the elbows, holding him up. He shook them off.

"I am sprung from the loins of an entire race of assholes."

"I can't love you—what part of that don't you fucking get?"

"Then scian'a'schian *let it be, until blades no longer thirst."*

"Is rejecting help wise, in your condition?" The female's voice was familiar, but for the moment the name attached to it was roiling around in Tiernan's head along with a very long lifetime's worth of other remembered things trying to find their places.

Before you all was dust
Without you all would be ashes
To lose you would leave my soul empty for a silent eternity

Planting his feet as firmly as he could, Tiernan drew a deep breath. In through the nose, out through the mouth. Again, and again. A simple, effective way to clear his head, to calm down.

When it worked.

It was not working especially well.

"The only help I need is my *scair-anam*. Right fucking now, if you please."

"I would if I could."

Unacceptable answer.

Hoping the ground would refrain from smacking him in the face, he opened his eyes. Aine—the adult Aine he had left behind with everyone and everything else, not the mocking adolescent Aine who had come within a heartbeat of ending him—was clearly exhausted, leaning on a dark-haired male with frosted-silver temples while she replenished her magick. A hand-mirror lay in the grass next to her, its surface spider-webbed with cracks.

"Why can't you?" Out of consideration for her condition, Tiernan tried not to snap.

Aine's lips pressed together into a thin line. "We have been unable to find a way back to the human world since the Demesne of Purgatory destroyed the Pattern."

* * *

Anyone who saw Tiernan Guaire might have been forgiven for thinking him a Fae at ease with himself and his world. A large, flat stone by the lakeshore still gave off the heat of the now-setting sun, and he lay back, propped on his elbows, watching waterfowl glide to landings and set the water to rippling.

Any such hypothetical observer might have been forgiven, that is, if Tiernan weren't exuding a fuck-with-me-at-your-peril mood potent enough to scare off the local fish. Even Cat gave him a wide berth, after an exploratory pounce nearly earned him a swimming lesson.

He remembered so much now. How long had he yearned for this peace, this supernatural beauty, after he'd been exiled from it the first time? He wouldn't have admitted it then, of course, even to himself—and who else would a wary Fae in the human world ever have admitted it to?—but he had known, whether two centuries ago or 12, or 20, that his heart had only one home, and that home was the Realm.

I knew nothing.

His heart wasn't here.

"May I join you?"

Tiernan didn't bother to look up. "Suit yourself."

Instead of sitting beside him, Aine went to sit on the edge of the rock, gathering up the layers of her skirts and dangling her toes in the crystal-clear water. She, too, looked out over the lake in silence, her unbound hair flaring even redder than usual in the rays of the setting sun.

"What happened to the *Marfach?*" she asked at last.

Memories of the battle under Purgatory slid into place alongside memories of his reawakening. "We tried to trap it, to send it here for you to destroy, or bury. And this is just a guess, but I think we fucked with time so badly when we trapped it that we broke it. Broke time."

"And you broke the Pattern in doing so."

"We had to. We couldn't kill the *Marfach*, and while I may never remember those few minutes' *bod-snadhaem* clearly, I'm pretty sure the timestop you and yours set up to keep us from sending it back here was going to blow everything straight to hell if we didn't do something about it."

Aine inhaled sharply. "Go on."

Tiernan shrugged. It didn't matter that she couldn't see him. "The *Marfach* had me when the trap closed. And all the time-fuckery threw us back in time, to before the Sundering. Maybe before there were Fae."

"I saw you go, I think." The Loremaster stared at her toes in the water. "I was the only one not in the Pattern when it was unmade. And I saw every moment of its making, and every moment of its existence... and the moment hell itself hung suspended in the middle of it."

"Hell itself. Sounds about right." Tiernan's throat tightened around his words. He waited out the spasm, watching a V of geese pass between the horizon and the setting sun. "The *Marfach* forgot what it was, and I killed it."

"And you forgot who you were."

"Yes." The sudden rawness of Tiernan's voice surprised even him. "But I never forgot Kevin."

287

Aine half-turned to look at him. The tears standing in her eyes were a shock. "When I told you we have been unable to find a way back to the human world, I did not mean that no way exists—only that most of us have been in no condition to search for one. And those of us who are, are needed to care for the others."

Tiernan sat bolt upright.

The Loremaster nodded, as if Tiernan had spoken. "Most of us survived the unmaking of the Pattern. But only a few of my colleagues remember what it is to inhabit a physical body... and it is a thing that takes getting used to."

Kevin.

I'm coming, lanan. Tseo mo mhinn ollúnta. *This is my solemn oath.*

Chapter Twenty-Four

How long before I can get out of this damned penguin suit? Black silk heated against Kevin's hooked finger as he yanked at his bow tie, leaving it to dangle around his neck.

Purgatory didn't seem to notice its owner's discomfort. The re-opening night crowd was practically elbow to elbow, men in leather brushing up against men in sequins and lace, or latex, or not much of anything at all. And while the fire marshal was never going to find out about the packed house, the HVAC people were going to hear from the management first thing in the morning. Or the next day. Even Fae money might not be enough to get the air conditioning looked at on New Year's Day.

Kevin hitched himself onto a bar stool, swiveling to eye the crowd. The cock pit was full to overflowing, and the patrons in the new VIP area certainly seemed to be enjoying the view—though Kevin was pleased to see that the ones who were enjoying it most were following house rules and had draped their oversized linen napkins across their laps. *Public or private—no in-between*, the signs all over the club read, in a half-dozen languages. Conall's security channeling could only hide what was in public view.

The bartender—not Mac, the new assistant manager of Purgatory was out working the floor—set a drink on the bar next to Kevin. He picked it up without noticing it; he didn't need to notice it, Mac had instructed the bar staff well, and he knew it would be his usual Jack and Coke.

"Tiernan would be proud."

Speak of the devil. Conall was wrapped in a black silk robe with the Purgatory logo embroidered in red on the left shoulder. Kevin guessed the coil of rope in his hand and the eager anticipation in his peridot eyes meant he was on his way to meet Josh in the dungeon.

"I'd like to think so." Kevin did his best not to choke on the words, or let his eyes well over. Again. The rest of the Demesne still thought they'd talked him out of his plan to turn the club over to Mac and his husbands, and he wasn't ready for any of them to figure out his true intent just yet. And he still couldn't hear the name of—couldn't even think of—Purgatory's real owner without feeling like someone had slipped a keen cold blade between his ribs.

Conall noticed something, of course. The ginger mage rested a hand on Kevin's shoulder. "Let us know if you need anything."

Us. The whole Demesne, plus Kevin's dad, had circled wagons around one of their own in a most un-Fae way.

But for all their efforts, the only thing Kevin needed, they couldn't give him. Still, he owed them thanks for trying. "*G'ra ma agadh*, Conall."

He watched Conall work his way through the crowd, skirting the stage and heading for the curtained doorway giving access to the dungeon.

The hallway leading to the dancers' dressing room—undressing room, really—was still more or less where it had been, off to the left of where Conall vanished; the room at the end of the hall, though, was as different from the old one as it was possible to imagine. Sloppily painted cinderblocks, thrift store folding chairs, and metal mirrors bolted to the walls had been replaced with a lounge at least as sybaritic as the VIP area, lacking only a hostess and personal bartender. Tiernan believed in taking care of the men who were the soul of the club, in a way the previous owner never had.

Had believed. Shit.

Kevin's eyes burned. His chest felt tight. Ice cubes jingled in his glass with the shaking of his hand.

Distraction, I need a distraction. Preferably something other than reaching over the softly glowing bar and fumbling around for the leather portfolio containing the deed to the club and the paperwork proving the satisfaction of all the contractors' liens, then finding Mac, handing him the works, and leaving Purgatory behind for good. No matter what he'd told the others, told his father. He couldn't stay.

But he'd promised Tiernan's memory that he was going to see opening night through, and fuck if he was going to break that promise, no matter how it ripped him up.

The dancers warming up the poles would have been a decent distraction, he supposed, if he'd been in any other mood. Garrett had hired two Hungarian brothers who specialized in dancing in stiletto heels that would have given Kevin a nosebleed if he'd ever tried so much as standing up in them.

291

As he watched, the lights went down, the DJ punched up the bass on the house music to the point where Kevin felt like he'd swallowed a vibrator, and tight spotlights lit up the two front poles, catching Tibor and Nikolasz halfway up. White light from the bar flared, too, flickering over the nearly-naked dancers.

Dear God. This is where it started. Where everything started.

Exactly here, on this same barstool. Kevin had been sitting right here, nursing a drink, numb and wondering what the hell he was going to do with the rest of his life after being denied partnership a second time. He'd been watching the dancers...

Kevin clenched his jaw against the groan trying to rise out of the ache in his chest. He'd been wrapped up in the dancers, then—hadn't even noticed the presence behind him, until that first soft murmur in his ear.

"Enjoying the show?"

Kevin's glass fell to the floor, shattering into a shrapnel grenade of crystal shards.

Warm breath caressed his ear; a hand rested lightly on his shoulder. Exactly the way it had that first night.

"The show? Remember?"

I'm not going to turn around. I don't dare. If he turned, he'd know he was dreaming. Hallucinating. Insane. *Just let me keep the dream a few seconds longer.*

A warm tongue-tip ran around the curve of his ear. "Come on, *lanan*, I've been living for this for the last six or seven hundred years, could you at least look at me?"

There was no denying the raw hunger in the voice Kevin knew so well. But it seemed as if the room turned, spun, rather than he himself. And before he could make out any more of his husband's features than a fall of golden hair, piercing blue eyes and a scruff of beard, he was crushed to a leather-clad chest.

And he was kissed. Jesus God, was he kissed. He could feel himself dissolving into that kiss, everything he was, everything he'd ever been, all the newborn effervescent thoughts of who he might be...

Christ, I'm thinking in threes. To the extent he was thinking at all.

And Tiernan, it seemed, was reading what was left of Kevin's mind, whispering the Fae verse he'd written for their wedding, in threes-meter, between kisses and nips and soft involuntary growls.

"Before you all was dust, without you all would be ashes, to lose you would leave my soul empty for a silent eternity—"

An ungodly yowl cut off Tiernan's urgent whisper; Kevin caught a glimpse of silver fur and impossibly long ears as something raced past the two of them and off into the crowd on the dance floor. And somewhere out in the throng, a puppy barked.

Kevin barely had time to brace himself as Tiernan sagged against him, laughing. "I should have known Cat wouldn't be intimidated by a Fade-hound."

"You brought a cat home with you?" The sight of Tiernan, the sound of his laughter, the scent of him all flowed into Kevin, filling places he hadn't even realized were empty because he'd been so focused on the obvious ones. He was floating, flying, falling headlong into arms outstretched to catch him. Arms he'd been certain would never hold him again.

"I hope you don't mind." Fae laughter faded to a Fae smile that tried to be innocent and missed the mark by a mile. "It would be hard to figure out how to take him back."

"Back? You mean, to the Realm?" Kevin caught at the edge of Tiernan's soft leather vest, the easiest thing for him to grab at the moment, and tightened his grip till his knuckles went white. "If you think I'm letting you out of my sight for a second, for any reason—"

"Oh, but I do. You're going to let me go long enough to let me Fade back into my office before anyone else notices me." Tiernan's hand closed over Kevin's. "So you can welcome me home properly." The smile was still there, but Tiernan's voice was tight.

Kevin swallowed the sudden large lump in his throat. "Go."

* * *

Tiernan's recovered memories still sat oddly in him. The dimly-lit office with its glowing computer monitors was familiar, yet not, a place he had seen yesterday, and had not seen for centuries.

One memory, though, had never left him.

Hurry the fuck up, lanan.

The office—his office—was like a cocoon. He'd asked for it to be built that way, and the contractors had obliged. Outside, the pole dancers' music shook the floor and the walls. Inside was as quiet as snowfall on water.

Not for long, though.

He leaned back against the desk, gripping the edge until the knuckles of his flesh-and-blood hand turned bone-white, staring at the wall.

He'd been able to feel the pull of Purgatory for

days. Not the ley energy he'd sensed back when the site of the club had been a stable for carriage-horses, but the call of channeled magick. But it had been elusive, like the flicker of a flame.

Until a few minutes ago, when a sexual siren call had echoed between the worlds and stepping through had been as easy as Fading.

And then he'd been standing at the end of the bar, looking out at the dance floor over Kevin's broad shoulder.

The door clicked open.

Closed.

"I thought I was dreaming." Kevin's voice was low, charged.

Taking a deep breath, Tiernan turned.

Kevin was leaning against the door, as if he needed help to stand. His eyes were red-rimmed, but the intensity of his gaze made Tiernan's breath catch in his chest. "I've been standing out there, afraid to open the door."

"Afraid?"

"Afraid there was no one in here. That I'd imagined you."

Tiernan crossed the room in two strides, sliding between Kevin and the thick soundproofed door and turning Kevin to face him. "If you want holding up, *elafantabod,* that's my job, not the fucking door's."

"Oh, God." Tiernan could feel a shiver run through his *scair-anam*'s body. "It really is you."

Tiernan had spent the last thousand years searching for the combination of lust and laughter and love in Kevin's dark brown eyes. And every moment of the search had been worth it.

"All it took to convince you was an f-bomb?" He traced his tongue-tip along Kevin's lower lip, nipped gently at it.

"That and being called *elephant-dick*. Nobody else—" Kevin's voice wavered, caught.

"No one else has the privilege."

It was the most natural thing in two worlds to turn nips to kisses, a line of them searching down the rough column of his husband's throat. Tiernan slid both hands under Kevin's suit jacket, around to the small of his back, and drew him closer.

Close enough to feel the heat of a certain *elafantabod,* even through however many layers of clothing separated them.

A thousand years of waiting, searching, longing were a heartbeat from being over. All he had to do was unbuckle Kevin's belt, unzip him, probably do something about the lower six inches or so of his dress shirt...

"Oh, fuck me senseless."

"I thought that was the general idea, yes." Kevin had let his head fall back to give Tiernan better access to his throat, but Tiernan could hear the smile he couldn't see. "Or was that an order?"

Tiernan drew a deep breath, filling himself with all the scents of his *scair-anam*. Cologne and sweat and tears and musk, warm skin and thick dark hair and a hint of Jack and coke on breath as familiar to him as his own. "You're going to laugh."

"Would that be a bad thing? I've gone a very long time without."

"I've been searching for you, waiting for this, for something like a thousand years. And now that I have you, I can't make myself let go of you. Not even long enough to get you out of this monkey suit."

Kevin's head came up at this. "A thousand years?"

"Close enough. Time does strange shit in the Realm."

Kevin seemed to be having trouble finding words. "You looked for me. For a thousand years."

To lose you would leave my soul empty for a silent eternity... How little he'd understood when he penned those words to be part of his wedding vows. "I couldn't lose you."

The silence stretched out. And then Kevin's hands, warm and strong, slipped down his back to cup his ass and hold him as close as skin, leaving a thrill of living magick in their wake.

"Funny thing... I don't want to let go of you, either. Ever."

A single perfect diamond fell from Tiernan's eye.

"Never," he whispered against Kevin's already kiss-swollen lips. *"Tseo mo mhinn ollúnta."*

This is my solemn vow.

Epilogue

Welcome to Purgatory.

If you've made it as far as the black glass doors, you knew what you were looking for, the unremarkable staircase tucked in among the dance studio and the tattoo parlor and Big Boy Massage. Or maybe you felt a call, the way others have before you.

And you aren't an officer of the law with surveillance or worse on his mind, because if you were, you couldn't make yourself descend the stairs. But if you're a square-jawed detective and you're not quite sure why you came, you might find someone who's been trying to get an appointment with you for the last few hundred years.

Open the doors. Let your eyes adjust to the dim light, the occasional pulse or flare or strobe. Let the driving beat from the dance floor settle into your bones.

Take in the huge tank, past the doors and around a corner. Stare in wonder—or in something else—at the erotic ballet of Purgatory's famed mermen. You can buy tokens to toss into the tank, to tip the performers. Pick your favorite, if you can: an R for the tall blond-crested god, an M for the handsome ex-Marine whose single leg seems right and perfect and graceful in the water. Or, as most patrons prefer, an L for the stocky bald bear who finds his own performance in the tank as comical as the eager onlookers find it arousing.

Make your way to the bar, and place your order. Watch the play of light under your glass, the dull red flames that come from nowhere and create no heat. And sometimes the flames leap and writhe and flare orange and yellow and sometimes a brilliant blue-white that leaves you blinking.

You'll find out what causes that, eventually. If you're among the lucky few.

Don't see anything you like at the bar? Work your way through the crowds on the dance floor, to an alcove just past Purgatory's infamous cock pit. Stop there if you like, for a few minutes, and enjoy the view; anyone who ventures into that black leather playground knows he's on display and loves to show off. And no matter how loud the music gets on the dance floor, you can almost always hear the groans and the cries from the pit.

Once you've had your fill—if you ever do, the owner is reported to be thinking about adding some high-tops to the corner by the alcove to accommodate watchers wanting to make a night of it—the shallow steps rising out of the alcove will take you up to the VIP suite overlooking the action below. A discreet tip to one of the young men at the head of the stairs will see you escorted to a table; another long-dead Founding Father speeds the delivery of a bottle of champagne to your table. And if you're fortunate and favored, Falcon, the suite's exquisite hostess, will deliver it herself.

The suite has its own bar, too, of course, manned by a silver fox uninterested in flirtation but so affable in deflecting passes that even his most ardent admirers don't mind that he's straight. He's family—his son gave Purgatory to his son-in-law as a wedding gift. And when the former Marine first sergeant finally grew sick to death of retirement, his son-in-law convinced him to take up a new occupation. The tips are incredible, and the way the suite is set up, he can't see when his son and son-in-law take to the dance floor or the cock pit. Which, he figures, is just as well.

Purgatory is full of stories, told and yet to be told. See the redhead in the silk robe, the one who looks like he needed a fake ID to order that drink in his hand, disappearing through a curtained doorway leading off the dance floor, walking backwards to catch one last glimpse of pure sex with curly blond hair wrapped around a pole on the stage? He's at the heart of both kinds of stories. His past left him with a longing for the kind of delicious ornamental bondage his partner's waiting to administer in the dungeon on the other side of the curtain. And his future is going to see him trained into the ranks of the keepers of his race's history and magick.

Oh, and his trainer? She'll be in for a surprise or two herself, courtesy of the silver fox upstairs. Purgatory seems to attract the unexpected.

Keep an eye on the bar downstairs.

On the special nights, when the mermen are lost in one another and the untouchable Falcon is nestled in the lap of a dark handsome man with wandering hands and the owner and his husband are learning one another's bodies by touch in the cock pit... and the redhead is bound to perfection and pushed past the limits of pleasure... the light in the bar, not fire at all but the tethered lust of a master mage, flares up.

And the back door of Purgatory opens, the door into the Realm, and the Fae come through, called by living magick and pure desire. They have legends of their own, new legends of Purgatory and its sweet decadent pleasures, and they come willingly to sample those pleasures when summoned.

Anything can happen in Purgatory.

Welcome.

Glossary

The following is a glossary of the Faen words and phrases found in *Hard as Stone, Gale Force, Deep Plunge, Firestorm, Blowing Smoke, Mantled in Mist, Undertow, Stone Cold* and *Back Door into Purgatory*. The reader should be advised that, as in the Celtic languages descended from it, spelling in Faen is as highly eccentric as the one doing the spelling.

(A few quick pronunciation rules – bearing in mind that most Fae detest rules—single vowels are generally 'pure', as in ah, ey, ee, oh, oo for a, e, i, o, u. An accent over a vowel means that vowel is held a little longer than its unaccented cousins. "ao" is generally "ee," but otherwise diphthongs are pretty much what you'd expect. Consonants are a pain. "ch" is hard, as in the modern Scottish "loch." "S," if preceded by "i" or "a," is usually "sh." "F" is usually silent, unless it's the first letter in a word, and if the word starts with "fh," then the "f" and the "h" are both silent. "Th" is likewise usually silent, as is "dh," although if "dh" is at the beginning of a word, it tries to choke on itself and ends up sounding something like a "strangled" French "r." Oh, and "mh" is "v," "bh" is "w," "c" is always hard, and don't forget to roll your "r"s!)

a'bhei'lár	lit. "to be the center"; an extremely charismatic person
ach	but
adhmacomh	wood-bodied. An insult.
adhmam	admit, confess
a'gár'doltas	vendetta (lit. "smiling-murder")
agean	ocean
agla	fear(n.)
agór	wrongness, dislocation
állacht	beautiful. Can be used to describe persons of any gender.
m'állacht	my beauty. Fiachra's pillow-name for Peri.
amad'n	fool, idiot
amaic	away; away from
anam	soul
m'anam	my soul. Fae endearment.
n'anamacha	their souls
aon-arc	unicorn
asiomú	'reversal-vengeance'. The act of making oneself crave whatever is being done to one as a punishment, thereby turning one's punisher into one's procurer.
asling	dream
át	spot
át mil (pl. *átenna milis*)	sweet spot
atráth	postponement. As close as *Faen* gets to a word for 'truce.'
batagar	arrow
beag	little, slight

Rory Ni Coileain

bi'scaol'e	"be unbound" (v. imp, antiquated)
blas	taste (v. imp.)
bod	penis (vulgar)
bod-snadhm	dick-knot. An unpleasant situation.
bodlag	limp dick (much greater insult than a human might suppose)
bragan	toy
breathea	judge
briste	broken
buchal alann	beautiful boy
cac	excrement
ca'ain	when
ca'fuil	where
cairtas-óntais	surprising/unexpected/improvised justice. In a word, revenge, Fae style.
callte	hidden
caomhnór	guardian
carn	pile
ceangal	(1) chains
ceangal	(2) Royal soul-bonding ceremony in the Realm (common alt. spelling *ceangail*)
cein fa?	Why?
céle	general way of referring to two people

	le céle	together (alt. form *le chéle*)
	a céle	one another, each other

304

chara	friend	
cheanglá	(masc. form *ceangell*) beloved one, consort. From the alternate Fae timeline.	
cho'halan	so beautiful	
chort-gruag	"bark-hair". Derogatory way of referring to a dark-haired Fae	
Clo'che	living Stone	
cnasaigh	heal (v. imp.)	
coladh	sleep	
comart'	symbol	
comhrac-scátha	mirror-foe; a magickal duplicate of the bearer whose only purpose is to fight to death or dismissal	
cónai	live	
coromór	equalizer	
co'salach	lit. "dirty feet." Implies feet growing in the dirt, like tree roots.	
crangaol	tree-kin	
crann	tree	
	a'chrann	a tree
craobód	twig-dick. Insult, occasionally lethal.	
crocnath	completion	
	m'crocnath	my completion. One of Cuinn's pillow-names for Rian
croí	heart	

Croí na Dóthan		Heart of Flame, the signet of the Royal house of the Demesne of Fire
Cruan'ba	The Drowner. Name given to the *Marfach* by the Fae of the Demesne of Water.	
Cu droc!	Bad dog!	
cugat	to you	
cúna	aid, assistance	
cúpál-macnas	mate-lust	
dalle	blindness; verbal component of an Air mage's blinding channeling	
danamhris	Lit. "to be done unto." One of the darkest words as'Faein for torture.	
daoir	1. beloved; 2. expensive	
d'aos'Faen	Old Faen, the old form of the Fae language. Currently survives only in written form, with a very few exceptions.	
dara-láiv	lit. "second-hand". Euphemism for masturbation.	
dar'cion	brilliantly colored. Conall's pillow-name for Josh.	
dearmad	forgotten	
deich	ten	
	deich meloi	ten thousand
derea	end	
desúcan	fix, repair	
dhábh-	lit. "two-become-one." Rare Fae	

archann	euphemism for sex.	
dhó-súil	fire-eyes. One of Cuinn's pillow-names for Rian.	
dóchais	hope (n.) (alt. spelling *dócas*)	
dolmain	hollow hill, a place of refuge	
domhnacht	depths	
	Domhnacht Rúnda	the Secret Depths, Rhoann's refuge in the Realm
doran	stranger, exile	
d'orant	impossible. Josh's pillow-name for Conall.	
draoctagh	magick	
	m'dhraoctagh	my magick. Rhoann's pillow name for Mac.
	Spiraod n'Draoctagh	Spirit of Magick. Ancient Fae oath. Or expletive. Sometimes both.
draoi	teacher	
dre'fiur	beloved sister	
dre'thair	beloved brother	
	dre'thair dtuismiorí	beloved brother of my parents (beloved to the speaker, in this instance, not

		necessarily to the parents)
dubh	black, dark	
dúrt me	I said	
dúsi	Wake up (imp.)	
ecáil	will see	
	a'ecáil	I will see
eiscréid	shit	
Elirei	Prince Royal	
fada	long (can reference time or distance)	
Faen	the Fae language.	*Laurm Faen* – I speak Fae
	as'Faein	in the Fae language. *Laur lom as'Faein* – I speak in the Fae language.
Fai'mhal	feral Fae, also called Wyld-Fae. Legendary Fae who supposedly survived the Sundering without being sheltered and changed by the Loremasters.	
fan	wait (imp.)	
fánadh	wanderer	
farthor	sentry	
fedair a	may/must/can be (comp. v.) Almost impossible to translate accurately; it can mean that a thing is permitted, required, or possible, depending on context.	

féin-dúltú	self-denial	
feol'marh	dead meat	
fiáin	wild	
fiánn	living magick	
	fiánn sachant!	magick forbid (it)!
fior	true	
fiur-mhac	nephew (lit. "sister's son"; see *thair-mhac*)	
flua	wet	
fola	wounded, injured	
folabodan	Fae sex toy. Derived from *fola*, injured, and *bod*, penis	
fola'magairl	bloody testicles. A common epithet.	
folath	bleed	
folathóin	bloody asses. Anyone sensing a pattern here gets a gold star.	
fonn	keen, sharp	
fracun	whore, Comes from an ancient Fae word meaning "use-value"– in other words, a person whose value is measured solely by what others can get from him or her.	
ful-claov	blood-sword; a magickal weapon usually formed from the channeler's own blood	
gallaim	I promise	
galtanas	promise (n., archaic)	
gan	general negative – no, not, without, less	
	gan derea	without end, eternal

gaoirn	wolves	
gastiór	binder, The One Who Binds	
g'demin	true, real	
g'deo	forever	
geal	bright, brilliant	
	cho'geal	as bright
geal'le'mac	almost-son, as dear as a son	
g'féalaidh	may you (pl.) live (see phrases)	
g'fua	hate (v.)	
glanadorh	cleanser, The One Who Cleanses	
g'mall	slowly	
grafain	wild love, wild one. Lochlann's pillow name for Garrett.	
gran	sun	
	an'ghran	the sun
grasán	a master-hunter's net, truesilver with a binding channeling woven in	
halan	beautiful	
haricín	hurricane; a form, or style, of Fae swordplay	
iasc	fish (n.)	
	iasc'in	little fish. Rhoann's mother's pet name for him.
impi	I beg	
inní-cnotálte	lit. "knitted-guts." An intestinal disturbance brought on by nerves.	
laba	bed	

	as a'laba!	(Get) off the bed!
lae	day	
laghda	debasement, groveling	
lámagh	hot (v., p.t.)	
lán'ghrásta	graceful, implying flight.	
lanan	lover. Tiernan's pillow name for Kevin, and vice versa	
lanh	son	
laoc	warrior	
laród-scatha	mirror-trap. Essentially a magickal ball with no exterior, only a mirrored interior. And the sweet revenge of all of us who failed solid geometry in high school.	
lasihoir	healer	
Lath-Ríoga	Half-Royal. A name for Rhoann.	
laurha	spoken (see phrases)	
	related words – *laurm*, I speak; *laur lom*, I am speaking, I speak (in) a language	
lobadh	decayed, rotten	
lofa	rotten	
mac	son, son of	
	mac'fracun	son of a whore
macánta	honesty	
machtar	desperation; root word of *macánta*	
madra	dog	
magarl	testicles (alt. spelling *magairl*)	
ma'nach	mine	

311

Marfach, the	the Slow Death. Deadliest foe of the Fae race.
marh	dead
martola	beef
marú	kill
Mastragna	Master of Wisdom. Ancient Fae title for the Loremasters.
milat	feel, sense
minn	oath
mo mhinn	my oath
misnach	courage
nach	general negative; not, never
nachangalte	unbound
nartú	strength
né	not, is not
ngarradh	sundered, The Sundered
nidantór	unmaker, The Unmaker
n-oí	night
'nois	now
ollúnta	solemn
onfatath	infected
orm	at me
osclór	opener, The One Who Opens
pian	pain
pracháin	crows
prasach'te	hot mess. Means almost exactly the same thing to a Fae as it does to a human.
rachtanai	addicted (specifically, to sexual teasing)
réaltaí	star (pl. *réaltaí*)
Ridiabhal	lit. "king of the devils", Satan. A borrowed word, as Fae have

	neither gods nor devils.	
rílacha	(it) rules	
rinc	dance	
	rin'gcatha gríobhan	"labyrinthine dance." A euphemism for Fae sexuality
	rinc-daonna	"human dance", a game of teasing and sexually overloading humans
	Rinc'faring	the Great Dance, an annual gathering of hundreds of Fae light-dancers
	rinc'marh	"dance of death," a blade-master's footwork
	rinc'lú	little dance
rochar	harm (n.)	
rúnda	secret	
sallacht	extremely stubborn	
saor	free	
sasann	we stand	
savac-dui	black-headed hawk, Conall's House-guardian	
scair'anam	SoulShare (pl. *scair-anaim*)	

313

	m'anam-sciar	my SoulShare
	scair'aine'e	the act of SoulSharing
	scair'ainm'en	SoulShared (adj.)
scian	knife	
	scian'a'schian	blade to blade; a duel
scian-damsai	knife-dances. An extremely lethal type of formalized combat.	
scian-omprór	blade-bearer	
sciana-Clo'che	knives of living Stone	
scílim	I think, I believe	
scol-agna	lit. "school of wisdom", school for children with high magickal potential	
selbh	possession	
sibh	you (pl.)	
síofra	changeling	
slántai	health, tranquility	
	slántai a'váil	"Peace go with you". A mournful farewell.
snadhm	knot	
s'náthe	strand, necklace	
s'ocan	peace, be at peace	
soladán	channel	
sol'fiáin	(v.) complete, make complete	
spára	spare	
	spára'se	spare him

spiraod	spirit
suait	turbulent
súil	eyes
sule-d'ainmi	lit. "animal-eyes," dark brown eyes
sule-speír	lit. "sky-eyes," blue eyes. Méalla's pillow-name for Suan
sumiúl	fascinating, beguiling. Lasair's pillow-name for Bryce
sus	up
s'vra lom	I love (lit. "I have love on me")
taobhan	diversion, plaything. Term for a non-Royal Fae who occupies the bed of a Royal before the Royal is pair-bonded
ta'sair	I'm free (exclam.)
tástimhór	'great test;' a cross between a vision quest and a final exam
tátha	bound; verbal component of an Air mage's binding channeling
téighras	go home (v. imp.)
thair-mhac	nephew (lit. "brother's son"; see *fiur-mhac*)
thar	come (imp.)
	Thar amaic. Come away.
	Thar lom. Come with me.
thogarm'sta	answer (imp.)
Tiar'na'Slete	lit. "Mountain Lords"; a mountain range usually in the far south of the Realm
tobar	wellspring (archaic)
toghairm	summoned, called
Tirr Brai	Folk of Life, or Folk of Power. Living beings with magickal

315

	essence.
t'mé	I'm
tón	ass (not the long-eared animal)
tón-grabrog	ass-crumb (of the clinging variety)
torq	boar
tráll	slave
tragód'mhan	Fae dramatic form, relating in often lurid detail the consequences of lust unfortuitously expressed.
tre	three
	Tre... dó... h'on... Three.... two... one...
tréan-cú	strong hound. Lasair's nickname for Setanta, his blind runt Fade-hound puppy
tróhi	fight (imp.)
trora	the V of muscle over the hips of a Fae or human male. A noted aphrodisiac.
trych	an unspecified eyeless creature
tseo	this, this is (see phrases)
turran'agne	mind-shock, the effect on a Fae of magickal overload
uisca	water
uiscebai	strong liquor found in the Realm, similar to whiskey
veissin	knockout drug found in the Realm, causes headaches
viant	desired one. A Fae endearment.

Useful phrases:

...tseo mo mhinn ollúnta.	This is my solemn oath.
G'féalaidh sibh i do cónai fada le céle, gan a marú a céle.	"May you live long together, and not kill one another." A Fae blessing, sometimes bestowed upon those Fae foolhardy enough to undertake some form of exclusive relationship. Definite "uh huh, good luck with that" overtones.
bragan a lae	"toy of the day." The plaything of a highly distractable Fae.
Fai dara tú pian beag. Ach tú a sabail dom ó pian I bhad nís mo.	You cause a slight pain. But you are the healing of more.
Cein fa buil tu ag'eachan' orm ar-seo?	Why do you look at me this way?
Dóchais laurha, dóchais briste.	Hope spoken is hope broken.
Bod lofa dubh.	Lit. "black rotted dick". Not a polite phrase.
Scílim g'fua lom tú.	I think I hate you.
S'vra lom tú.	I love you.
Sus do thón.	Up your ass.
D'súil do na prácháin, d'croí do na gaoirn, d'anam do n-	"Your eyes for the crows, your heart for the wolves, your soul for the eternal night." There is only one stronger vow of enmity in the Fae language, and trust

Rory Ni Coileain

oí gan derea.
me, you don't want to hear that one.

Lámagh tú an batagar; 'se seo torq a'gur fola d'fach.
"You shot the arrow; this wounded boar is yours." The equivalent *as'Faein* of "You broke it; you buy it." Often used in its shortened form, "*Lámagh tú an batagar.*" (or "*Lámagh sádh an batagar*" for "they shot". It's probably only a matter of time before some Fae in the human world, taking his cue from "NMP" for "not my problem," comes up with "LTB."

Tá dócas le scian inas fonn, nach milat g'matann an garta dí g'meidh tú folath.
Fae proverb: Hope is a knife so keen, you don't feel the cut until you bleed.

G'ra ma agadh.
Thank you.

Tam g'fuil aon-arc desúcan an lanhuil damast I d'asal. G'mall.
"May a unicorn repair your hemorrhoids. Slowly." One can only imagine....

Magairl a'Ridiabhal.
Satan's balls.

Se an'agean flua, a'deir n'abhann.
The ocean is wet, says the river. The pot calling the kettle black.

galtanas *deich meloi*	"promise of ten thousand". A promise given by a Fae, to give ten thousand of something to another, usually something that can only be given over time. Considered an extravagant, even irrational showing of devotion.
Támid faoi *ceangal ag* *a'slabra* *ceant.*	We are bound by the same chains.
Né seo *a'manach.*	This isn't for me.
mo phan *s'darr lear sa* *masa*	my favorite pain in the ass
Dúrt me lath *mars'n*	I told you so
Bual g'mai, *aris.*	Well met, again.
An'Faei a *ngaill,* *ta'Fhaei an* *tráll.*	The Fae who needs, (that Fae) is a slave.
lasr, s'oc as *fola*	Flame, frost and blood. A Fae oath, a little milder than the ones involving hearts and eyes and wolves and suchlike.
Do dalat- *serbhisach.*	"Your saddle-servant." The equivalent of "at your service". Usually sarcastic.
Fan lel'om. *Bh'uil tú* *ag'eistac* *lom?*	Stay with me. Do you hear me?
An-bfuil tuillt *aige*	Is he worth saving? Or does he only have use-worth?

*a'hartáil? Nó
an-bfuil sé
a'fracuin?*

*Sé ar 'chann
de dúnn.*　　　　He is one of us.

*Ca' atá tú
a'rá?*　　　　What are you saying?

*Ní fed'r lom
an'uscin lat.*　　　　I can't understand you.

*Tá cúna saor
in asc
is'daoir.*　　　　Free aid is the dearest.

*A'buil gnas le
lom ar-gúl.*　　　　Fuck me backwards.

*A'buil gnas le
leat a's
a'madra
dúsigh tu
suas leis.*　　　　Fuck you and the dog you woke
up with.

Blas mo thón.　　　　Taste my ass.

*Sasann muid
le chéle.*　　　　We stand together. Unofficial
motto of the Demesne of
Purgatory.

Tá'siad marh.　　　　They're dead.

draoi ríoga　　　　royal wizard (actually Irish,
rather than *Faen*, Rian's title for
his court mage)

*Bei mé tú
a'ecáil g'deo.*　　　　I will see you forever.

*Tá thú
toghairm.*　　　　Thou art summoned. (very
formal)

*Cac'iasc
i'uisca suait.*　　　　Fish-shit in turbulent water. An
expression of frustration.

*Tá tú
cho'geal an
ghran a*　　　　As brilliant as the sun on a
strand (necklace) of stars.
Heavily sarcastic.

320

crocta's 'náth e de réaltaí.

Bain trall ascomath chu 'garradh a 'chrann. — As well try to un-cut a tree.

Cnasaigh croí le m 'anam- scair. — Heal (the one who is) the heart of my SoulShare.

Cadagh dom a tacht ar 'shúl ó anseo le... — Allow me to come away with...

Ta 'bhar mé fhéin le... — Take me with....

in loco scintillans braccis — Latin. "In place of [the one with] twinkling trousers."

Magairl snáthith ar 'srang! — Testicles threaded on a wire!

mac 'fracun fola 'the — Bloody-assed son of a whore. And yes, Conall did kiss his mother with that mouth.

Gafa id 'r cú- cémne a 's tine. — Caught between (the) Fade- hound and (the) fire. An unenviable position.

Céd d 'chacairt tabh i 'r den chosa, a 's ná iarr orth sluasad a 'fál ar isacht. — Pull your shit-cart around back of the stable, and don't (bother to) ask to borrow a shovel. A common Fae response when asked for a less than convenient favor.

Básagh gan 'anma! — Die nameless!

321

Slán abhaile, agus Dia a bheith in éineacht bheirt agaibh.

Irish, rather than *Faen*; Go safely home, and God go with you both.

Gan cé g'vratheann m'croí.

Not while my heart beats.

Ní fed'r le dhá rud a léiv: dilan bragan 's'intinn di'cat.

Two things may/must/can never be read: the diary of a courtesan and the mind of a cat. (The *Faen* compound verb *fedair a* is extremely ambiguous in this context; death sentences have been imposed—or commuted—depending on the particular shade of meaning applied.)

Slán'abhonn, slán'aslán, slán'abhal.

Safe met, safe parted, safe home.

About the Author

Rory Ni Coileain majored in creative writing, back when Respectable Colleges didn't offer such a major, so she had to design it herself, at a university which boasted one professor willing to teach creative writing, he being a British surrealist who went nuts over students writing dancing bananas in the snow but did not take well to the sort of high fantasy she wanted to write. She graduated Phi Beta Kappa at the age of 19, sent off her first short story to an anthology being assembled by an author she idolized, received one of those rejection letters that puts therapists' kids through college (Ivy League), and found other things to do, such as going to law school, ballet dancing (at more or less the same time), nightclub singing, and volunteering as a lawyer with Gay Men's Health Crisis, for the next 30 years or so, until her stories started whispering to her. Now she's a lawyer, a legal journalist (and thus a card-carrying Enemy of the State and darn proud of it), an Associate member of the Order of Julian of Norwich, a proud mother, about to go back to school to become a spiritual advisor, and engaged to the love of her life, and is busily wedding her love of myth and legend to her passion for M/M romance.

Books in this Series by Rory Ni Coileain:

Hard as Stone: Book One of the SoulShares Series

Gale Force: Book Two of the SoulShares Series

Deep Plunge: Book Three of the SoulShares Series

Firestorm: Book Four of the SoulShares Series

Blowing Smoke: Book Five of the SoulShares Series

Mantled in Mist: Book Six of the SoulShares Series

Undertow: Book Seven of the SoulShares Series

Stone Cold: Books Eight in the SoulShares Series

Other Riverdale Avenue Books You Might Like

The Siren and the Sword: Book One of the Magic University Series
By Cecilia Tan

The Tower and the Tears: Book Two of the Magic University Series
By Cecilia Tan

The Incubus and the Angel: Book Three of the Magic University Series
By Cecilia Tan

The Prophecy and the Poet: Book Four of the Magic University Series
By Cecilia Tan

Spellbinding: Tales From Magic University
Edited by Cecilia Tan

Mordred and the King
By John Michael Curlovich

Collaring the Saber-Tooth: Book One of the Masters of Cats Series
By Trinity Blacio

Dee's Hard Limits: Book Two of the Masters of Cats Series
By Trinity Blacio

Caging the Bengal Tiger: Book Three of the Masters of Cats Series
By Trinity Blacio